MY LIFE ON EARTH AND ELSEWHERE

Praise for Peggy Payne

"Mesmerizing..."
--*The New York Times*

"She tells an incredible story incredibly well"
--*The Baltimore Sun*

"...Real emotional power..."
--*The Atlanta Journal-Constitution*

..."Beautifully intense."
-- S. Kelley Harrell, author of *The Teen Spirit Guide to Modern Shamanism* --*Huffington Post*

"...Entrancing and unsettling..."
--Angela Davis-Gardner, author of *Butterfly's Child*

"Her writer's eye sees to the center of things—to the spiritual center of our beings, whether we're from this side of the earth, or the other."
--Clyde Edgerton, author of *The Night Train*

Praise for My Life on Earth and Elsewhere

Peggy Payne has written a completely original novel which grabbed me from the beginning and never let go. Absolutely, achingly REAL--and it's funny too! Both teen and "adult" readers will love it.
--Lee Smith, *New York Times* best-selling author of *Dimestore, Blue Marlin, The Last Girls*

For my brothers, Franc Payne and Harry Payne, with love and admiration

CHAPTER

ONE

F loating up, away from myself, away from my body. So easy, it's the softest feeling. Light and swimming in air. I'd forgotten I could do anything like this. Now I think I did when I was little, but never for more than a few seconds and only a quick blur, not the way it's happening now. From here, maybe thirty feet up, I can see the three of us down below, Mom, Dad, and me, sitting in the white metal patio chairs.

Dad has his hands on his knees, leaning forward a little, Mom all formal and stiff in a way she never is. From up here, I look so skinny and young, like I'm thirteen instead of sixteen.

But I'm not there. I'm here, my mind and my senses hanging steady in a spot near the top of the big backyard sycamore tree. Up here everything is so IMAX I can't believe it—all amped-up, hyper-real. I'm stunned into a state where I'm almost calm, taking it in. I hear every little bird and insect and the slight breeze fluffing the nearest branches. But only a murmur of the conversation below.

The three of us…I can hardly bear to look. Mom sits with her legs wrapped tight around each other, her dark blonde hair fallen forward. I see a little of her face. The sun makes her hair shine like twenty shades of beach sand, unlike mine, brown and ordinary. Dad is still talking. My body is turned in his direction, and I'm pulling at my sleeves, stretching them down over my hands. My raspberry-stripe top, which I never want to see again after this day. How can I be sitting there—my shoulders looking hunched and tense—when my mind is up here? Is this what it means to lose your mind? To simply float away? From this angle, I can see my feet, my sneakers, balanced on the toes, pushing hard against the bricks under my chair.

All this started fifteen minutes ago when Mom stuck her head in the door of my room to tell me to come downstairs for a talk with her and Dad. It was semi-worrisome. That's when I first got a strange buzzy feeling. We're not usually so plan-ahead about having a conversation.

I'd have jumped right up, but I'd gotten into this spooky old book I found, *The Magus*, about mysterious games in an island villa called the Waiting-Room. It was so fascinating that I'd already ignored a couple of beeps from my phone. Also, it was way weirder than I've ever imagined being, which was making me feel better about myself.

"Let me get to the end of this part," I said. "Four or five pages. Okay?"

Mom didn't say okay. She didn't say, You come right this minute, Darcy. She didn't say anything more. She waited motionless, with a slack expression like I hardly ever see on her, staring out the windows on the other side of my room. She's usually so supercharged and busy. But there she stood, holding on to the doorframe, not even looking at me, with her mind who-knows-where.

"I'm coming," I said, slinging my legs off the bed. She disappeared from my door.

Stepping into my low-tops, I left the book where it fell. Her face had looked flushed, the way it would if she were excited. She'd sold a big painting? She hadn't seemed happy, though. She had a fever? Or maybe she was going to tell me what's been going on around here lately. Do I want to know? There's a change in the house's personality. The air seems different, the light, too, like it's pulled too thin, every room feeling gray around the edges.

Downstairs, the two of them—she and Dad—trooped along behind me toward the back door. I was outside by the time I realized they'd stopped, had gotten hung up talking in the kitchen. So either this conversation wasn't all that urgent or it was so important that they had to stop and discuss strategy.

I sat rocking my chair back and forth, metal grating against the brick, waiting for the Family Summit Meeting to begin. Through the window I could see Mom's silhouette, Dad's shoulder and arm. I wasn't getting a good vibe from the sight of them. I thought maybe if I stopped watching, they'd hurry up—although science-guy Dad has jokingly pointed out to me more than once that a watched pot actually doesn't take longer to boil. He has such a clear view of how everything works, which is how I'd like to be: sure about what's going on and what results to expect.

Behind me the garden gate into the alley rattled. Mr. Frederick, our peculiar neighbor, peered over the top of the fence. "Thank your parents, please," he said.

"Okay, sure, what for?" I almost expected him to say for giving me life. He drops odd bits of advice, like, "Double-knot your shoelaces. Always." Really, he's kind of nice, a lonely old guy, but some of the little kids in the neighbor-hood make fun of him.

"For turning down their musical volume," he said. "Not that I don't like opera, but enough is enough."

My parents were asked to turn their music down? How juvenile! "I'll tell them, Mr. Frederick." He flung his arm into an overhead salute and disappeared.

Then the house door *click-clicked* open. There they were, Mom and Dad, both of them staring at their own feet as they carefully came down the back steps.

"Mr. Frederick was here," I said as they settled into chairs. "He thanks you for turning down your music. I guess you guys are just too loud and wild." I was trying to keep this conversation light.

They shrugged at each other. "He never mentioned anything about music," Dad said, "to either of us." It was then I realized that there'd been no music lately. Was that the change I'd felt in the house? It wasn't the only change. I was getting a worse feeling.

"Darcy?" Dad's voice shook. Suddenly I didn't want to be here. Without looking, I felt Mom getting jumpy.

Whatever he was about to say, I didn't want to know. For

4

months the whole house had felt off somehow. Dad in the wing chair "thinking" for hours, his eyes closed, or jotting notes. Mom working out so much it's ridiculous. The sound of her jump rope at night going on and on: *swoosh-thump swoosh-thump*. . . .

"Darcy, for complicated reasons, your mother and I are going to live apart—"

Apart? Live apart? Not them. Not us. I stopped hearing him. Like I had water plugging up my ears. Mom blurred at the edge of my vision. The boards of the fence behind her blurred. I don't have to listen, don't have to hear any of it.

I was dizzy, ears stopped, my head full of wind. What's going on? The oddest sensation, like starting to stand up from the chair. But I wasn't.

No, I was.

I was rising, weightless, lifting off of the seat. How could this be happening?

All the heaviness in me vanished. I was floating completely outside of myself, like shooting up from the bottom of a pool. Up and up. Happening so fast I couldn't know what to feel.

I slowed, hovering now, my body's still down there though, the three of us sitting in the white metal chairs like everything is normal.

Normal? No. This isn't supposed to happen.

It *is* happening. I've slipped out of my body and stayed out. Maybe the shock of the news damaged my brain.

Dad puts his hand to his forehead, as if he's trying to get his thoughts straight, but he always has his thoughts in order. Even sitting down, he looks tall and thin, like a sculpture made out of one long piece of wire. Squiggles of gray show in his dark hair. He's down there explaining. Looks like now I'm gripping the arms of the chair. But I'm not listening. If I'd really wanted to know, I could have asked weeks, maybe months ago. The only thing I wanted to hear was that everything is fine.

At this altitude I can look out across the rooftops all the way down Hillsborough Street to the university. Music blasts from a car going by a block or two away. The bass feels like it's thumping at the bottom of my throat. I still have my senses. At least there's that.

Everything is nice up here, the air smooth and perfect. In fact, this whole experience feels weirdly natural. I've always been fascinated by weather, meteorology, and of course trees; now I'm getting a whole new view of the sky and the highest twiggy branches. The September greenery around me still looks like summer: the star-shaped leaves of the tree, a fat-belly squirrel running and jumping on limbs that shouldn't be able to hold him. Little ripples, what Dad would call pressure waves, keep coming from the far side of the tree.

There, in the shadows beyond the trunk, something's moving. Someone is there, sending out the invisible waves. I feel its presence like a hum. Twenty feet away. In the patchy light I can barely make out a person-shape, taller than I am, much too big for the branches up this high. Ten seconds ago I was by myself. My whole mind shivers. I stare and strain toward what I'm seeing. Big shoulders—it's a guy, a boy, I'm pretty sure, though branches interrupt his silhouette. His dark hair is a pile of curls, unless it's the leaves around him I'm seeing.

I could call out. No, and I mustn't blink—I'll lose sight of him. Or I'll find myself back on the patio with my parents, wondering what made me think—

He's moving. His bare upper arm, deer-colored, flashes past at a spot where light breaks through.

He's turning away. My brain screams him messages: *Move into the sun so I can see you! I have to see you!*

He turns back and sees me, and his dark eyes flicker with a brightness that looks like wild happiness. Or is it shock? He's almost too surprised. This is not a regular guy. Is he someone who slipped out of himself, like me?

None of this is possible. I have to be imagining it. Yet I can't look away—I might lose sight of him.

A scratching sound, repeating, like he's trying to light a match and having trouble. A little hiss as fire flares, and I see his cupped hand, the glow on his face. Heavy dark eyebrows. His skin looks so warm. A ball of flame the size of a tangerine, too big for one match, drops straight down, dying out near the ground like a shooting star. My parents don't seem to notice.

In a burst of panic, I realize: I looked away from him. But he hasn't disappeared. Instead, he walks away from me, out on the branch—he's a jumble of shadows changing every second— out into the mesh of twigs, at the far leafy edge of the tree. How is that possible? How is any of this possible? I hardly see him now, only motion; he blends into the shifting bits of light. Gone.

Gone where?

I almost expect to see him on the ground, walking over to where I sit with my parents. But my body is looking slumped and pathetic down there right now. As I look, the brick paving zooms closer and—No, wait! Stop!

A rush of rising sound. I slide back into my ordinary self. Like being sucked into a narrow tube. Shit! Once again I'm tight-packed into my skin.

Dad is still talking. He has on his methodical look, like when he's trying to patiently explain some math problem. I can't think—I'm too woozy. The edges of everything wobble. Ordinary sound feels rough, like waves crashing around me. But Dad's coming into focus. The wavering eases. I'm starting to get what he's saying: we'll still see each other and they both love me.

He's going on and on. I hear him now, can't stop hearing him, saying the predictable stuff: there's never a good time, he knows it may be a shock. His professor voice has gone away.

It *is* a shock. It knocked me out of myself. Or made me hallucinate. Although practically everybody else has divorced parents.

"How can you be splitting?" My voice still works. "You haven't even been arguing." There's a very off-key feeling about this split. Something else is going on with them. Or is it me feeling woozy?

I want to go back up in the air, follow the make-believe boy out into the leaves, and escape. I haven't recovered from whatever that was, and I'm being clobbered by whatever this is. I feel like I've just gotten off a state fair ride. Even sitting still, I'm staggering. Maybe I'm getting sick. Closing my eyes,

I imagine myself pushing upward, hard as I can, squeezing stomach muscles, trying to go back up there. Like I know how to make it happen. The effort seems to plant me even heavier in the chair, all the airy feeling gone.

Mom clears her throat. She's tearing up the bottom of a paper match with her fingernails, though why she has a match I'm not sure, since they both supposedly quit smoking long ago. "Darcy, your father will be staying with the Milners until"—she pauses—"for the moment." Her face looks older, the crow's feet and neck wrinkles more obvious. Dad's nose is red. He has tears in his eyes, like when he told me Gran died. They both look wrecked.

"Not far away," Dad says.

Staying at the Milners until when? For sure, I would have noticed if one of them was having an affair. He already has a place to stay?

I ask, "Whose idea is all this, anyway?"

They both start to answer. They both stop. They don't look at me; they stare at different spots on the ground.

I do the same thing, tipping the chair back and forth, harder and faster. These chairs have never sat level since Dad put the brick down in the backyard. "Put down" is the way he says it. Mom says "bricked up."

"Some things we don't get to choose," Dad says finally. "Some things simply appear, seemingly out of nowhere."

Appear? Like the boy in the tree?

"Some parents stay together for their kid," I say. My chest feels so tight I can hardly talk. I hate them both—for wrecking everything. It's not like they were ever in perfect bliss with each other, not since I've known them, at least.

Now all of a sudden they have to destroy our family? "This is so not right." Dad looks like he's practically dying. He might as well be, since I'll hardly ever see him anyway. Now all at once I'm crying big-time. I want them to see what they've done.

Dad reaches out his long arm and gives me a Kleenex. As if that will do any good. As if anything they do from this moment on will do any good. Mom comes over beside my chair, gets down on her knees in her white jeans on these bricks she hates, and puts her arms around me. She's crying, too. Hard. Although I would bet anything this is her idea; she's an extrovert and gorgeous.

Maybe we'll all three sit here and cry forever. Already I know it's going to be worse when we stop. It'll sink in and I'll be embarrassed that I've acted so completely immature—like a three-year-old—when I should've said, "Yeah, whatever."

"I didn't think you'd do this," I tell them. Mostly I didn't think it could feel this bad.

CHAPTER

TWO

"I'll be at Cup A Joe," I say when I walk into the living room. After the big conversation, I dragged myself upstairs and texted Martin that we had to talk. "Back in a while," I say to them, my former family. There they are, Mom and Dad, sitting on opposite sides of the room. Dad's legs reach about halfway across the space. So now all of a sudden he's single, going off to live somewhere else. They both feel lost to me, like they're flung out of our family and into the world. My dad, Perry Colvard, PhD, scientist at NC State, researcher on water behavior: erosion, tsunamis, stuff like that. Now completely separate from my mother, Gail Fitzpatrick, the artist. No longer a couple. My stomach feels twisted tight, like a towel being wrung out. Nothing will ever be the same.

Before today, we always hung out in the kitchen. The silence in this living room is big, full of whatever it was that I didn't listen to out on the patio and will eventually have to find out.

Mom looks unhappy, also nervous, which is not like her —repeatedly opening and closing her sunglasses. "Your father is going over to Chapel Hill. We thought you might want to ride with him." Forty-five minutes away from our Raleigh neighborhood: the UNC campus, and downtown: ice cream, pizza, Carolina T-shirts,

"I told Martin—"

"That's fine, honey," Dad says. "We can do it another day."

"A weekend outing with my father. The routine begins." He looks hurt. I wish I hadn't said it. I feel bad. Here I am rejecting him when he's probably already feeling crushed. Can't look at either of them or I'll get upset again. I stare at his scientific journals on the end table so I won't start to cry: *Physics of Fluids, Flow, Turbulence, and Combustion.* As if he chose his field to try to think logically about my mother's personality. Or his own deep-down undercurrents.

Don't think; look at the mirror. Check your eyelashes for clumping. Imaginary tree guy had wonderful eyes. I loved the expression on his face. So happy and amazed—and looking straight at me! If I made him up, I did a good job.

I want to be up in the tree now. I do know the tree is real at least. My insides feel stirred up, as if something is pulling me to be up in the branches... Or maybe I just want to get out of this room.

My being up there, seeing him—it's no more unbeliev-able than my parents splitting. My mind races back and forth between the two shocking events. My whole being is churning into chaos; it's possible that I've had a breakdown and can never trust anything I see or feel again.

WHEN I OPEN the door to Cup A Joe, the coffee-roast smell hits me like heat. I can't get three feet inside before I see most of the group at a table: Sydney, Bink, Susan, Lisa. They were supposed to be at the pizza place, not here. Drake in his goth eyeliner, with his girlfriend who goes to private school. Tony Llewellyn, who mostly acts like he doesn't see me. He's such a back-of-the-classroom type, dirty black hair, always leaning on walls because it's too much work to stand up, looks like he's smoking even when he isn't. I don't know why he bothers to show up.

When I get within reach, Bink—the great Bink Halliday —snaps the rubber bands I'm wearing on my left wrist, which I would normally count as a tiny social victory. Lisa says, "He-ey," in that singsong two-syllable way girls do in the hall at school when they're not super-interested in speaking to you. Susan is checking her phone. Charlotte's not here, which is good; could be hard to handle more than one best friend at the moment.

"Gotta go," I say. I grab a caramel coffee and head for the side room where I'm meeting Martin. None of the gang tries to stop me. My social standing is: Included But Not Pursued.

Past the inside doorway, I'm relieved to see him, standing near the wall like he's studying the Sundance poster. Even from the back, I recognize his khaki cargo shorts, the tire-tread flip-flops, his legs. Martin runs track, and he looks like a sprinter: wiry, though taller than most, or so I'm told. He is also a tiny bit older than everybody else, and very tuned-in emotionally. He's possibly gay but so far undeclared. His social status: Gets Invited, Gets Respect. Goes his own way and doesn't pay a price for it.

He sees something is wrong and hugs me. I don't want him to let go. I need his smell, his acne concealer and Mentos and the IcyHot they rub on his legs after a meet.

"Full update," he says, staring at my wrecked eyelids as he lets go of me.

What hits me: I can't tell him about anything but the parents, only the devastating news. No floating up in the air. No tree boy. If he told me about flying up in the air and meeting someone, I'd think he was having serious problems. Maybe I am. Did I lose my family and my mind in the same day?

"Dad's moving out." It hurts to say the words out loud. Can't let myself start sobbing in the middle of Cup A Joe.

Martin leads us to a table to sit. We flump down into the chairs. "Darcy, I'm sorry."

I can't speak, can't look at him.

"This makes no sense," he says as I grip my mug with both hands and stare hard at the tabletop. "I always thought your parents were cool together. Maybe it's temporary?"

I shake my head. He shouldn't try to get my hopes up—it's too painful.

He runs a hand over the top of his head, like he's trying to shake loose the right thing to say. "Did they give you a reason?"

"It's for the best." Did my parents say that trite phrase?

How would I know? I wasn't there. I hate not telling him what happened to me. But I can't. It's too weird.

"This is when it's worst, Darce. When mine did it, I was in fourth grade, didn't go to school for three days. Upset stomach. Now it's a matter of keeping up with where I'm staying. You lose track of what it was like before." He hesitates. "Are they going to court? Mine did."

Court?! Martin has managed to make this worse. "No way." Dad wouldn't talk about stuff in public; he'd rather do whatever Mom wanted. Then he'd zone out listening to tragic Bach cello music.

The mural on the wall in this room is depressing: distorted faces and dark colors. They should have hired Mom to paint it. It would be pink and orange. "What kills me," I manage to choke out, "is that I always thought it couldn't happen. I feel so stupid. Now my life is split in half. Permanently."

I was ridiculously sure we were different, that my family handled things better and wouldn't allow something like this. Plus, there were only three of us, too small a unit to break. Mom and Dad do argue and sulk sometimes, but their problems feel like the long scratch on the living room coffee table: been there forever, and what's so bad about it all of a sudden? Probably Dad will get the scarred table.

"Also, here I am at the age where I should be focused on my friends and getting independent and instead now I have to worry about my parents." I really don't want to start crying in the middle of Cup A Joe.

Martin reaches over and drags my chair, with me in it, up close beside him. His arm, brushing against mine, feels so physical, especially compared to floating up in the air and staring at a boy who disappears. Bumping up next to Martin seems familiar and warm and comforting.

I couldn't see Tree Boy well enough to guess his age. Sixteen? Eighteen or nineteen? I'm thinking like he's real and has an actual age. My mind is bouncing in every direction.

"You know you're talking to yourself?" Martin says.

"What? What did I say?" I'm panicked that I said too much. He'll think I've lost it.

"You were counting off numbers. It's okay, you're under stress. It'll pass."

If I tell him about the boy he'll decide I need help. He has it in him to tell my parents. He's so conscientious, he'd think he was doing the right thing. I might want help if I were only dealing with the parents. But floating up in a tree? No way. I'm not in the mood for someone giving me a diagnosis. I'm going to figure this out in private.

Saying nothing now feels wrong, though. When did I ever hold out on Martin? But I can't say I flew up into a tree. "I suppose I could act out, get into drugs, graffiti, long-sleeved tattoos." Being joke-y makes it easier to talk.

"Wouldn't fit," Martin says. "You could be selling opioids in the school parking lot,"—the hipster-nerd at the next table twists around to look at me—"and everybody would still think you're seriously Honor Society. And nature-y, like the close personal friend of pine cones and ferns."

I should be sitting alone with pine cones now, because this is too hard: talking about my destroyed family, and at the same time making sure to leave out that the shock threw me out of myself and up into the air. I can't sit here pouring out half of what's happened today with my brain clamped down tight on the rest.

"Let's go hang with the others," I say. I'm on my feet in an instant.

Martin looks rattled, like he did wrong. He didn't. It's me. I can't tell him everything and it feels so lonely and traitorish.

"It's okay, Martin. Don't worry. You've cheered me up. See?" I put on an exaggerated smile. "Come on. I've recovered from the family drama. I'm ready to get back to regular life."

CHAPTER

THREE

N ot exactly a first, but surprising: Dad picking me up from school. Four days he has been out of the house. There's his silver hybrid. Kids stream across the lot, between and around cars, the whole crowd of us moving like water parting and coming back together. He's pulled into the area for School Buses Only, being a hundred percent unaware of the rules for parking. He'd move instantly if he knew. He likes things "systematic." The word he loves most is "rigorous." He always uses it when he's talking about his favorite students. His eyes look warm and admiring when he talks about those kids. I try to be rigorous, but it's hard to apply to everyday life. It's super-hard to apply to a boy walking out on flimsy twigs in the top of a tree. Everywhere car doors slam, people yell across the lot to each other, engines crank up. "Bye, guys," I call out to my last-period buddies, Wendy and Jamal.

"Hey, honey," Dad says when I get in. "Good day?"

"Pretty much."

Then silence settles heavy, like something immovable, before he has even finished turning us out onto the street.

"No news?" he says after a block or two, in a trying-too-hard voice.

My mind goes blank. "Not really."

I want us to talk. I need us to talk, like normal. But for the first time ever I don't know what to say. Getting a pop quiz back seems trivial. It would be silly, fake conversation, which we don't do. I lean my head back and close my eyes, like I'm tired, let myself drift.

The first moment I noticed Dad taking a conversation with me completely seriously, I was maybe four or five. I remember so clearly. It's sad to think about now. We were all in the kitchen. I was standing on a little stool at the counter, doing my own "cooking." The cupful of mush I was making —out of flour, Cheerios, water, corn meal, etc.—was supposed to be cookie dough. I reached for the orange box, called baking soda, though it wasn't a soda, it wasn't even liquid. This was supposed to make the cookie big. I said to Dad, "If cookie dough gets bigger, is there more cookie or does it stretch or what?" The idea that there would be more seemed magical. He turned toward me with an expression I'd never seen, as if he was looking at a me he'd never seen. He smiled like everything in the world had suddenly turned out right and I was his best surprise. "Same amount of cookie," he said. "It just gets bubbles in it." The look on his face more than made up for no extra cookie and no magic. What I'd done: I'd asked him a science question, a logical question. I'd learned how to impress him.

Maybe I could devise an experiment to test whether Tree Boy is real.

Eyes still closed, I hear Dad punch from public radio over to my hip-hop station, which he used to complain about. Charlotte, my primary BFF besides Martin, said there'd be a lot of this trying-to-please-me behavior. I think she wanted to make the split seem less bad, when she's almost as shocked and upset as me.

This ride, if I let myself think about it, is painful. I'm scared the not-talking might be hurting Dad's feelings. Every afternoon since he left he's come back to supposedly get stuff but really to gaze worriedly at me. Four days I've been out on the back patio, trying to rise and getting nowhere. I'd like to rise out of this car and float somewhere.

I remember more now about a couple of almost-floating moments when I was small, once in kindergarten riding a tricycle fast in circles on a basketball court. Once in second grade when I was listening to thunder with the window open. A couple of years ago, I thought I saw someone fly past my second floor bedroom window; but when I checked, it was obviously the shadow of a guy working up high on a utility pole. There was never anything like flying up into a tree.

I already knew that sycamore tree pretty well, the way its bark breaks up and peels. I love trees, and this one started my leaf collection in third grade, a nerdish hobby that I'm quiet about these days.

"I'll look after your little Japanese maple," I offer, waking from my fake nap. We have to break the silence. And I want to say something nice. Maybe I could fly out of my bedroom window and hover like a news helicopter over the scraggly little stick. I haven't been able to make the lifting thing happen again. What if it was one time only, or didn't happen at all and I imagined it? Did Tree Boy show up because I was in the midst of the worst angst ever in my life and he's like some kind of guardian angel?

"No need to worry," Dad says. "I never should have planted it so close to the walk. I wasn't thinking." He thanks me embarrassingly extra much for offering. It didn't used to be like this a week ago. Also, last year he'd have planted that little tree in the exact right place.

The sun visor in front of me is pulled down, mirror in view, which could mean some woman has been riding with him. I won't think about it. Can't help seeing myself: my almost-sexy lips, the too-big pores on my nose. My shoulders look skinny. I'm very petite. Last year a loud, stupid boy in a movie line said I looked like a ten-year-old with tits. I ignored him.

My eyes ought to look different, mysterious, from my Tree-Boy experience, or wounded and deep from the family breakup. But they're the same ordinary brown.

We ride along, quiet again. The silence feels ominous. I keep thinking that if I'd talked to Dad earlier, maybe he and Mom wouldn't have gotten to this place. I could have pointed out things that would have helped him be more her type: if he would be more enthusiastic and outgoing. I know a lot about him and her, just because of my own personality. I have an awkward combination of their traits, Mom's intense emotion, Dad's being so hyper-analytical and research-y. I tilt somewhat more toward Dad's type. I like specific answers, usually. I'm sure I'll major either in atmospheric science or botany. Mom's loosey-goosey-ness is fine for her because, 1) she's an artist and 2) absolutely everybody loves her, which means she can get away with whatever. I'm out of luck on both those characteristics.

Now that I think about it, since the Mom and Dad halves of me don't work together all that well, why should the two parents get along? Probably I need to be more supportive, but it's extremely hard.

"At what point," I say, "are you going to start dating, if that's what you call it? I need to know what to expect." We've pulled up in front of the house. He lets his breath out, as if it's almost a relief that I've asked a real question.

"That's complicated, Darcy."

"It's important to me to know, Dad. I don't want any awkward surprises."

"Well, as I said when your mother and I talked with you —I have some decisions to make. Your mom wasn't patient with waiting."

"What waiting? I didn't hear anything about decisions." I hadn't heard, of course, because I was up high overhead. Not listening. "What decisions? You already made your decision."

He gives me an odd look. In the afternoon light angling in the car, his eyes look more muddy green than brown. "Like I said, I've been feeling more and more uncertain about my calling, my mission in life."

"Your calling? You mean being a professor, studying waves?" My mind shoots out in a dozen directions.

"I'm not ready to say more. I'm not clear. As I've repeatedly said to your mother. As I said to you." His voice has an edge that I haven't heard aimed at me, ever.

I can't admit I wasn't listening to their big announcement. I definitely can't say why. Not to Dad.

"Darcy, I'm sorry. I don't mean to snap at you."

"I know you're going through a lot, Dad." I try to say this sympathetically, though my throat feels tight and hurt.

"Forgive me," he says.

"Okay." I keep looking straight ahead. I'm not sure how much this forgiveness is supposed to cover.

CAN'T GET STARTED on homework and I've been sitting here at my desk staring for an hour. Trying not to think about this house without Dad in it. It's now been nine days since the split, over a week. I've redecorated my room in my head a dozen times. In the real world it's still the same: pale green walls, sheer white curtains that riffle from a breeze or the heat vent, clothes heaped on the little daybed under the windows. Moderate clutter that has been building since maybe eighth grade. It needs a change, since everything else is changing. Might be nice to have a change that I'm in charge of. So, time to dump the wall display of ancient album covers: Smashing Pumpkins, Nirvana, Pearl Jam.

Once again around the room: keep or toss? Definitely keep the comforter, silvery-blue-green that looks like a mixture of sky and water. Keep Mom's three little weather paintings— cumulus, stratus, and cumulonimbus clouds. I still love my vintage perfume bottles, most of them with a dab left of the smell. Don't need the Instagram printouts of my friends' selfies tacked to the back of my door; I know what those guys look like. Don't need the Mardi Gras beads when I've never been to Mardi Gras.

Maybe I need a snack.

For supper tonight, Mom and I ate grocery-store ready-made frozen lasagna. We used to "have dinner" every night and it was always a big deal. Dad did the cooking; he finds it relaxing. I could easily drown in the guilt that I'm *not* going to miss his Algerian stew, among other specialties. Mom and I talked at the table as if things were somewhat routine, which they're not.

Afterward, this stalled attempt at doing my homework. We're supposed to do a brief essay on one of a list of topics comparing different cultures' mythologies. I don't want to write anything. I'm not in the mood. I should be allowed a time-out from all obligations since my life and all my assumptions have been dumped on the floor. Martin warned me. For a while, he said, everything is too much trouble. You don't want to open your eyes.

I could think better if Mom would stop banging over-head. She's upstairs in her studio hammering on metal, working on jewelry—and probably cracking the plaster in my ceiling. Until recently, she didn't work up there so much at night. The metalworking is also new. If I had an umbrella or a long stick, I could get up on this chair and rap on the ceiling like an answering call. Looking around for something I can use, I'm so shocked that I practically knock my chair over jumping back.

He's here, Tree Boy, three feet away, sitting on the edge of my bed but not looking at me. I don't think he sees me. Grabbing the back of the chair, I regain my balance.

He reaches down to rub one ankle, like he has a bug bite. His legs are bare almost up to his knees—the hair springy and dark; he's wearing a long loose pullover-shirt-type thing. He's in my room. The boy from the tree. Am I imagining him? Am I seriously not well?

I'm scared to move. He might disappear.

More banging from overhead. He doesn't seem to notice the noise. It's like he's on the other side of a glass wall. Or I am.

"Who are you?" I say in a whisper. "Are you real?" I doubt he can hear me, even if I yell.

He turns in my direction, as if he's searching, and finally looks toward my face, though not exactly at me. My heart is beating like a mad parakeet. His eyes are like dark ocean.

No answer. He seems confused, as if he just woke up. His black curls are smooth and glossy like each one has been polished, his expression so open-looking—like nobody at school ever.

"I'm Darcy," I say, keeping my voice low. He stands without making the slightest sound.

Taking one step toward him, I reach out my hand. My fingers touch his bare arm. He startles. I jump back.

I felt him: he's there. I ask again, "Who are you?" The question surprises him more than the touch, his eyes cloud with alarm. I don't know how to tell him not to worry, that I'm not dangerous, my question isn't dangerous. I glance at my hand that touched him. What I felt was not exactly cloth or skin or the hair on his arm; it was more like a column of turning air, a slow warm tornado. I look up quickly—he's gone.

But he was in my room, not in a tree. And I was in my body like usual. He was standing here in the middle of my regular life. Like a normal real-life guy. He couldn't have gotten in through a window. They're both open, but the screens are fastened and they don't open from the outside. Could he have hidden in the closet? He isn't in there now. I'd have heard the door open if he'd gone out into the hall. There is no explanation for this.

What is happening? This is seriously bizarre. It has to end. I can't let myself slide into fantasy, no matter how real it seems. I'd lose everything else. I'd be sitting and staring, imagining I'm having a life.

This whole episode—the boy, the floating up in the air, his presence in my room—was a temporary blip. It happened because of extreme stress from my family falling apart. A perfectly natural, maybe unusual reaction. But now it's over. I'll make sure; I'll be keeping a careful watch on myself.

FOUR

All day at school I was careful to be completely alert and in touch with the outside world. It has been three weeks now since the parental divide and it's time for me to begin to act somewhat normal. I didn't daydream for one moment, not about anything. Not even about an ordinary boy like Ethan in front of me in math, the twisty little curls on the back of his neck, or me giving a graduation speech where I explain what's wrong with high school and it goes viral and makes me a huge influencer, or being an extra on a movie and being noticed by Timothée Chalamet and him going with me to a ballgame with his arm around me the whole time—I don't know why I ever think about actor-guys anyway. Silly and juvenile. In the halls today, when I said, "Hi," to people I made sure I said their names and looked straight at their eyes. I paid attention in every class. I sat up straight. So much effort. Too much. Very tiring and unnatural.

Now that I'm home, I can relax a little and google for better information on how to stay balanced and in control when under extreme stress. There has to be a better way than hyper-alertness. I probably seemed even weirder than usual. I'm embarrassed to think about it.

The first site that comes up is "The Scientific Way to Stay Sane," on an American Express page, of all things. Quick skim: doesn't look so easy. It's a huge list. Do a grounding exercise—whatever that is. Listen to Mozart, connect with people, breathe slowly. "Curtail discretionary activities." I guess that means don't go overboard on the extracurriculars. Lots more suggestions. Too many. I definitively close my laptop and put it aside.

Maybe I'm already sane, just like I've always been. The list also said I should learn to recognize my response to stress. Flying up into a tree, seeing an unreal boy. Apparently that's my response.

So when the stress goes away, then probably that will, too. I could decide to not worry about it and enjoy it while it lasts.

But the stress isn't going to end. My parents aren't going to get back together, and I'll never again go around assuming things are okay. I don't know what to do about my mental health. Maybe there's nothing to do but hope nothing even more outrageous happens.

At dinner, Mom decides to tell me what went wrong with the marriage. It has been a month.

"People have different needs," she says. I dabble in my

bowl of Cinnamon Toast Crunch and wait. Lately I mostly want to eat cereal at every meal, and she's been letting me. I'm almost too tired to have this conversation.

"Of course your father is a fine man. You know that." She watches me closely. I nod. She looks tired too. She has on a T-shirt that's Dad's, like she's trying to keep him around. She seems as road-killed as Dad over the split, though she's obviously the one who made the decision.

"But he's unhappy," Mom says, "and burdened so much of the time." I'm drawing circles in the bowl of milk with my spoon. She doesn't try to stop me. The way the milk swirls makes me think of what I felt when I reached for Tree Boy, like a current spinning against my hand. Is that really something I would make up?

"And it's as if he's pulled in different directions," she says. "Sometimes suddenly so exhilarated for no apparent reason."

"Did you ask him what was going on with him? Why he's spaced-out or pulled in or whatever he is?" I'm not asking him. I'm a little uneasy asking her.

"Of course I asked. As he said when the three of us talked, he's rethinking everything he was taught. He apparently needs a lot of silence to do that. And he seems to need something bigger than me."

"Bigger?"

She doesn't look at me.

"When you first got together, was he happy then?"

"He was moody, introverted, though not like in the last couple of years. He wasn't so searching back then." A hurt look crosses her face.

Searching for what? I shouldn't ask, since he's obviously searching for something that's not her. Although I'm pretty sure it's not a girlfriend. So what could it be, then? Maybe he doesn't know. The way he's been acting, it seems like it's something inside him. She's rubbing her arms with both hands, like she's trying to get warm. "I guess it was pretty hard for both of you, Mom. Since you're so different."

She lets out a big sigh, as if she has been declared innocent. That was so simple and easy for me to say and such a big deal to her that it makes me sad. Would have been good if I'd said it sooner.

NIGHT AFTER NIGHT I sit here, propped on my bed, trying to do homework, looking at Instagram, not posting anything. I can't possibly post.

Even though he hasn't come back, I sit here thinking any minute Tree Boy will appear. I'm scared he will. It's possible I could stay deluded permanently, sitting here with him, and never come out into the real world again. I might forget that my regular life had ever existed.

Another horrible possibility: something—or someone—truly scary and evil could appear. Why haven't I thought of that before? I ward off the giant wave of fear, force myself to breathe slowly, to think rationally: if it's not real, if I only imagine it, it cannot hurt me.

I close my eyes to prove I'm not afraid.

Open them. Everything looks normal. My same room, backpack on the floor, today's shoes lying on their sides.

Eyes closed again, I breathe slowly.

Jolt to attention, eyes wide. Something just brushed across my face. I felt it. But no one's here. Clock says 3:14 a.m. Light's still on, I must have fallen asleep. Still in my skirt and tights.

Getting off the bed, I give the room another search. He's not here. He could have been, though, and I missed him. No, I'd still be feeling the way he disturbs the air. What am I thinking—disturbs the *air*? I'm the one who's disturbed. I leave the light on, climb under the covers in my clothes, pull the bedspread up to my chin. I think he is real, and all the stuff that's happened is real. But the scariest thought: that's probably how people with schizophrenia feel.

By THIRD PERIOD Advanced Biology mid-morning, my brain is like our compost pile, eggshells and rotting vegetables. Couldn't get back to sleep last night. Now I want to put my head down on the table and pass out. I could say I'm not feeling well. No, I think somebody has told my teachers I'm going through "a difficult period." I don't want to play into that. I resist the label, especially all these weeks from the actual trauma. Also, I need to seem hyper-okay, not a hint of unwell in the head. I need to convince myself.

Yawns keep coming from the deepest part of me. Justin sitting beside me is twisting his chair; the coil under the seat makes a rusty whispery sound that has a nice rhythm.

Teacher voice: "Can someone tell us about the discovery of DNA? How did this come about?"

My dad has discovered things. About the movement of liquids. He should get more credit. The Colvard Ripple? The

Colvard Wave? Sounds good to me—like flavors of frozen yogurt. I put my forehead down for one moment on the cool top of the lab table.

"Darcy?" Teacher voice, directed toward me. Mrs. Moore, who I usually like a lot. "Do you need to go to the infirmary?"

I lift my head. Her glasses make her eyes too large.

"I'm fine," I say. The whole class is looking at me. My face instantly heats. I probably look like I have a fever. Or like one of the stoner kids. "I was up late. Studying."

She nods in that you're-full-of-shit way. Also, her feelings look hurt; this is my passionately favorite subject, and she takes some pride in me—I told her privately about my obsession with tree leaves—and now I'm disappointing her. I want to say I'm sorry, but how? She turns back to the front, her diagram of Nucleotides: Four Types.

The thought flashes, to say out loud: I was studying how a stranger can appear in a tree and in my room and then disappear like vapor. I was studying how to know what's real. But I don't want to hurt her feelings even more. I don't want her to worry about me.

SEEMS like I caught up on sleep at school today, because I stopped being tired as soon as I got home. Afternoon light from the bedroom window is at the angle now where it gets in my eyes. Shifting to get out of the glare, I see him! The boy! Oh my God, it's happening again. Standing near my dressing table, like he's been here the whole past hour I've been sitting here reading. Global warming and giant sequoias— and all the time him standing near me. How could I not notice? That spooks me. I did hear a muffled *whump* sound a while back but thought it was from a car. He's staring at the door that's a little ajar, as if he's never seen a door before. He turns a little and looks straight at me. This time he seems to see me.

This is not real, I tell myself. I need to think clearly, make sense. At the same time, I'm fascinated—amazed! Getting up carefully, I take a step toward him, making no sound at all. Every move in slo-mo. Like walking toward a bird landed on the grass. I'm humming a lullaby-type tune, hoping slow music will put him at ease, will keep me from freaking.

He darts a glance toward the ceiling, as if he can't tell where the music is coming from, which gives me a chance to quickly check out the rest of him without his noticing. He's wearing a sort of tunic, burgundy-colored. It looks a lot like what he had on before, but shorter. As I get closer, the material seems alive, thin living tissue with a rusty glow to it.

He's staring at me now—no question he sees me— intense curiosity, eagerness on his face. I like his face, his narrow chin and wide forehead, his long skinny nose.

"I'm Darcy." I keep my voice slow and level, enunciating deliberately.

He blinks fast like a wind has hit his face. I'll stand here all night if I have to, staring back at him until I understand what's going on.

He makes a low sound, starts to clear his throat. Does it again, like he's testing his voice box, trying it out for the first time. I like it—a deep rumbling guy sound. I want to smile. But no, I have to stay still, composed, not startle him, not let myself be distracted.

What kind of person wouldn't know about voices? About facial expressions? What *is* he? If I were just imagining him, he would know how to talk.

I make a raspy sound, imitating him. He laughs.

Laughs! And his face is so alive and shining. It's like he holds nothing back. Every grain of feeling shows. I'm laughing, too, of course. I can't help it, it's contagious. Relaxing my statue pose, I flop back down onto the side of the bed. He sits, too. We've broken the sound barrier. We settle into silence and I almost relax.

That's the last thing I remember. It seems like two seconds later I'm waking up, fallen over from where I was sitting. The clock says I've been asleep for two hours.

How did this happen? What did I miss? Sitting up, I try to make sense of my hair with my hands. I feel him still here in some form; maybe he can see me.

Knock, knock. Mom sticks her head in the door. Her coming up the stairs must have woken me. She looks surprised. "You took a nap."

"I guess."

"You okay?"

I nod. The grogginess is lifting. I don't feel like talking. I lie back down as soon as the door closes again. The boy is definitely gone. I don't feel his presence at all.

I need to think, replay his whole visit as much as I can. Make sense of it. But my memory has to reach too far to grab hold of all that happened. Or maybe this is a sign my brain isn't working right. I need to remember and get good information—what causes him to show up. I need to know what's going on, scientifically. So far, no common denominator in the moments when he appears. Except maybe different kinds of banging noise?

As Dad is always saying, correlation is not causation. Just because two things happen together doesn't mean one causes the other.

I was baffled yesterday when I finished reading *The Magus*, because it wasn't clear on who and what was real.

I'm completely clear about what happened in my life this afternoon: he was here. I was awake, in my own body, so he has to be real.

CHAPTER

FIVE

T he hall of lockers looks grim. It's late afternoon, not many people still here. Martin is giving me a hard time: "Why did you agree to do this in the first place?"

"I was so happy to get elected. It was a complete surprise." What I don't say: it was the kind of change I need right now, good news in the normal everyday world. Near the stairwell a janitor is starting to mop the floor, the smell of the cleaner like a mix of nail polish remover and vanilla. Weirdly comforting because it's so familiar.

"How could you possibly have won, Darcy? A senior always heads Prom Decorations. Plus, you are not the type. You're not organized or a team leader or—"

"You don't have to be insulting. I might like being the boss of something for a change."

"I'm not being insulting in the least. You don't want to be a committee chair kind of person. How did this happen?"

He's leaning toward me in a worried parent way. He's such a protector.

I sigh. "It was a political fluke. Three of us were nominated. The winner should have been superpower Cissy or Layna but they have the same cool friends, so they split that vote between them. I apparently got all the other votes."

Martin is pondering this. My supporters were like me: probably came to the meeting thinking it was a chance to pass for normal. Lately, connecting with normal has become excruciatingly more important. For obvious reasons.

"I thought I could try out being extroverted and active, Martin. Anyhow, it's only decorating a gym."

He gives me a dubious look. It's prom we're talking about, after all. The prep takes months, almost until the end of the school year. He's right. I should never have agreed to this. But people actually trusting me with something so big-deal-ish in the ordinary world was irresistible.

"I could resign. If a few committee members hate me over it, that would be better than the disaster we're apparently facing."

"We?"

"Of course. If I don't quit, you'll be my first recruit. You obviously know what needs to be done. You can be in charge of bringing in volunteers and delegating jobs."

"I've been fearing this. For the last five minutes." He blows out a puff of air like he's already fed up and exhausted.

"It might be okay, Martin. We could come up with something amazing. We might wind up heroes with decorations everybody'll remember for years."

"They'll be laughing for years."

"But, Martin, my doing this is a way to superglue myself to normal, so nobody can wonder about me, no matter what."

He gives me a strange look. Did I say anything odd? I don't think I did. I have to be careful every second, watch what I say all the time. Otherwise, I might blurt out something impossible to explain away or take back.

"You're probably right, Martin. I should never have agreed." Of course he is, but I was so pleased, so ridiculously validated, by getting elected. It was like they voted me Normal Sane Person. He nods and looks away, like he understands why I, or anybody, would want that.

THE GREEN NUMBERS on the clock say 2:21 a.m. I finally fell asleep after hours of prom committee fears. The loud paper-crumpling sound coming from near my desk must be what woke me. The boy. He's here, in my room. I know it, though it's too dark to see.

I want to jump up, flail around until I find him. But I have to stay cool. Nothing to do but wait for him to show. If I go stumbling around the room or turn on the light, I'll scare him away. Why doesn't he appear? This is so hard. I've been lying here twenty minutes at least, totally tense, wanting him to come and, at the same time, thinking it'd be better if he never showed up again. A pipe rattles somewhere in the bones of this hundred-year-old house, which could be full of all kinds of mysterious beings in addition to this boy. Already there's Mom's "painting muse" she's always talking about. She doesn't see this woman; she just gets ideas popping up in her head and says they come from her hidden guide.

A throat-clearing sound from the dark doorway of my closet! I see nothing. Footsteps, hitting solid on the wood floor. Two. Three. Four. My heartbeat is just as loud. He's slowly moving in my direction. Pauses.

There. His silhouette against the window. He seems to be soaking up moonlight, brightening. My insides have turned to bubbling adrenaline. I hear him breathing. He pulls in each breath, pushes it out, like he has to think about it, remind himself how to do it.

His light is rising, his face visible, as if he's lit by a camp-fire. But the fire has to be coming from him. There's no other possibility; the light from the window is white and cold. Numbers on the radio, nasty green.

Again the throat sound. I copy it, though it doesn't come out the same. His is more animal-ish and male. Moving, moving toward me. With a faint warm haze all around him.

"I'm Darcy," I say, same as last time. Maybe hearing something familiar will let him feel comfortable.

"I'm Darcy," he says. He spoke! I'm sure that's what he said, though it sounded thick. Three syllables, same rhythm. He probably thinks *I'm Darcy* is a word that means hi. Or maybe his saying he's Darcy means he's a creation of my imagination.

I reach to turn on the lamp. That's stupid: he radiates like one of those *luminaria* bags that decorate yards at Christmas. I'm in shadow, which is where I want to be, given how bad I probably look after being asleep for hours. I point to myself: "Dar-cy."

He says it again, this time clearly. Perfectly.

"You," I say. He makes a puzzled face, in slow motion. I point to him. "*Your* name." I say it so it doesn't sound like a question, which seemed to scare him off before.

"Name," he says, and smiles. I fall back against the pillow. His smile is so gorgeous; it's the slow, warm, not-at-all-nervous kind that goes into your eyes all the way to the back and makes you feel flustered.

Now he's sitting straight-backed on the bed. When did he sit? I didn't see it happen. He's wearing that same short burgundy thing. Light seems to slide down from him like water pouring past in a smooth river. Every detail of him makes me question whether any of this could be real.

"Name. Risto," he says.

"Risto," I repeat, to be sure I understand.

He doesn't nod or make a sound, instead sits looking at me with the smile still going in his eyes. Like saying that much means everything's taken care of.

"Risto," I say again. No response. The edges of him blur into the dark, the way he looked in the leaves of the tree.

My feet and ankles go hot. We're touching! He has flopped backward, lying down across the foot of my bed, his mostly bare legs flung out in front of him. Lying across my feet, he feels more like a blast of heat than actual weight.

"Risto. Where are you from?" Am I talking to myself?

His face looks like he's struggling. He repeats my words, once again sounding growly and muffled. "Werrrh aa yooo fuhm."

"From," I say in one clear syllable, as if this will make more sense.

"Farr-uhm," he says again. Like the Christmas song —*pah rum pah pum pum*. I have no idea how to pantomime words like *where* or *who*. Or *how did you get here?*

Then I realize I've been asking him lots of questions, which could spook him. But if he's spookable, that means he's real. It would mean he's a being with emotions completely separate from me. "I don't know how to talk to you." This is so frustrating when he's sitting right in front of me. And he absolutely *is* here. "Okay, maybe you know some other words besides *name*. Here are some you might know. *Boy. Bedroom. Night. Tree.*" A wild shot: "*Heaven. Sky. Magic.*"

"You are speaking in the form of English language," he says, and grins in the most normal way, triumphant, as if he has figured out some knotty problem. I am stunned into temporary silence.

"English! Yes!" I say when I can make my mouth work again. "What is your language?" Now I'm the one who sounds like a foreigner.

"English. It arrived to me when I have heard you speak sufficient number of the words."

"I guess that means you knew it when you were little and when you hear it, it starts to come back to you."

He frowns. "I do not know."

"You do not know?"

"When I hear, this language in me come forward. From the place where languages live, it rises to my mouth. I will say the English better after greatly much speaking." This is exciting; we'll be able to talk. I can find out everything.

An idea for an experiment, a test of his realness, pops into my head. I hand him an empty glass from my bedside table. "Risto, will you put this on my desk, please?" I point, in case he misunderstands. I so want him to pass this test, to be real.

He takes two long steps and puts the glass down over where I'm pointing, then comes back to the end of my bed, flops again across my feet. Propped on one elbow, he lounges, comfortable as can be. His legs look like the track guys who work out running in deep sand. My legs—I don't know if they're there anymore or if they've melted into nothing except the hot feeling.

"I'm curious what language you speak usually."

"No language. I am only beginning."

"No language at all?" I move one foot, testing. His edges are getting pale. He's leaving. "No, no, wait." He dims, seems pulled from the back, growing farther away and fainter and in another second: gone. The dead moonlight lies across the floor, touches the edge of the bed.

Gone!

But he was here. We talked. We touched! I'm sure of it.

Turning on the lamp, seeing the room empty, I check my desk. The glass is still there, where he put it. I knew it would be. Throwing back the covers, I look at my feet. The tops of both are red. Like sunburn. Absolute proof he was here. Double proof—that I'm not imagining things. Instead of worrying about my mental state, I should think of myself as lucky.

Wonderfully lucky.

Unless I'm so over-the-edge that I make red splotches on my skin with my mind, and forget where I put the glass in the first place.

Hopelessness knocks me back on my pillow. Hopeless to think I'll ever know anything for sure again. He seems so real, but how is that possible? Tears leak out of the corners of both eyes and get in my ears and my hair. There's no one I could seriously ask about this. I used to think I was a semi-loner. I was wrong. Now I know what being alone really feels like.

CHAPTER

SIX

The next night I'm reading an econ homework
chapter about determinants of supply and
demand, my eye makeup refreshed like I'm definitely going to see him. I'm being ridiculous. Worse than
ridiculous, I'm acting completely insane. He cannot be real.
Waiting for somebody who cannot be real is proof of insan-
ity. I am slipping.

And it's not just the fact that he appears out of nowhere
—that's not all that makes him impossible. There's the way
he looks gorgeous and alive like nobody else I ever saw in my
life. I keep thinking about that Keats or Byron poem,
changing the "she" to "he": *He walks in beauty like the night /
Of cloudless climes and starry skies; / And all that's best of dark
and bright / Meet in his aspect and his eyes.*

But if I were only imagining him, I'd be able to get him
here any time I wanted. And I can't. Also, I've been doing fine
in the rest of my life, not being any odder than usual anyway,

no more than anyone would whose parents just split. Just a lot of crying, if I let myself think about it, and being irritable, which I have every right to be.

Throwing the book aside, I turn off the light, even though it's not late. Maybe dark works better. I'm tired anyway, probably from going over and over in my mind the question of who is this Risto, why is he showing up?

Voices float up the stairs and hum through the floor. Dad has come over and is downstairs arguing with Mom, although she's the one doing the talking. She seems louder now that I've put down my book. He's quieter than ever these days. I don't know what to make of that.

More than anything, I wish our family and my life had stayed together, all in one piece, not broken in half. They're both so hurt, and so am I. I'll probably spend the rest of my life expecting disaster to strike any minute in some totally unexpected way.

The only good thing about the split is the shock of it flinging me out of my body, showing me a boy with such sweet, honest eyes. That first day, his eyes had more feeling and life in them than most people ever show in their whole lives. And when he landed in my room, he didn't try to hide that he felt confused and scared.

Meeting him, I saw into another realm, a different form of life. How can it not be real? I put my hand into it!

I want to lie here in the dark, uninterrupted by the voices below, and think about Risto. He's no longer Tree Boy; he has a name.

But I keep getting snatches of the argument downstairs. "You have a responsibility...!" Mom's saying. Are they arguing about money? One academic plus one artist. Two homes. One kid. Not poverty, not mega-bucks. Mom does well for an artist. Still, she's not making millions. She does a lot of work she knows won't sell, stuff she passionately needs to do, and tries out new directions as she's "led by the muse."

"You're the one who made this decision, Gail." So it's not about money, it's more personal. I strain to hear more.

From Mom: "You shut down, backed off from me, like I'm untouchable. For so long. What did you expect exactly? Tell me that."

Untouchable? He literally doesn't touch her? Dad now, his voice so much quieter that I can't hear a word.

"Too late," Mom is saying. "I don't know why we're going over all this..."

I don't want to hear it. I'm getting a headache over my left eyebrow. My stomach feels tight. Their voices are dropping. I can't possibly hear. Which is good, because I wasn't going to be able to stop myself from listening.

CHARLOTTE's kitten heels clack on the slate stones of the path up to Jared's house as we head, closer and closer, toward the front door standing open. It's Friday night after Thanksgiving, which was dismal, vegan turkey with the family of one of Mom's New Agey friends. And now this party: My heart is full of dread.

"Extremely loud," I point out—about the party, not her shoes. She doesn't hear me. Anybody could hear the gang inside from three houses down the sidewalk: a tinkly roar with the occasional yell or playful scream. Three girls I never saw before spill out the side door into the open garage. From the look of them, Charlotte's dressed right: scoop-neck black leotard and a real-looking fake tattoo of a mermaid. She offered to pick out what I should wear; I shouldn't have refused. I look like I'm dressed for school or a club car wash: jeans and an ordinary long-sleeved tee. And no jacket in spite of the air feeling like forty degrees and damp because she said it would be too much trouble to keep up with.

"Come on," she says, grabbing my wrist like I'm a child.

"You are the bossiest person." She really is bossy. This is her strength and her weakness. Like me minding my own business is both good and bad about me.

"Well, you're walking slower and slower."

"I wasn't invited. You should never have talked me into this." We are on the front steps. Jared lives with his aunt and uncle, who are hardly older than we are. They let him do anything, even when they're in town.

"Everybody's invited," she says in her most absolutely-sure voice. "You need to get out more. You've gotten seriously spacey."

"This party is the penalty for spaciness?" She's right, though, about my recent peculiarness. I'm not a person who can afford to get any more out-there. Which is why I agreed to do this. I need to seem more connected. I need to keep my life in the real world.

We walk in without ringing the doorbell. The foyer is darker than the front yard with its streetlamp. Charlotte weaves us into the crowd in the living room, squealing greetings in every direction. She's good at this. Parties that feel slightly dangerous make me nervous. People are packed almost too close to talk. I look past whoever I'm jammed up against. Kids are semi-dancing. And smoking. I'll go home smelling like cigs. A few feet away, a tall guy is trying to crush a drink can with his teeth.

"Jax!" a girl calls out to him. "You can do it." All I see of her is a splotch of light from the kitchen on dark straight hair.

"No hands, Jax," someone else says. He jolts forward as if he's been bumped. The can pops out of his mouth and drops.

"Where'd it go?" A guy's voice. "Grab it. It's got to be worth something on eBay. Jax licked it."

Jax is a basketball player. "Is this a contest or something?" I say to the boy standing closest. "With the can?" It's Horton Godfrey, who sat near me in Spanish last year.

Horton gives me a blank look. "Uh, no." He looks away, takes a swig from his own can.

I hate this party.

"Excuse me," I say to the back I'm pressed against on the other side. "Can I get by you? Need to get over where the drinks are." Nobody hears or responds. The crowd keeps shifting, making little openings I can squeeze through.

Omigod. Against the far wall, next to the cooler. A guy who looks like Risto, yet wearing human clothes. His face is mostly turned away. His hair, though! His curls! It has to be him. No, not in the middle of a loud party. I have to see his face. Up on my toes, leaning far to the side. He's turning in the wrong direction. Crap!

From behind me: "Need a hoist?"

"Martin! You're here." His knit cap is pulled partway over

his ears. He looks completely relaxed in the middle of this party, which feels like a minor betrayal. It's very much unlike him and makes me wonder what he's up to.

"Passing through," he says.

"You smell like beer. I thought you were in training." That hat is so wrong on him. Knowing him, he wore it to be warm.

"Not at the moment."

"Well, I think the beer altered your vibes. I had no idea you were here."

"We should run a few tests sometime on your vibes. That could be my senior project: find out how reliable your flakey intuition is."

Flakey reminds me: How could I have forgotten Risto, even for a moment? I can't believe I looked away. Peering around Martin, I get a clear view of the location. The boy who looked exactly like him is not there. That person is completely gone.

Martin laughs. "Got your eye on somebody?"

"Sort of. Not exactly."

"I sense a love object. What have you not told me?"

So much I haven't told him and he's standing there completely trusting me. "Martin, you know you're yelling?" I glance around to see who's listening. A splash hits the side of my leg. A drink, I hope. It's cold, so it has to be.

He leans down, puts his mouth against my hair and semi-roars, "If we don't yell, we won't hear each other." His breath in my ear gives me a shiver. In the corner of my eye, I see Horton watching all this. Horton, who cold-shouldered me, is still standing by himself, while I'm successfully partying.

Beyond Horton, Risto is back again. He looks me straight in the eye for a fraction of a second and knocks the air right out of my lungs. He's here. He saw me. For one instant. Now he's back to listening to a clump of guys talking. Do they know he's there? I'm not sure they do. But he looks at each one who speaks in a way that nobody else here looks at anybody, like each guy is somebody he admires and cares about and he wouldn't be embarrassed to say so.

"Who are you staring at?" Martin says. I can't look away to answer. "Darcy? I'm seriously neglected here."

I fumble a hand onto Martin's arm. "In a minute," I say. Risto is wearing an old-fashioned red golf cardigan, like he's in costume, except for his face that hides nothing. There's the faintest brightness around him, or that could be my imagination.

What do I do? Knock people down racing over there? He knows I'm here.

"You should have brought yourself a folding ladder," Martin says, "to get a full 360 of the crowd."

A big blocky head and shoulders blocks my view as Kenny Broughton lumbers past. Again, Risto is gone. Not in sight anywhere in the room. I do see Charlotte, smushed against Davis Perez, who she came here to see.

"You are acting strange!" Martin says at full party volume, as a phone call causes the room to suddenly quiet so the caller won't know there's a party. Jared's aunt insists on keeping a landline. A couple of guys near us laugh: at me, I'm sure, since Martin has yelled out to everybody that I'm strange. The phone call is nothing. The noise level rises again.

Martin is saying something, I don't know what. The music feels like it's getting louder until it isn't music anymore, more like waves breaking, closer and closer together.

Risto is somewhere near, I can tell. The crowd heat is leaking out of the room, washed away by the sound.

All is suddenly quiet, the party far away, and now I'm hearing traffic off in the distance—as if I'm outside the house, but how could that happen?

Risto is beside me. Just the two of us. We're on the front lawn, the damp grass shiny under the streetlight as we're stepping down onto the sidewalk like two normal people. Taking a walk in the cold night air. I don't need to figure anything out right now while this is happening, only pay close attention. Make sense of it later—so unbelievable...

"Perhaps we will dine together," Risto says. It's the first time he has spoken tonight. Sounds like he's using a phrase book for tourists. He touches his hand on the lower part of my back. It feels better than anything...

The night around us contorts. Sparkles in the sidewalk come closer, the air thicker in some places than others. Am I falling? I reach for Risto's arm, and it's like I've grabbed a moving train, nearly yanks my arm out of the socket. I can't let go, and my hand is so hot. Thunder roars all around us again.

I'm sitting at a table, and Risto is taking a seat across from me, a waiter beside us laying down menus. Risto—I like his name, I like thinking it—Risto looks more beautiful close-up in the light. He has those thick black eyebrows and shining dark eyes. No stubble like a lot of guys have. Even clean-shaven, the shadow of his beard is faintly bluish.

He smiles at everything he sees around us, such a happy relaxed look on his face. "We are come to this fiesta."

"We're at Taverna Agora," I say. "It's about ten blocks from my house."

An armload of dinners sails by at eye level, carried by another waiter. Risto's face shines with happiness: "Pompano," he says.

The waiter pauses, says, "Tonight's special. You know your fish. Unusual."

"Of course," Risto says. "It is a creature of the water." The man looks like he's trying not to laugh as he moves on.

Wait a second! This is important! Another person can see Risto and hear him. I'm not the only one. So this is Proof-I'm-Not-Deluded Number 3. Right after my sunburned feet and the glass of water on my desk.

"Risto, how did we get here?"

"I choose to come to you." He says it happily, like he expected me to know that much all along. And he didn't even hesitate at answering a question.

"To come to me?" I was only asking about getting to the restaurant, but this is huge, what he's saying.

"Yes. Across distance, I have felt you, your spirit, like a tree. I hear so many times your spirit-voice like airs that whisper in the leaves."

He chose me. He came and found me.

"I come and I wait very long," he says, "then you are with me. I see you, so daring and also full of quietness." His face radiates joy, full-force happiness that he's not even trying to hide. The warmth in his eyes overwhelms me even more than what he's saying. It's the most beautiful thing I've ever seen.

"I'm so glad you waited." It's all I can manage to get out when my emotions are traffic- jammed in my chest and my throat.

We both get shy and look around the restaurant. When I glance over at him again, I see him staring hard at a spot somewhere behind me. He looks confused, worried.

"What, Risto?"

He shakes his head. "A being watches me," he says.

"A being?" I twist around to look but see no one watching.

"She is gone now. Woman spirit, very judging. Taking my measure. As if she will make some decision."

"Who is she? Why was she judging you?"

"I do not know."

"What does she look like?" I'm starting to picture horror movie faces.

"Clothing from human life, long blue skirting. She is strong. Her middle stout. She knows dust and soils of Earth, I think, her face more old than you. Brow is stern. "

"But she's not human?"

"No, not at this time." This gives me a chill. He looks surprised, says, "It is not to fear."

I want to trust him. And what else can I do? But I don't like the thought of some *being* lurking.

Our food arrives. Risto eats like a normal person. When we talk again it's about ordinary stuff, mostly him asking me questions about every detail he sees or hears, as if he's never imagined anything like it before. And I'm trying to seem daring and full of quietness at the same time, while I'm explaining what is ribeye and what is cocktail.

Something jars my shoulder.

"Darcy." Martin's voice is in my ear. The room, somewhere in the party house, is mostly dark. I'm sitting on the floor, knees pulled up to my chest, leaning back against the wall. When I slowly straighten out, my legs feel stiff.

"Come on, Darcy. Charlotte left a long time ago. I've gotten us a ride."

Risto is gone. I'm at this party in a back room of the house. Martin's pulling at my arm, trying to get me up.

"I can walk."

"You couldn't two hours ago. You were like a zombie when I hauled you in here. All this time passed out. How much have you had?"

"I had zero. Nothing." We cross the main party room. Over in a circle of lamplight, Horton is sprawled on a chair, dead to the world. Mostly empty, the place looks like an ordinary living room littered with plastic cups. It smells like the closet at school where volleyballs are stored.

"I wasn't back there two hours. It wasn't that long. I wasn't back there at all." He's right, though. My body was in the back room, at the same time another version of me—my spirit and all my senses—was out with Risto.

Martin doesn't bother to look at me. "Come on," he says, hustling us out the door.

SEVEN

The inside of this part of Crabtree High School is like an airport, wide and low with a big swoop of windows at one end. Except we don't fly away, we keep circulating. Round and round, through the school day routine in this long wandering flat building. All day people I barely know have been looking at me. Could be I'm exaggerating. But I like it.

All I did was park my ordinary body in a back room while the rest of me went elsewhere. As far as anyone who was in the party room knows, what happened is Martin half-carried me back there because I was looking sort of passed out. Not the biggest deal in the world. Like I'm the only person who ever disappeared into the back of a party house for a while. But it's not what people are used to from me.

I somewhat expected the attention today, wore my most body-con dress, horizontal stripes, giving them something to look at. And after all, Risto chose me, which makes me feel naturally deserving of attention.

Martin said at lunch that I'm walking around looking different—confident and like I know a secret—and that's what people are noticing. Charlotte said we'll talk this afternoon, in complete detail. I haven't told her about Risto, of course. The situation is too delicate, too unbelievable. All day she's been texting me, wanting to know: *WWY??* Where was I? I was in two places. Can't lie to my friend about where I was. Can't explain either, even to myself.

What would I say? In a calm reasonable voice, I could start gradually and tell her: the shock of my parents' split took me across some kind of border into a new world. Well, probably not new, but one I never would have discovered or imagined.

Do I believe that? I think maybe I do.

Mom's sautéing mushrooms and onions, the whole house smelling like butter, when I hear Charlotte come in the door downstairs. I can't tell her what she wants to know about the party. She clatters up the stairs to my bedroom, throws her purse down, and flings herself across the bed, the exact place where Risto was only a few days ago. She looks at me intently. "You don't look hung over."

I don't stir from where I'm leaned against the headboard. "I'm not."

"Then what?"

"Where were *you*, Charlotte? Who'd you go off with?"

"You're changing the subject. Your mother asked me to stay for dinner, by the way."

"She's on a cooking jag."

"Who would have expected that?"

"I know. You should stay."

"Can't. Anyway, the party. Do you remember Martin carrying you? You'd slumped against a wall, like you'd gone to sleep standing up. Martin carried you to the back like a lifeguard with a nearly-drowned person. You were draped across his back."

"Don't remember. He told me about it."

"There's probably a video online by now, which would spike up your reputation."

"No, I'd have heard."

"You're being extremely withholding, Darcy. Also, you've hardly said a word about your parent crisis since it first happened, which is not healthy. And it's not good if you drink half a beer or whatever and black out."

"I don't know how to explain. I really can't." I keep worrying that the whole story will burst out of me, no matter who's around. It's not that I don't trust Charlotte, but she's so talkative and she could say the wrong thing at just the wrong moment without meaning to at all.

"Well, if you don't want to talk to me, fine. I'm not going to pry into your business. If you're mad or something—I know, you're pissed at me for getting you to go to Jared's. You're blaming me for whatever you did?"

"It's not that."

"What is it?"

I'm dying to talk about him. If I speak at all, I'll blurt it out.

"Okay," she says, after a moment, "what was happening when you started waking up? Were you and Martin doing anything? A lot of people think he has an in-love-type-thing about you. Of course you know that."

"Nothing happened with Martin."

"I don't know how you can be totally sure you remember. Were your clothes all twisted around, any different from before?"

"No, and I would know."

"You don't seem to know much else." She grabs at her bag that dumps Jolly Ranchers, hair ties and Tampax all over the bedspread. Also, her signature Secret Orchid body mist has leaked. Probably a guy like Risto doesn't wear aftershave, whatever type of guy he is. I don't know, haven't gotten close enough yet.

"Charlotte, I can't talk about him."

Him?! How did that word get out of my mouth? Exactly what I was scared I'd do!

"Him? Martin? You talk about him all day." She has the edgy tone she uses when she thinks Martin has more influence over me than she does. They both think I'm somebody they need to look out for and manage, like I'm a total baby. A new thought changes her face. She's looking at me in the penetrating way my mother does. "Darcy, who is 'him'?"

"A guy I met. I might not ever see him again. I never know." My skin feels hot all the way up into my hair.

"But he's amazing, right? I can see from your expression.

You've honestly got a thing for him. Oh, I knew it! Did I see him at Jared's?"

"If you did, you'd have noticed. He has fabulous black curls, five-ten-ish with a big, wide chest and shoulders, wearing a dumb-looking sweater." I want her to say she saw him. "He always looks relaxed, Charlotte, like he's never been worried about anything. Even when he's serious, he seems like he's about to smile." I could go on and on: his heavy eyebrows, warm brown eyes—that's it, that's what gets me: the right-up-front heart-warmth of him, not just how gorgeous he is.

She shakes her head. "Didn't see him. Who is he? Like, his name? He's obviously not from school—"

"Definitely not."

In the quiet of the room, I hear Mom banging around downstairs. What would it hurt to tell Charlotte a little? More than anybody else, she could appreciate—

Louder bang. I turn toward the door. What is Mom doing?

Charlotte gasps, an inhaled shriek.

"What?"

"Did you see?" Her face looks sincerely shocked; she is not being dramatic.

Heat rushes all over me as I frantically look everywhere. Nothing. "Did I see what, Charlotte?"

"There was somebody in here, for one second. I swear to you there was!" She has sprung off the bed, turning and turning to see everything in the room. The look she gives me —for one passing second—is insistent that she isn't making this up.

"I believe you."

"You have a ghost in your house, I'm serious." She walks back and forth across the throw rug, combing the air with her hands like she's searching for him.

"What did the ghost look like?"

"A guy with black hair. So fast it was hard to see."

Charlotte saw Risto! This completely proves I didn't make him up, no further proof needed.

She stares at me. "It's obvious you know what I'm talking about. This has happened before."

"Yeah, it sort of has. Happened before."

"The way he vanished, he seemed surprised."

She saw enough to notice his reaction. Now she's scared him away. "He didn't expect to see anybody but me."

"Darcy, you have to tell me everything immediately." She has stopped searching the room, sits back down but is tense, like she's still ready to pounce.

"You can never say anything about this to anyone."

"I promise. A thousand percent."

"It's not like I understand what's going on," I say. "He shows up. I don't know how it happens. He tells me hardly anything."

"He talks?"

I nod. "But if I ask him anything much, he evaporates."

"Oh my God!" She lets out a long breath like she's trying to get calm. "This is too amazing. But," her expression turns to worried, "it can't be true." Now she looks like she's mad at me, as if I've done something bad to her.

"But you saw him, Charlotte."

I can almost see her mind clicking, trying to come up

with an explanation. There's no way around the the fact that she saw him.

"You think we're both seeing things, Charlotte?" She looks away. I don't stop. "If we were both hallucinating, wouldn't we be seeing different stuff? If we're both seeing the same thing, then..." I stop because the conclusion is so obvious. And I am so glad she saw him, even if it did scare him momentarily. This completely nails down that he's real, the time I've spent with him—it's all real.

"It's not possible," she says.

"Okay, well, you let me know when you figure it out," I say, as she somberly starts gathering her bag to leave.

"Your father would like you to call him," Mom says when I walk in after a stultifyingly routine Friday at school. Now and then a day feels like a long stretch of interstate with the same scenery start to finish.

When I reach him, he's in his lab, which has an echoing hollow background sound, unlike his cozy crammed-full office. I can picture where he is, near the long series of glass boxes for studying what currents do to sand—looks like the fish section of PetSmart without the fish. Again, I push out of my mind the stuff I overheard Mom say to him.

"Darcy! I was thinking you might be interested in going bowling."

"Bowling? Are you serious?" One thing I didn't expect about the new life was "activities." Next it'll be historic sites.

"I am. It'll be seriously fun!" He sounds hyper-energetic, which means he's feeling really down and trying to hide it.

Of course I'll go bowling with him. I'd play ice hockey if it would help.

Inside Kingpin Lanes there's a constant loud hum behind the knock of bowling pins falling; sounds like his lab, a hundred times magnified.

"Size six, right?" he says when we step up to the counter.

"I would never have guessed you knew my shoe size. You don't even notice clothes." His knowing makes me want to lean my forehead against the side of his arm where it's close to my face.

"I bought those cowboy boots we gave you last Christmas." He hands me a pair of red and green rental beauties, so ugly they distract me from sad thoughts of a Christmas that's coming again fairly soon.

We get a lane. I choose a ball that's white marbled with blue.

"You want any instructions?" he says. "I've practiced a few times."

Dad has practiced bowling. With who? "I've got it under control," I tell him. I've been watching these guys run with the ball, curtsy as they let it go. I stand still, hold the ball prayerfully, like the rest of them. Next, run and hurl it. It thunks down onto the floor, careens sideways into the gutter.

"It's all right, sweetheart!" Dad calls out. "It's a lot harder than it looks." When I flop down next to him, he puts an arm around my shoulders. Guess I'm not "untouchable" like Mom, although I now notice that he seems only half here, half paying attention.

Some kid drops a ball in the next lane. Sounds like the

air-slam in my chest when Risto arrives. "Dad, have you studied things like people appearing out of nowhere? Starting to see someone you couldn't have imagined?"

I shouldn't have brought this up. I blurted it out without thinking.

He slowly pulls his arm away, shakes his head. "I'm not seeing anyone. We told you, there were no third parties involved."

As my grandmother says, I don't know whether to laugh or cry. I was right; he's not completely listening. Though Dad has always missed the conversational point at times, regardless of his academic smarts. "No, I mean like a hologram, somebody who looks real."

"Holograms are everywhere, on credit cards for example. Light scattered by an object reconstructed. Why do you ask?"

"I ran across the idea." I can't possibly explain why I want to know. Dad sits staring off into space like he's thinking about third parties. I feel mucky unhappiness rising in both of us.

From behind me, a woman's voice: "Dr. Colvard!"

Dad stands. "Hi, Nell!"

Nell, obviously one of his students at some point, has long black hair that swings and shines. She looks like she wants to hug him. He takes a quick step back, introduces her to me. Is she another untouchable? Or is he being professional and careful?

When she leaves, I check his face. Unreadable, but what did I expect? He's like that a lot lately. I haven't even seen the new place he finally got—his "room" as he calls it. He gets up to bowl again, though I don't think it's his turn. He knocks them all down in two tries. A spare.

"Beautiful," I say, clapping, when he slings himself back into his chair to write down his score. He looks somewhat cheerful again. I won't ask about his room, or anything else. Instead I'll give him a house-warming present next time I see him, a plant, something upbeat and splashy, like a painted-leaf begonia....

A rush of noise: middle schoolers are flooding the adjoining batch of chairs for the next lane. A girl with gleaming lip gloss is giving a boy a noogie. He grabs back at her. Lots of screaming. No untouchables. Middle school seems like a different lifetime, a much better one on the home front, back when my father was an understandable guy, who was nothing more worrisome than over-serious, back when my family was unbreakable.

CHAPTER

EIGHT

ll around us, the noise of the school Student Union
clatters at party volume. It's one o'clock, busiest
time of the day in here, and Martin is telling me
he's worried about me. "Your partying blackout or whatever
it was isn't the only strange thing about you lately, Darcy.
You seem stoned a lot of the time, like nothing's worth bothering with, everything's beneath you."

I laugh. He doesn't.

"Oh, Martin, I've always seemed dazed or daydreamy,
out-of-it. You've been telling me that for years. Remember
that day I came to school in mismatched shoes?" I run my
hand over his buzz cut, the part I can reach. "There's no need
at all to worry." I pull my hand back fast, because he has a
seriously irked look, like he thinks I'm being condescending,
somehow insulting. I didn't mean it, I was just being affectionate and reassuring. I hate how I screw up emotional
stuff.

He backs off and turns away before I can try to explain what I can't explain. So I'm left alone here, among the various social clumps, after driving away my friend. Fighting off the fear that I've somehow really messed up. Okay, I'll make this a test. Can I handle standing here by myself in the middle of the Student Union at lunch?

Counting seconds: one alligator, two alligator ...

My conclusion after nearly a minute: I can do this. Not that I'm completely comfortable and confident, but I'm okay. I'm sure it's because of Risto choosing me out of all the world —a few months ago I couldn't have done this. Or maybe it's not confidence at all, instead I'm standing here torturing myself, feeling bad about Martin.

On the positive side, though: I'm getting new respect from people since my supposedly wild party experience, including a sort of awe coming from Charlotte. Since she learned about Risto, she's been a bit subdued, watchful, the way you might be with someone who's seriously ill. She can't think I'm hallucinating, though, because she saw him herself.

"French fry?" Bink, who is always so tall, has come up beside me holding what's left of his lunch—ketchup-smeared mess—toward me.

"Charming," I say, staring at the soggy fries.

"I am, aren't I?" Bink Halliday is actually aiming his fire at me. I'd look around to see who's noticing, but that would be shallow. It's not that I'm so wowed by Bink, but he is so famously cool and it's hard to be completely immune to people's opinions.

"Well, maybe a little." Weak response. Not charming.

His turn to say something. He's concentrating on eating fries.

"So," I say, "I have to go drop off some stuff before the bell."

"You're a serious girl."

"Because I need to drop off stuff?" I'm starting to move away. Probably he's heard the recent reports that I'm not as serious as everyone thought. Wow! He's walking with me. He'll find out I have no stuff to drop off, that I made that up because I was nervous. This attention is nice. I want it to end before I have a chance to mess it up.

"What do you have this period?" he says, not answering my question. I have to remember this technique.

"Numbers. Pre-calc."

"Like I said: serious."

"Taking math doesn't make me serious. It's required."

"There you go, doing what's required."

"I give up," I say, though I hate it when I'm viewed as a rule-follower. Risto wouldn't think of me that way. Although I don't know what he thinks about anything. I don't know the most basic facts about him. Except he travels mysteriously, has a major knack for languages and such a sweet warm personality. And he looks at me as if he sees everything about me and is thrilled and delighted.

Bink is making a turn that I'm not, he's already six feet away. "See you, Serious."

"Sirius is a star," I say. He laughs. I can't believe it: I successfully bantered. It popped out. I didn't think about it. This is what comes from my new confidence.

Here's my classroom. It's empty, I'm early. Dropping

onto my desk the books I pretended I had to drop off, I collapse into a seat, feeling both revved up and exhausted. And worried. Because Martin is mad at me and I'm pretty sure I know why. The huge stuff I'm not telling him is getting between us. I hate hurting his feelings, cannot let us get distant from each other. I can't handle my life being broken into more pieces.

SHANEQA WALKS into the prom meeting late, carrying a mirrored disco ball-type thing that hides her whole upper half. She puts it down on the closest table.

Leaning against the front of the teacher's desk, I stand in front of everybody trying to act like a normal decorating committee leader-in-chief. Already today, my anti-prom smudgy-eyeliner friend Drake texted me his "favorite link" for buying black crepe paper and horror party supplies; I sent back a "ha-ha" emoji.

"Where'd you get that?" Bink says to Shaneqa. He's added himself to this committee of mostly girls.

"She got it at Year 1970," says Nan Prioli who is way too cool to be on a committee chaired by me. Bink grins meaningfully at Nan and waits for her to notice him, while Shaneqa explains how she found it at a swap shop and there are only a few mirrors missing.

"What if we got a lot of those," Martin says. "We could have dozens hanging at different heights and some on the floor. It could be a light show the whole time."

"I like it," I say in an authoritative way. "We could blow

mist into the whole place so the shine gets sort of soft and diffuse."

"Too skating rink," Nan says.

"I'm googling mist blower. " Bink jabs away at his little screen. "Here's an Italian company. 'Orchards, pesticide, livestock ...' "

"Pesticide! The blower would have to be cleaned out extremely thoroughly," Nan says, twirling a strand of her hair.

A new guy I don't know is telling everybody about ways we could use some special earth-moving equipment to make the gym floor into dramatic new terrain. A bulldozer in the gym? Layna wants to do something with mermaids. Dress as one, probably.

Now somebody's talking about movie-quality snow. But prom is in May.

"Too much like detergent," I tell them. I may have interrupted, but we're really on the wrong track here. "No fake snow. Only real stuff. Real clouds. Real...." With everybody watching, I don't know how to say it. Magic? "Real mysteries. Like maybe shadowy shapes of people moving through the crowd. Sometimes you can see them and then they're gone and you don't know how they got there or where they went....Spirit-creatures....Beautiful, mysterious, you don't know how they could even exist."

Nobody's saying anything. I went too far, let myself forget where I am.

The classroom is so quiet I hear the rattle of the janitor's broom cart out in the hall. I was only trying to get people thinking, to expand the possibilities. I wasn't suggesting real ghosts for prom decorations; that would be preposterous. They're looking at me, Martin especially, his face hard to read. Somebody starts doing the *The Twilight Zone* tune.

"Okay wait. It's possible," Martin says. "We use a projector, throw images. It could be high-impact." People start talking, Martin egging them on. Martin cuts a glance in my direction: to say, in case I don't know, that he's covering for me, for my spacey weirdness. I send him a thank you with my mind.

I keep my mouth shut and the discussion rolls on to New Orleans and Spanish moss and balconies and it starts getting late and I am so ready to be out of here. "Well," I say, "maybe that's enough ideas for now. I'm going to declare this meeting adjourned." Then Martin is on his feet so fast it's like a track meet. He doesn't wait for me. He's the first person out the door.

SITTING IN SECOND PERIOD, all I can think about is yesterday's embarrassing meeting where we made no progress. And my *Twilight Zone* moment: now everybody knows I'm even weirder than they thought. Well, good. Fine with me, except for Martin.... Of course I texted him as soon as I got home. No answer from him last night or this morning. I'm a little worried.

At least I know I'll see him after this class. We're always going in opposite directions in the same hall between second and third periods. I have everything ready to leap up and get ahead of the traffic. The instant the bell rings, I'm moving, dodging elbows.

There he is, approaching our regular intersection. I wave. He doesn't seem to see me. I pick up speed. He doesn't stop. Instead he hurries around the corner before I can get there.

I don't understand. He thinks I've gotten odd in a seriously bad way? He's still bothered by my zone-out at the party? He never ran from me before. There's something he's not saying, that much is obvious. Could he have stuff going on that *he's* not telling *me*? He's always told me everything, but then I've always told him everything, up until now.

Hours later, sitting with Civilizations homework in study hall, I run it all through my head: stuff that could be making Martin mad at me.

1. He sort of carried me out of a party room—he's never had to do that before.

2. He didn't understand why I'd even be on the Decorating Committee, much less the chairperson.

3. In the meeting when I said how I thought we should decorate with real stuff, real mysteries, he looked embarrassed to know me, and angry.

4. Maybe at lunch a few days ago he thought I was patting him on the head in a condescending way. Or I wasn't taking his complaint seriously.

That's all I can think of. No, wait—of course it's not. The biggest thing of all is I haven't told him about Risto. Probably he can tell there's something I'm not telling him. He is after all a *sensitivo,* what I call a guy who is more emotionally plugged-in than the average one. Obviously that's it and I just don't want it to be because it's too hard to handle. The other items are only making it more clear to him that there's something he doesn't know.

I have to talk to him. Now. This cannot wait.

But what can I say? I can't tell him. He'd be completely convinced I need help. It would be like telling scientist Dad.

I don't need help, not the kind he would think. What I need is for things to be normal and good between him and me, like they've been forever.

At the door of his sixth period class, he almost walks past me. I grab him by a handful of his shirt sleeve. Even though I don't know what I've come to say.

"Martin, please."

He stops. At least there's that.

"Martin, I'm upset."

"So am I. There's stuff going on with you. I don't know what it is."

I was right. He does see. "Martin, I can't—"

"Yeah, I know. Whatever it is, 'you can't' or won't. So I gotta go." He pulls away from me, leaves me standing beside the door in the almost-empty hall. Classes are starting. I'll be late. I don't care.

I lean against the wall.

Have I traded the way we were for Risto? And where is Risto anyway? He might not ever show up again. It's not right to have to make a choice. I love Martin. He's been my friend for a thousand years. Maybe this is scaring me more than it should, but we've never had an argument.

CHAPTER
NINE

Mom has a date. I can*not* believe it. She tried to deny it, off-handedly mentioning yesterday that "a friend" would be coming over. Of course she tried to downplay it: it's too soon. Only ten weeks since Separation Day, and I get home from school and find the crystal wine glasses sitting on the counter and a little wheel of brie cheese set out to get runny. While I'm staring at this still life, she comes downstairs, smelling all Prada by Prada, not a whiff of turp or linseed oil on her from her studio.

"Who is he?" I say when she hits the last step. When I see she's looking embarrassed, I know it's going to be bad.

"A friend," she says again. "You may have met him in passing."

"If he's a friend, I would know him."

"Not necessarily."

"It's way too early for you to be inviting some guy into our house, Mom." Remembering her accusation to Dad—"

you act like I'm untouchable"—only makes this worse. "What's his name?"

"Darcy, my timing is up to me. I'm in charge of who I have a conversation with. You have not become the parent around here." I remain sternly silent. She says: "His name is Webb. Llewellyn."

My face falls into my hands. Oh, God! I'm bent double with the shock of this; I'm not exaggerating: "I can't believe it." My cheeks are scorching. The worst possible ... "Tony Llewellyn's father." Hostile Tony who hates me. "I can't believe you're doing this. You have no idea ..." I head for the stairs.

"Darcy!" she yells after me.

"I'm going to my room, if you don't mind. I have to 'process' this news."

MR. LLEWELLYN. Did she think twice about this? No, she didn't. She doesn't process, no matter what her therapist says; she takes action.

I've seen this Webb person exactly once, when he came to Career Day last year. He's a Jaguar dealer, showed up at school like he was dressed for a drink on a movie star's yacht. Soft loafers, a linen sport coat and black tee. He talked to our class about tariffs—wandering, obviously, off the topic of careers. I can't imagine Tony loved his coming to school. More urgently: does Tony know about this date tonight? This elder-tryst?

God, let it be a one-time thing.

Don't let Tony know.

I can picture it: Tony Llewellyn as my step-brother. In the same house, using the same bathroom, where I could never leave a single personal item. The possibilities are hideously embarrassing.

In addition to being unfriendly, Tony seems semi-dangerous. Martin heard he's seriously into online gambling. If you so much as say hi to him, he acts like you're trying to sell him Girl Scout cookies.

Mom and I would wind up being the ones to move in with them. Their house is no doubt bigger. Tony would arrive for his weekends with his father and stare at me with pure loathing because of being forced to have someone as odd and barely popular as me for a step.

I could refuse to go. This is my home, and I won't leave it. My chest hurts at the thought.

She's still in the kitchen when I go downstairs, doing things that don't need doing. Like sorting the big forks from the little forks, waiting for the Creature-in-Slip-Ons to arrive. The wine glasses still sit empty.

"First of all," I say. She jumps. I'm still getting used to Mom being nervous. "You can put away your artsy wine. This guy is going to want a martini." Maybe she already knows what he drinks. That had better not be true.

"This doesn't concern you," she says, all starchy.

"The main thing is: I'm not moving to their house."

Her face goes sweet and warm, which suddenly makes my throat tight. "Oh, sweetheart, nobody's moving."

I refuse to cry. "You say that, Mom, but I know how impulsive you are."

In a millisecond, the look of sympathy is gone. She sucks

in a breath and launches into me. She "experiences me as disrespectful." I've heard it before. The doorbell rings. No way to get upstairs without passing the front door. I run, ducking through the foyer, flying up the stairs to my room. I don't care if Mr. Jaguar is peeking through the little window-pane and watching. I don't care if he hears me. I will not be introduced.

"I'm not moving from this house!" I yell at Mom. There's a catch in my voice when I throw the words down the stairs.

I grab my phone and put a pillow over my head so I won't hear when he comes in, and then the murmurs and footsteps and Mom's rippling laugh from below. I speed-dial Char-lotte; if I text, I'll still be able to hear them. She picks up, first ring. "Mom has a guy downstairs. Already. He's the worst in so many ways."

Charlotte starts madly spinning off questions at the other end: "Who? Who? Could you tell how well they know each other? What does he look like?"

"He looks like somebody I need to get rid of."

CHAPTER

TEN

I t's after midnight before I hear Webb leave and I finally get to bed. The house is quiet. I already know it's impossible to sleep. Too much to think about and try not to think about. The sheet feels like miles of fabric all tangled around my feet. If Risto were here, my mind would be calm.

That's when I see him, sitting in my desk chair, lit by the moonlight coming through the windows. I could tell myself he appeared because I thought of him, but I've been thinking about him for days and that hasn't caused him to show up. He picks up my phone, turns it over and over in his hands. He checks out my block of sticky-notes, then the scissors. Makes a mark on his hand with a highlighter. Turns and looks over his shoulder and smiles at me.

"Risto." I keep my voice low.

"I learn of you at your desk, MyDarcy. While you have your sleep." His voice has such sweetness, like his whole heart is speaking to me. Regular day-time people aren't like this. If they were, everybody would fall in love with everybody.

"I practice at your desk seat to be like you, a student person." I think that's what he said. He wants to be a student? He tells me his feelings, but not why or how anything works. "I am making more understanding of you," he says, "then I can bring for you all of the best happiness." That makes me smile: the best happiness. I so want to stay awake and be with him, but my eyes are sleepy. I'm tired. With him here, I'm so relaxed. I may be fading....

THE ROOM IS LIGHT AGAIN, my phone alarm blasting. Crap! Morning! No Risto in sight.

Clothes. School. Homeroom. The whole week-long day ahead.... I hit snooze to get a few more minutes sleep, but my eyes won't close. The room is so bright, I give up, get up and get dressed. Wasn't the forecast gray-sky-chance-of-rain?

Downstairs, Mom is drinking coffee. She motions for me to sit; she already has the milk on the table and the box of Lucky Charms and a bowl. "Darcy, I have a question. About last night."

I wait—agitated—though my insides feel heavy and tired.

"Were you talking on the phone late in the night?"

"No." I stare in actual surprise. She's looking so suspicious—and Risto and I said only a few words.

"Okay."

I want to say: why do you ask? But that might make her

suspect me more, like I'm trying to find out what kind of incriminating evidence I need to hide better.

I'm relieved when I finally get out the door, heading toward the privacy of school, where I can sit and think about him. His sitting quiet at my desk in my room—that was so nice. And all he was doing was being there with me.

Walking down the hall for first period, I feel like I'm flying, though I'm bumping along with my backpack in the traffic of everyone else. Every single person passing—super-popular Brooke and her two besties; golden Tim Jensen; Anjana, all regal and oblivious; the Aspie guy, Horace; Joey with his leg still in a cast—seems friendly and nice, all of them my friends. The clang and roar of classes changing feels sweetly familiar. Everything is good and anything is possible.

Charlotte comes rushing toward me. She scurries in a crouch as if she has something urgent to tell me, making herself shorter so she won't waste time leaning over when she gets here.

"You are not going to believe who asked me to hang out on Saturday," she says. "An actual ride-together date."

"Okay, I won't believe you. Who is it?"

"Bink! Halliday!"

My stomach does a double-flop. "Well, yeah, I guess that is a surprise. Cool, though."

Charlotte looks blissed-out in a way that's different, softer than her usual excitement. I liked it when Bink was semi-firing on me. But she looks tender, the way I feel when I think about Risto. Nice that we're both on the edge of a new kind of happy at the same time. Knowing that puts me in a super good mood for the rest of the day.

THE THREE LITTLE candles on my bedroom floor make a wobbly yellow triangle of light.

Something is going to happen here tonight, and I want it to be Risto showing up. Being with him has made me realize what's amazing about being with somebody. It's when they let all the doors be open between you. Suddenly your life and the whole universe are twice as big as they were before.

But it's been too many nights since the one when he sat at my desk, and I was falling asleep and missed out on what could have been time together. All these wide-awake nights of waiting since, and being groggy the next day. I'm tired of waiting for him. I have to try to reach him.

Mom being out tonight means this "ritual" I read about won't be interrupted. Thank God, she didn't leave with Webb. I haven't heard his voice recently, and she's been around the house a lot, being extremely nice, which is maybe her way of apologizing. I think I convinced her the whole Webb thing was wrong. So I have my mother back, which I'm happy about.

All afternoon I was googling and meditating and soul-searching on methods to contact someone like Risto. I'm not the only one something like this has happened to. A lot of people have guardian angels and spiritual guides, which isn't the same but it's still spirits connecting with live people.

I try the chant again, but I keep getting distracted. The

directions on eHow said to send out a message with rhyme and rhythm to "radiate into the cosmos" and draw him in.

"Boy from the tree, come to me," I say. This is silly. I feel ridiculous. But I say it again, and again, upwards of fifty times, until it has no meaning.

The smell of the candle wax in the dim light gives my room the feeling of one of the little side alcoves in that empty church where I went with Dad once. Although he's pretty much an atheist and into being rational, he says he has to leave his lab now and then to sit and concentrate where it's quiet. He probably wasn't thinking about his research at all, but instead worrying about things between him and Mom.

Back to the chant: "Risto, find your way. Risto, come today." Over and over.

My skull feels hollow and windy, full of nothing except the shaky candlelight. It's about to happen: something is. I don't sense Risto, but I'm starting to float, the candles bright spots below me. I'm going to bump the ceiling. I'm about to smash— No, I drift through it like it was never there. I can't believe this is happening. I'm outside. Over the house. Rising like I'm weightless. There's our chimney. There's the big oak branch scratching against the roof. There's the tree where I first saw him. Higher and higher, as if I'm made of wind. Tears slide out of the corners of my eyes. I'm so excited I'm crying.

Darkness is closing in below me. Can't see the house any more, or the street. I feel a ping of fear, but it goes away in an instant. Soft air pours past my face, down my back. I'm traveling fast, still going up, the air so dark and smooth... And warm. I've left the December night behind. I wish I could see all this happening. I wish I could tell somebody.

A faint hint of light ahead, the sky over me starting to pale. I see my arm, my hand. I still have on my same ratty sweater. I have no idea where I'm going. Or how I'll get home. The light's getting brighter, the sky loaded with stars. They're bigger than usual, like little white fires have been set all over the sky. Feels like I'm breathing them in, a cold drink full of them, my chest full of sizzling stars, my chest and my eyes.

Now a hissing splitting sound—

And all at once, Risto is beside me, the night sky gone. We're sitting in a splash of light beside a little creek that throws off sparkles like daytime stars. The ground smells like Christmas trees, but the air is summer. In my ordinary life, it really is almost Christmas, but it's cold back there and the air outside smells like cars and mud.

"You're here," I say.

"No, I think it is you who are here."

I'm sitting on the ground, acting like this is a normal place. But these woods seem too bright, like pictures doctored with software, the grass so green that I want to chomp into it and taste lime Jelly Belly. The leaves I squeeze between my fingers feel overly alive, as if juices are rushing through their veins, not like any leaves I ever touched before. Pulling off a few, I put them carefully in my pocket and look back at Risto for some explanation of all of this. He smiles as if he's already answered every question I could possibly have and he knows I must be completely satisfied. And I do feel answers arriving in my mind, so familiar that it's as if I have always known them. We are in a realm that has always been here, even before the Earth. And there are other realms, more magical, and realms beyond those, unimaginable. This is a place that a human can reach, but the methods are as hard to grasp as clouds. Still, this one, where he seems at home, is closest to human Earth, which makes me feel good. I want him close.

He touches my hair. Or at least I think he does. It feels like a sunny beach breeze. It's definitely not December here. "You have arrived to me," he says. "Thus my heart soars like a mighty bird."

"Risto, I love—the way you talk." I want to say so much more.

"Also you use the English words most expertly," he says. I can see he's thinking about something else in a very concentrated way, as if he's trying to understand. I'm trying to understand all of this—this place, and flying out of my house and through the stars. But being next to him like this — He moves his face closer to me. He kisses me, slowly and carefully, fits us together like he wants to get it exactly right. I feel it all the way down to my feet. Like nobody has gotten this close to me before. It's the most personal, intimate thing imaginable.

He pulls back and looks at me, his eyes so happy. "You are the beautiful friend of me. You give to me such joys."

Before I can speak, we kiss again. This time he doesn't stop. As if he was uncertain before and now he's sure what to do, as if the human guy part of his nature has completely kicked in. We're lying back on the underbrush, which feels as hyper-charged as he does. His mouth is real. And his chest.

His breath on my cheek. Every detail of him is better than real. He smells like the ocean and a wood fire and snow all at the same time, which sounds like an exaggeration, but it's precisely true. I feel like I'm doing slow backward flips.

"Darcy." The voice is far off. Risto doesn't hear, doesn't stop, his hand traveling up and down my side. Good. I won't hear either.

"Darcy!" Louder now. Yelling.

I'm standing up. In my bedroom at night. The door is shaking. I locked it, of course.

"Coming, Mom!" Quickly flipping on the lights. The candles. I kick at the mess on the floor, melted wax turned hard everywhere. Char marks on the floor!

"What is going on in there, Darcy? You didn't hear the smoke alarm?" A man's voice is coming from behind her. Not Dad. Red light flashes from the window all up on the ceiling, filling up the whole room with swirling light. Blast of a horn.

Ambulance? Firemen? No. Please, no. I throw my coat on the floor and a pillow on top of it. My lips feel swollen from making out. I flip the lock, open the door. Mom seizes me in a death grip, like it's our last moment together. She's shaking. "I'm okay, Mom."

From behind her, a beefy, ruddy-faced guy walks past us into my room. "Hello, honey," he says, daring to pick up my coat from the floor. "We were worried about you." We? My eyes fall shut like they're never going to open again.

Tony's father. Mr. Llewellyn, way older-looking than when he came to class, calling me honey when he's never met me. Mom, beside him, all glammed-up in tight jeans and her shawl with gold threads running through it. He's talking about them as "we".

Banging and crashing from below. "I thought we left the door unlocked, G," he says to my mother.

G? She has a nickname? She's been seeing him all this time!

The banging—Risto? No, he must not show up now.

A huge clomping man appears at the top of the stairs. Fireman. Dressed like Darth Vader. Another one behind him.

"You didn't hear the siren?" Mom says to me. "How could you not hear?" She's searching my face, staring at my pupils to see if I'm on drugs.

I put my hand in my pocket, feel for the twig, the leaves: they seem dried and fragile. When I touch them I feel where I've just been: the air, its breeze that feels like a whispered hum. A word comes to mind—astral—and stars spin out before me, then are gone.

"My mind was elsewhere." If this guy weren't here, Mom would be shrieking: what were you thinking? You could have burned the house and yourself! She's holding back.

One of the firemen pokes at the hard candle wax. Mom is staring at me. "Is this a ceremony?" she asks. "Some Wiccan pagan thing?"

She's hoping. It's an explanation she'd prefer to arson or drugs. "I lit some candles, that's all," I say.

The larger fireman says, "Looks like we're okay here, ma'am." A fairly young guy, standing in my bedroom in those Batman boots. This whole night has been unbelievable.

"Mom, I'm sorry I caused all this trouble. I'll be much more careful in the future."

"How about: you'll never light a match again in this house."

But the candles worked! I found Risto! I made it on my own to the astral zone. And she shouldn't speak to me like this in front of a stranger. I throw a cold glance at Mr. Llewellyn, who should not be here. He sticks his hand out. "We haven't officially met," he says, suddenly smiley-smooth. "I'm Webb Llewellyn. My son is in your class."

I manage to squeeze out a "hi."

CHAPTER

ELEVEN

F irst day back at school after the holidays and it feels
good to be back to normal, though we got through
Christmas morning okay. Dad was already in the
living room by the time I came downstairs. The main thing
different was that Mom was in clothes instead of a bathrobe.
Apparently she never told Dad about the firemen coming,
maybe because of Webb being there.

Standing with my homeroom out in the hall, I break a Kit
Kat and pass a piece over to Charlotte, who's close by in a
different line. "A little caffeine to keep us awake during
assembly," I say.

"Like I'm going to sleep sitting on bleachers with no
back," she says. "Not that I turn down chocolate. Thanks."
This morning everybody's heading into the gym, first thing.
Assembly! No need to take notes, instead a chance to think.

Charlotte's teacher is pulling her group toward a

different entrance. "See you," we both say at slightly different instants.

My class files into the gym, up onto the stair-step bleachers. Hollow clunking from the sound system. The student body president starts talking, kids still shuffling into place. He's saying that a couple people are getting awards, seniors I hardly know.

The place quiets down. A boy, Hugh Chen, walks to the center of the shiny basketball court. He gets told he's going to Washington, D. C. next summer to work in an epidemiology lab. Would Risto find me if I went to Washington? Next, Cassie Friedman—such great hair, sun-streaked—goes out to get recognized for winning a Young Filmmaker award: a documentary about the polluted creek not far from my house. Good—she deserves a prize. I should have already been over there picking up litter.

Although nothing anybody can do to that place is going to make it like Risto's creek, with leaves trailing in the water that are so green every one of them looks juicy and brand-new. If I made a video of that, I'd be on talk shows. Or, more likely, people would think I staged it, made it all up.

"Sorry," I whisper. Seems I bumped the elbow of Carter, next to me, jostling her while she was texting. Worst thing ever. She gives me an oh-please look, glances around for a friend to agree with her about how out-of-it I am. I don't care. It's so trivial what she thinks of me. I'm starting to feel buzzy, getting The Feeling. Light and full of soft static. Is this possible? Right in the middle of Assembly? Oh, wow—wow! —going up, the bubbles start sliding into smoothness. I can do this right here surrounded by people at school!

I'm a few feet above where I was sitting, not in a tree or off in some magic place. I can stare at everybody on the rows behind me, see what they're doing without their knowing I'm watching. Carter is still texting: *M back with L again!!! Hate! Kill!*

The reply arrives in two seconds: *He was always vile 2 you*

Carter hits the keys again: *Im 100% over it*

I can't tell who she's talking to. Probably her chief side-kick, Hannah. I drift backward, leave Carter and Hannah to work it out. Reading over shoulders—this is an amazing extra benefit of my flying ability. I could learn so much, things I would have no normal way of knowing. If I wanted to run into someone, I could invisibly lurk around their conversations and afterward show up where they're going to be. Oh, Charlotte would *so* love to be able to do this. It's wrong not to teach her—if I knew how I was doing it.

Here's another person tapping into a phone: Tony. Big surprise, when is he not online? He's probably playing some slasher-type game. I float around to the back of him to take a look, see exactly how bad it is. His neck and shoulders are mega-skinny. An Ichabod, like Dad calls himself. His hair is solid black.

He's texting. So he has a friend. I judged him wrong. Sinking a little closer into reading distance, I can see it.

"UNC -2.5 Ntr Dm 5000"

Notre Dame? On his screen: *CNFRM.*

Confirm? A bet on a UNC-Notre Dame game. Basketball. So this is the illegal gambling people say he does. I'm watching a crime in progress? I'm pretty sure I am.

This is creepy. Not the gambling part which doesn't seem

like a huge deal to me. But watching is like peeking through blinds into somebody's bathroom. I don't want to be watching this. Turning back toward my physical self, I float away from Tony. There I am in my rust bulky-knit sweater, sitting on the second row—the back of my head, anyway. And such little shoulders. I look so small. I seem to be sitting completely still. Coming close, I see Carter is still texting her friend: *dead? druggd??? turned to stone!! she so wacko.*

Wacko! They're talking about me! I'm sitting too still. At the end of the text is an emoji: a girl sticking out her tongue in disgust.

I zip down, a whoosh of dizziness, a tiny hissing I can feel. I'm back inside myself again. My left leg has gone to sleep, my lips and eyes feel dry. Carter, rummaging in her purse, glances toward me with a reasonably friendly look, like she wasn't just talking trash about me.

Enough spying! Never again. I don't want to know what people are saying about me in secret. Normal communication is hard enough.

More important—a truly big deal—how do I make sense of what just happened? The range of what's possible keeps expanding.

HALF A DAY LATER, homework done, I try out my new skill of solo floating. It starts instantly. The ceiling seems to be coming closer, like happened before. I automatically reach to cover my face as if I'm going hit it. There's no bump at all; I float through, up into the night.

So quickly, everything changes. A sound like water

pouring or huge wind in the distance and light, getting brighter, too bright. I can hardly look at it, the fuzzy patch, getting closer, a whole enormous swirl of stars. Turned up on its edge, rolling through the sky. A spiral galaxy. Millions of miles high, millions of miles away, rolling past in front of me, so many stars that they're blended together. I'm dizzy. The sound is so loud, this enormous roaring whisper. I feel the breeze from it, this far away: a cold wind that goes through every pore of my sweater. I feel like I have nothing on at all, am carried in a carbonated liquid, sparkling water, tiny bubbles clinging to every pore and hair of me.

The galaxy is passing, farther and farther away. So beautiful. The whispery wind dying down. I'm lying on my bed, on my back. The light is yellow from the reading lamp. I'm staring at the ceiling. Back so quickly. Doesn't time mean anything up there? My phone is buzzing. Not a text, a call.

"Hello?" Clunk-a-chunk sound in my ear. "Hello?" I say again. All I hear is a dial tone. Whoever it was hung up. The number isn't one I recognize. Probably a wrong number. Or Martin from a borrowed phone. Or Risto, coming to me in a different way. I don't know what to expect, from him, from me. The more that happens, the more it's all a mystery.

CHAPTER

TWELVE

"Risto, I remember nothing of how we got here." He smiles his radiant smile that seems to shine in the silvery air as if it's reflecting on cloud particles. It's two days after my solo trip, and I'm glad he's with me on this one.

"It is extremely easier to be here than in your home world. I have great work and efforts to come to your place of residence at this time."

I'm beginning to see familiar sights through a clearing haze, but so strangely. My familiar neighborhood, distorted. It's unnerving. The inner workings of objects are as visible as the outsides; I can see the front and back and sides of that little green house all at the same time. I could get seasick. He puts his arm around me. The contact is so intense it feels radioactive, as if his arm is faintly vibrating. He wasn't like that in my room, but maybe he was at that creek bank because that was all pretty intense.

I'm getting vertigo, sliding around on what is supposed to be ground I'm walking on. I think I'm walking. We're on a sidewalk, of sorts. I could sink into it or float above it.

"Risto, exactly where are we?"

"We are astral. We came through world of stars to return and enter here my astral home."

"It's my neighborhood—in Raleigh, North Carolina — all jumbled and distorted." Flowers have started to bloom in the yards, too soon. Some of the blooms look too big.

"Of course. Astral is in the same place as your life." We are walking, I'm pretty sure. Semi-walking. I feel like I'm halfway weightless, the sidewalk as limber as boards. Lying on the creek bank, I didn't have this problem. I'm getting somewhat used to the feeling. "Most times," he says, "you see only your layer. I see mine."

"These layers are on top of each other."

He laughs as if this is hilarious. "No. Upon the same location."

"So, my regular town is full of your invisible world all the time."

"This is certainly correct."

Too much. I need to get oriented. start at the beginning, with the most ridiculously basic info. "Risto, where do you live? Do you live in a house with parents?

"Parentage," he says. "This is not taking place at this time."

"Parents long ago?" I say.

"I cannot know."

"Could we sit down a minute, Risto? On solid ground? It's too hard to navigate." I can't tell how much effort any movement will take. Like opening a door that jams some of the time but not always; you don't know in advance how hard to push. "Is it like this for you, Risto, when you come to my place? Do you get dizzy? Is this what you mean by great work?"

He shrugs. "It is some disturbing. Human Earth is very heavy life."

So he has had to struggle to come to see me and be with me. More than ever, I know I have to learn to cope. Sitting feels better, leaning against this little wall between two yards, next to a bed of zinnias. My head is settling. The nearest bloom feels completely real except, like Risto, a little more than real. I put my hand on his leg, on the white wrap thing he often wears. The heat of him feels good all the way up my arm and into my chest.

He looks relaxed with the sun hitting his face, his eyes closed. I'm always torn between trying to find out who and what he is —what world/layer/universe this is — and forgetting all that to effortlessly be with him.

For this moment I'm going with being with him, aware of his whole long body beside me.

The street seems almost ordinary and quiet. That dog crossing the street is by himself, looks fox-like. Someone is following the dog. At least I think so. What am I looking at? A shadow? An adult-sized thing, see-through, shining, moving toward me, following the reddish dog.

My hand squeezes Risto's leg. He opens his eyes. "Risto, what is that?" The dog trots up to us, fixes his gaze on me.

A sort of shade falls over us. The shadowy creature is before us. "Risto?"

He raises his eyebrows at me like he has a question. I jerk my head toward the wavering shape, as if you could possibly not notice it. "What *is* it?" Risto blinks himself completely awake and smiles toward the thing; they speak in some language that sounds like a broom sweeping on the back patio. A ghost broom. The hairs stand up on my arms.

To me, Risto says, "This entity is a person who is dreaming. In his sleep, he has come to visit the spirit of the dog called Trixie."

"He told you this?"

"Yes, you have heard him say."

I heard only breathy brushing sounds. No human language. The thing is still hanging there. I shrink back from it. It's spooky and I don't want it touching me.

...I open my eyes. Wait — my eyes weren't closed.

Risto and the silver thing are gone. All I see is the fence around me on our brick patio at home. I'm sitting slumped in one of the uncomfortable metal chairs. The back door to the house opens and closes. "Darcy...?" Mom says. She sounds uneasy. "What are you up to?"

"Day-dreaming." I say. She gives me a long look. She can probably see I'm rattled. Because I just screwed up. I let myself get scared away from where I wanted to be. I'm not letting it happen again.

THIRTEEN

C harlotte's going to update my hair. She likes to improve me, has been suggesting this for a while. I finally agreed after I saw how it looked from the back: wavy and neat like somebody's mother. Charlotte's come in downstairs. I hear the staccato pat-pat-pat up the steps toward my room.

"Darce," she says, flinging herself in the door, looking more swingy-haired than ever. "I brought my mom's salon kit she uses on my brothers."

"Red alert! I've seen your brothers." Charlotte puts what looks like a pink plastic tool box down on the floor and starts unpacking it: scissors in several sizes, flat iron, curling iron, big round brushes. There's more to her mother than I realized.

"Some terrific product," Charlotte says, holding up a plastic container in each hand. "And your boyfriend Risto is going to love your hair." She says it a tiny bit sarcastically, rolls her eyes like she's sure I've only imagined Risto and she's indulging me.

"You saw him, Charlotte. I'm trying to figure out how to get him to show up here in my regular life."

"I personally would love to have a secret life." She's started fooling with the top of my hair, moving strands around.

"But you wouldn't want the most exciting part to be hidden. Or to feel like your life is sort of split into two pieces." Her expression says that she doesn't think it would be such a bad deal. "Something else I've discovered is rising up above my actual body. Not just floating up in a tree. I can fly around. I can read what somebody's texting and they don't know I'm there. At least I did it once anyway."

"Seriously? If you can really do that, you absolutely have to show me how."

"I don't know how, except by accident. Besides, what's important about the rising is the amazingness of it being possible—and being with Risto, of course—not reading people's texts."

"If you won't teach me, you can definitely find out some info for me. Like, did Bink see Joanna again since they broke up?"

"Not doing it, Charlotte."

"Why not?" She whacks three inches off of one side. She's irritated because she's left out of my secret life, which she doesn't believe in anyway. Now I'm worried about my hair.

"Reading over people's shoulders is too weird, Charlotte.

You don't know what you might see. People say things they wouldn't say to your face."

"That's so unadventurous, Darcy. You usually have more curiosity."

"I have enough strange activity in my life. I mean, I'd like to find out good stuff to tell you, but suppose I see things that would just make you unhappy."

Now she's moving in a way that's jerky and harsh. "How's your mother's boyfriend?" she says. To ask me that, she's in her most seriously shut-out offended mood.

"I thought he was out of the picture. He's still around."

"You need to let your mother go."

"Go? That's a little extreme."

Charlotte makes a so-what face.

So now my weird double life, my flying life, is making trouble with Charlotte. I can't let things get screwy with her. Already Martin is unhappy with me. I sure can't "let my mother go." I need my closest people more than ever. When truly wild things are happening, you need your people to help you hold on.

WITH CHARLOTTE'S pissy mood and the way haircuts too often go, I was semi-prepared yesterday for bad results, that Charlotte's idea of how I should look would ruin my Earth life. But when I see myself in my mirror, I look pretty terrific. The back and sides are straight wisps, the bangs and the top stiff and raggedy. And the color, the color! Or lack of it. It's ash blond with gold tips, the whole effect a bit like the singer Pink. Fluffing the ends, I feel the points of the different lengths against the palm of my hand. Without the confidence I've gotten from Risto and flying and all, I wouldn't have had the nerve to agree to any of this.

When Mom saw it, she stared, then said, "O-kay," in that slow two-syllable way that means you have serious doubts.

Studying the outcome in my mirror, I'm happy. If Mom hates it, she can think of it as a revenge hairdo, me getting back at her for Webb and for throwing Dad out. We could call it even. Then I wouldn't have to be mad at her anymore.

This gold is really nice with my eyes, the light flecks in the brown irises. I've stared at myself so long that I'm losing track of what I'm seeing; the whole mirror is starting to seem like my brown eye color. Wavery with gold light. Something darker is moving in it, getting larger.

My eyes feel dry from staring. I mustn't blink. The darker shape is filling up the whole space, emerging. Risto. Standing in front of me. I feel like all the liquid in my insides is sloshing.

"You," I say. "Coming out of the mirror? I can't believe it."

"It is a helpful procedure, in English called scrying."

"Never heard of it."

He's staring at me now like he's scared.

"You are a different being," he says. He's looking at my hair. "You are not MyDarcy." He's not joking.

"Risto, I'm not different. See, my face is the same. My voice is the same."

He's shaking his head, stepping back from me. What have I done? I should have thought. He obviously doesn't know how hair works if he thinks a new cut means I'm no longer me. "Risto, hair grows back, color grows out. Nothing about hair is a big deal."

He's fading.

"Risto, my hair grows fast. It will *change*. It'll go back to the way it was!"

So pale now he's transparent.

He's gone. Because of a haircut. I do not believe it. If he thinks it won't change, that I'm not me, he'll never come back. I've lost him. My stomach drops like I'm falling fifty stories.

I can't let this be true. Over a haircut?

"Risto!" I yell into the mirror. But he's not in there, I know that. The mirror's nothing but some kind of door. Eyes shut tight, I lean my forehead against the glass, call him silently with my mind: "Risto!" But he doesn't come.

He doesn't come. All the hopes I had, everything good is broken into pieces.

I'VE BEEN LYING HERE for an hour—hating my hair, hating Charlotte, hating my parents for splitting and Risto for running away without listening, and hating myself, of course, for not *thinking,* not figuring out in advance what he couldn't possibly know. How did I let this happen? How do I get him back? We have to talk. I push myself up into a sitting position. Moving, jostling my insides, makes me feel even more wrecked.

But I have to deal with this. Groping my way to my laptop, I hit Google with "define scrying." Hope I have the word right. I have to know how to follow him into the mirror. I have to find him and explain in a way he can understand. This computer is acting so slow I want to crash it through the window.

Here's the word. I had it right. Scrying. "Also called seeing or peeping..." A lot more than peeping, I'd say, when his whole self steps completely out of the mirror into my room. "...A magic practice... Involves seeing things psychically..." Done by staring into reflective surfaces like glass or water. The visions "are thought to come from God, spirits, the psychic mind, the devil, or the subconscious."

Correction: Risto is not a vision. He is warm, physical, real.

The doorbell does its little buzz. Omigod, Dad's already here; I almost forgot. Grab my purse and shades, grab the begonia I bought for his place. Speed-scuffling down the stairs, I see through one of the little windows at the top of the door, the side of his head. Having to wait on the porch at his own house! Hurts to see him there. If I were him, I'd be furious, every time. Though maybe he wouldn't want to risk walking in and finding a Webb-type-person making himself at home. Nothing is fair.

"Hey, Dad." I start moving us toward the car.

"Whoa, hold on," he says, grabbing my elbow as I head past him down the porch steps. "Let me look at you."

I stop, turn slowly toward him. For a moment, I'd forgotten: my hair. His face is doing twisted things. "You don't like it either?"

"So your mom's seen it?"

"Well, she didn't really say much." Risto is the one who didn't like it. I suddenly want to cry. But I can't tell Dad about any of it, obviously. Changing the subject: "Charlotte did it."

"Charlotte," he says. I once overheard that he considers Charlotte "quite something," whatever that's supposed to mean. "You're happy with it?" he says in careful-father mode, still ignoring my request for his opinion.

I do a shrug, the kind where you hold your shoulders up at your ears for seconds before they drop. "Mixed."

He laughs.

"White with gold edges," he says when we get into the car. "Christmas-y, I guess. Does the new do mean I should worry?"

"Completely unnecessary. And it's *blonde* with *gold* tips, Dad." He's the one whose life is in upheaval, who has no home. "Should *I* worry about *you*? It's obvious there's stuff no one is telling me." I'm not just changing the subject. I'm pointing out what really needs attention.

He stares down the street, eyes zoned out. I hate when he gets like this, does his far-away thing. I know it's part of what bothered Mom.

"Okay," I say. "Forget I asked. Here. This is for you." I hand him the plant. I meant this to be a nice thing and instead it's turning out awkward.

He takes the little pot in both hands. His eyes have zoned back in, tender and sad. "Thank you, Darcy. This is thoughtful of you." He seems uncertain where to put it.

"I'll hold it," I say, taking it back. "So you can drive."

He starts the car. "I'm okay, honey. No need to worry. What I'm doing, I'm just letting my new situation reveal itself to me."

"Reveal itself? What does that mean?"

He shakes his head, hooks his seatbelt and glances to be sure mine is on, then tries to get me to talk about school. Or Charlotte. Or "my new look". Or the snow we were supposed to get and didn't. I do not like the raw-egg-in-my-stomach feeling this is giving me. Already I was full up to my throat with what happened with Risto.

CHAPTER

FOURTEEN

N ot even a year after the split, hardly more than half a year, and Webb is downstairs, having breakfast. An outrage!

Mom warned me yesterday that he was going to stay over. She was nervous and snippy, telling me a complicated plumbing-problem-at-his-house reason for why this sleep-over was necessary. She even tried to act like he'd be sleeping in the guest room.

"This is so irresponsible," I said to her. "Everybody knows you shouldn't expose your children to short-term boyfriends."

Soon as I said it, horror swept over me. She thinks Webb is long-term? Before the split, was she cheating on Dad with this ghoul? I walked out of the room. We haven't spoken in the eleven hours since. Now I am about to walk straight out of this house without pausing for one second.

Downstairs, as I approach the kitchen, his voice is ever

clearer, definitely Webb-ish. Authoritative yet jokey, like a morning radio announcer. I start getting a wild feeling: like why is this reptile here, when Risto is not here and probably never will be again? I think I'm going to be sick. He stands when I come into the room, as if manners will help.

"Good morning, Darcy," he says.

Mom looks around from the stove. She's making banana waffles—on a weekday.

"Hi," I say, looking nowhere near his red face and his double chin. "I've got to hurry."

"But, sweetie," Mom says. "You haven't—"

I'm straight out the back kitchen door, far down the alley before she can turn around. And, to the beat of my feet hitting the gravel, I'm chanting *Risto Risto Risto*. Calling him, the way I did with candles burning in front of the mirror. The way I've been doing whenever I'm alone and it would be safe for him to appear. I can't give up.

MARTIN WAS RIGHT. I shouldn't be involving myself in chairperson jobs or prom decorating. I don't know why prom planning is supposed to start this soon anyway. But everybody says it takes months. I'm sitting with the few people who've shown up for the meeting, instead of standing in front of them like a real leader. Worst of all, Martin hasn't shown up. I'm ending this meeting as soon as I possibly can.

"Because *I* think," Mary Ella Sanchez is saying, "that a Hollywood theme is limited and everybody in the world does it and we should go with something like mythical kingdom which has so many more possibilities."

Shaneqa jumps in, "*I think something more futuristic...*"

This discussion has been going on for like twenty minutes by the clock, and it seems like three hours. These meetings have been happening for weeks. I could call for a vote, but there's no theme that more than a couple of people would vote for. All the ideas are ordinary or too difficult to pull off.

They're all waiting for me to say something. A teacher-type person pokes her head in the door: how long will we be using this room? "A few more minutes." I am so grateful to her. She has given me an excuse! "We're ready to wrap this up for today," I assure her. A couple of kids in the group shoot each other a look, questioning my quitting so early, but it's not like we were making progress. These people deserve better leadership, somebody who is excited about the job. I'm too sad to get excited about anything, especially decorations for a supposedly romantic night. They have to be hating that they elected me, any of them who voted for me.

"Okay, all you creative minds," I say to them, "let's each come up with three good themes and we'll meet up here next week..." I don't look at them as I throw together my stuff. This time I'm the first one out the door.

I HAVE to get things back to normal with Martin. I can't stand to lose my steady buddy. Sitting in homeroom the next morning, I'm anguishing over the situation with my loved ones. Risto is probably permanently gone. The air goes out of me when I think these words. Martin is avoiding me—and he seems preoccupied when I do see him. Charlotte is acting distant, Mom's with Webb, and Dad's in some strange touchy state of mind. I get upset about them one after another, and then another and another. It doesn't stop. My life is a bunch of broken glass. Risto thinking I'm someone else, Risto disappearing, hurts the worst.

But our goth warlock friend Drake has given me an idea. He's planning to go to a parapsychologists' conference two hours away. He knows somebody who can get him in. Drake must already be a little psychic, or why would he have told me about it? I've pretty much decided: going to this may help me learn to communicate with Risto, to reach him and explain haircuts and get him back with me. I haven't been able to make chanting or scrying or anything else work. Plus, if Martin will go with me, then being together for all that riding can give us a chance to be normal with each other again.

"Tell me again why I've driven ninety-five miles for this meeting?" Martin says as the four of us get out of the car to go into the parapsych meeting in some conference-center-type-place.

"Research," I say. "Like I said before, on other realms. Other kinds of beings different from us. How we can communicate. How we can have a relationship with them." I still feel hideously bad that I can't tell him more.

"Like aliens, extra-terrestrials," he says it in a flat tone. Not a question.

"Right. The whole range. You have to admit that the possibilities are exciting."

He gives me a sullen stare. He thinks this is a stupid trip and something I would never have thought of doing in the past—it probably makes him more suspicious that I'm hiding something. It kills me to let this go on, but he's too rational to understand. He would think I've seriously flipped out. It's one thing to go to a meeting to listen to people talk about spirit beings, and another to say you're hanging *out* with one. Although, sudden thought: maybe Martin will learn stuff here that changes his attitude, that makes it possible for me to tell him my secrets.

Drake is already close to the door, Charlotte loping along beside him. The other people going in don't look like I expected: ordinary adults in normal coats and shoes, none of them faux-vampire like Drake in his midnight blue velvet and dingy lace cuffs.

In the lobby, fifty-year-olds mill about drinking coffee. The few younger ones look like a lot of Dad's grad students, pale as if they never leave the lab and never sleep. Drake, flagging us from an inner doorway, is the only alchemist-Druid-type in the whole crowd. I have on this old hoodie of Dad's, which I love, but it's too long.

We do not fit here. We look shady. Doesn't matter; this is where I urgently need to be. To learn about Risto-type beings and how to make it possible for him and me to be together like normal falling-in-love people. If I ever see him again.

I'm determined I will.

If we were together like normal, he could go places with me in the regular world: school stuff, games, parties. We could walk down to the shopping center together like humans and get a cappuccino—*and* fly around the universe and go places like Tahiti and the Norwegian fjords. The two halves of my life would be pulled together into one. That's what I need to make happen. It's probably completely impossible.

That doesn't stop me. I'm more determined than ever.

On the home front, though, I don't even try. I'm making no attempt to pull the "Mom and Dad" halves of my family back together. At least I'm not naive enough to think I can do *that*.

Am I completely deluded to think I can find Risto and explain about hair? I've stopped asking myself if I'm delusional in knowing he exists. He exists. And anyway, a person could drive herself crazy going round and round trying to answer a question like that. He exists and I want him to come back.

The parapsychology program, it turns out, is academics reading papers in different rooms all over the building. The map takes me to a little meeting room where a dozen or so adults sit in scattered school-library chairs waiting to hear about Spontaneous Incidents Presenting Features from a Diverse Range of Types. In such a small group, it's obvious I'm not a professor of anything, which feels slightly dangerous, although I can't see how there could be any real risk.

The speaker arrives toting an armload of papers. She's short and hefty. Not ethereal. None of these experts look like they'd believe in any suspect ideas. I pull my hood up. Somebody has to be a little spooky. Plus, I feel like hiding.

Throat clearing from the front of the room. Dr. Halterman has her papers in order and her PowerPoint ready.

An hour later, my head is ready to fall to the floor like a brick. She's still talking about experimental protocols, field resonance, transduction. It has zero to do with Risto. Nothing I've heard here will make it possible for me to find him, for us to do ordinary everyday activities together, like going for a normal walk. That is, if he ever comes back. His timing was never predictable before, but now, with the way he vanished, his absence is ominously longer. At least two weeks—I don't want to think about how long it has been. I miss him. His sweetness makes me feel excited and calm at exactly the same time. I don't know how that's possible.

"Lastly," she's saying—I'm so relieved that this is almost over—"I like to end with the kind of story that fascinates, the sort of anecdote that drew many of us into this research in the first place."

She smiles. "In an old office building in Chicago, a man is getting papers out of his briefcase, alone in a conference room before a meeting. He looks up and sees a woman standing silently on the other side of the table, though the door hasn't opened. There's no way she could have come in. She's wearing dark red lipstick, a 1940s-type suit and a little hat with a pouf of a veil. He's sure he's seen her in an old family photo, standing with others beside a two-toned Packard Clipper. She has something like a pack of cards in her hand. He starts to say, who are you, how did you get here? But at the first sound, she evaporates backward, getting paler and paler until she's transparent and finally gone and all of that happens in about three seconds.

"After looking around the room, he steps to the other

side of the table. Lying on the floor is an empty crumpled pack of Chesterfield cigarettes."

Chesterfield? A brand they had back then? So the woman dropped the package. Evidence! Like the twig I brought back from Risto's woods. It hurts to even think his name.

"These are the stories that draw public interest and support," Dr. Halterman is saying. "Especially since this man later reported further contact with the woman he saw."

Further contact? Like her showing up, having conversations with him? Finally we get to the important stuff!

"Spiritualist baloney," somebody mutters. I whip around to see the fifteen-watt dim-bulb who said this. Can't tell which one.

Another voice. "The artifact would be expected to dematerialize..."

My leafy twig has not dematerialized.

"They're still smoking those in Europe." A third voice. What's with these people? They're researchers who should be the most open-minded to the possibilities!

"We must never ignore anecdotal evidence," Dr. Halterman says. Hurray for her!

"I have a twig with leaves on it," I burst out, "from a similar phenomenon." Did I actually just say that? The baloney voice murmurs something about weed. I'm furious. "I know a little something about the scientific method," I say. "My father is a big deal in hydraulics; he invented a wave-force measuring gadget. So I know you can't laugh off evidence in any type of science because it doesn't match your expectations."

My face is on fire. My heartbeat is so fast I could vibrate

off this chair. The man I'm talking to seems mildly amused. But this leader knows about other people who've had experiences like I have: mysterious otherworldly contact. I'll never doubt myself for a second again.

"My goodness," Dr. Halterman says. "You must be Perry Colvard's daughter. I'm on an interdepartmental committee with him."

Oh shit! "You know him?"

"I do."

He's going to find out I left town, told no one where I was going. What do I say about why I'm here? I'll have to get to him before she does, come up with some kind of reasonable excuse, explain I'm working on a project...

OUT IN THE lobby during the break, I wander across the room. "Very cool that you said that stuff," a voice says from my left, a guy in the grad student age range.

"Thanks." Didn't notice him before—a youngish guy in jeans and running shoes. Crossed over into adult, but not too far.

He sticks out his hand. "I'm Great Hawk Wing."

"What do your friends call you? Great?"

He laughs like he's embarrassed, rubs his elbows like he's cold. "Hawk. It's pretty new. My shaman gave it to me."

"I'm Darcy. My parents gave it to me."

"What brings you here, Darcy?" Inevitably someone was going to ask. Maybe a shaman could reach Risto. I picture a man in buffalo robes beating a drum and dancing in my bedroom.

"I'm doing a bit of research," I say. A science project is probably what he's thinking. I feel Charlotte and Martin over at the wall keeping an eye on me. Probably because there is something disturbing about this guy. He's twitchy-nervous, his motions jerky. He blinks too much, his gaze skittering over my face like he's scared to look at me for long. And what my friends are too far away to notice: the air around him feels damp and charged the way it does before a thunderstorm.

"What is your area?" he says. He wears the kind of glasses you see on scientists with crewcuts, like maybe the guys who developed the atom bomb, but his hair's stringy blond.

"Out-of-body experiences." I've just learned the term, turns out I'm not the only one who's had those either. "What are you interested in?"

"Energy fields," he says, doing a quick move with his head to toss back a strand of hair. "I'm developing a theory of everything." He says it like he's angry, as if he expects to be laughed at or attacked.

"Exactly what I need. A simple explanation that somebody could actually use." Suddenly there's a funny quaking feeling to the air. He's glancing around in every direction.

Bang! Like metal cracking. Again, the same slam. I know these sounds. Risto? Oh, please, yes! Be here. Find me!

No sign of him. Hawk's searching the crowd still. The same clusters stand around talking. There's Martin, texting, Charlotte looking bored. No one else seems to have heard the crashing.

Hawk is giving me a questioning look. "You, too," he says. I nod.

He heard what I heard. This is big! Another proof that I'm not making things up. Though I don't need proof at this point. I know I'm not insane. We do seem to be the only ones, though. Do I seem as weird as he does? Maybe we're both a bit off and that makes it possible to hear stuff. "Your theory of everything, Hawk, does it explain the noises we heard?"

"I have some thoughts about this." He does that quick side move with his head again, like it's a habit. Like he's shaking off a bad thought.

"It's good I came to this meeting today," I say, "because I have a bunch of questions that urgently need answering."

"Cell?" he says. We swap numbers.

"When I've heard that banging before—" I hesitate. How much can I say? I can't think. My head feels too full. People are heading back toward the meeting rooms. "We'll talk," we both say at pretty much the same time. He looks as stunned and off-track as I feel. In fact, a lot more so.

CHAPTER

FIFTEEN

"Honey?" Mom is coming up the stairs. I'm at the mirror looking for Risto, and trying to make my hair seem longer. The instant I see her face I know there's a problem. The hoodoo conference two days ago—I still haven't gotten hold of Dad to make an excuse. But my taking a secret road trip—I'm in trouble. No, wait: she's giving me her innocent look, like she doesn't know I'm going to hate what she's about to say.

"We have an invitation," she says.

"From who?"

"From whom. It's from Webb. He'd like to grill steaks for you and me one night soon."

My Mello Yello crashes to the floor, pee-colored drink everywhere. "I'm not going."

She sits down on the bed, ignoring the mess. "Is it Webb? Or do you not like his son?" She hesitates. "Or is it the idea of me dating?"

"I'd say it's more than an idea at this point. With him cruising around here like he belongs. I never know when there might be some beefy guy in a fancy sport coat walking into my room."

"Darling, you've hardly seen him."

"Fine with me."

"Do you and Tony talk at school?"

"Are you serious? No. We do not talk at school." No, I read his text over his shoulder and watched him engaging in illegal gambling, technically committing a crime.

"Tony's shy, I think," Mom says.

"He's hostile. Oh, God! Is he going to be at this cookout? Anyway, who fires up their grill in winter? We're going to sit outside eating with temperatures down to thirty degrees?"

Mom assures me Tony won't be there and that Webb's patio has outdoor heaters, then gets up to leave, now that she has dropped this crap bomb on my head.

She comes back with a towel, wipes up the drink. Doesn't ask me to help.

Two seconds after she leaves my room again—I still have my face in my hands, cursing them all—Dad's number rings on my cell. First time since I got back from the conference. I haven't called him— What I could say without incriminating myself? I wasn't supposed to be in another town.

"Darcy, it's your phone," Mom yells from downstairs.

"Got it!" I yell back. Now to find out if the parapsychologist woman told on me already.

I pick up, start jabbering: "Hi, Dad. Dad, did I tell you about my new research project? It's so interesting, about people being outside of their bodies and—"

"Darcy, I already heard about it." Stomach quavers.

"Oh, yeah?" My voice sounds too high-pitched.

"At the bowling alley. Remember? You asked me about holographic images. I meant to do a little checking about that. It slipped my mind. I'll do it for sure. I want to hear more about this."

"You do?" Of course he does. But talking about anything even close to Risto feels seriously dangerous. Dad is not on this wave-length. He'll think the separation trauma has damaged my brain. And of course for a while I wondered about this myself. As we talk for a while, I gradually calm down. Turns out he only called to say "hi."

Two days later, Mom sits in my room telling me I need to "see someone." A doctor. Just to be sure. You know, that all is well with me. She looks sympathetic.

"Why are you saying this? I'm not having problems." I just got home from school after a perfectly routine day.

"Darcy, you've had a shattering experience and you're not quite yourself lately."

"You're talking about the divorce/separation? Back in the fall? I am un-shattered." I'm permanently disillusioned and depressed if I let myself think about it, but that's different from shattered.

She reaches over, touches my hair, the spiky ends that are longer and limper now. She's being affectionate, not trying to improve the look or remind me of it, which gets to me. "The truth is, Mom, I've been too busy to think about it." So glad she didn't bring up me seeing a therapist back when I was doubting myself. I can just imagine trying to explain Risto to a therapist. Having to stonewall would only have made me feel worse.

"You don't seem busy. That's what worries me. You're alone in your room so much." She hesitates. "Look, I want to rule one thing out."

"What thing?"

"Drugs."

"Are you serious?"

"I am and I would like a serious, honest, complete answer."

"No drugs. No weed. Nothing."

She looks doubtful.

"That's all I can tell you, Mom. It's hard to prove you're not doing something."

"A few days ago when I came in to bring your laundry, a couple of drawers were standing open." A hot feeling is rising in my chest. She came in here and poked around? "I touched nothing, Darcy. The drawer was open. What caught my eye was a little baggie with crumbled leaves..."

I can't keep from laughing—at the same time, I'm horrified. My Risto leaves! How could I have left that drawer open? "Leaves, that's all. From a tree. You know, I've always loved trees. Anyway, wouldn't a person in your generation be able to recognize the real thing?"

Silence. I shouldn't have said that. "All right," she says. She looks weary. Long pause. Maybe this conversation is over. "One more question, Darcy. What is this I hear about you going off on a jaunt across the state last week?"

My whole body does an inner quiver. "A scientific meeting," I say, like this will make any difference. That woman must have talked to Dad. I thought I was home free.

"A trip with a carload of kids to a city two hours away? Without a word to anyone about where you are?"

"I had my phone on." Another weak defense. If I'm grounded, I'll be alone. No Risto and nothing to distract me from the loss of him—and all because of a haircut.

"I am to know at all times where you are. You know that."

No need to remind her of the partial truth of what I told her that day: that I was studying with Martin. My breath stops halfway in. That woman who knows Dad didn't know about any carload of kids. So, it's Martin—he's who did this! So he "protects" me and gets revenge for my secrecy at the same time. Clever. And I dared to hope he would learn enough to be open-minded, so I could talk to him. "Martin told you this, didn't he?"

"That is beside the point."

I know it was him. If it were that lady at the conference who knew about Dad, I'd be having this conversation with him. Martin, who's always been so straight-shooting and loyal. I can't believe it.

"The point is that you are not to take trips without my knowledge. So, five days grounded: no phone, no going out with friends, and absolutely no hanging out in your room. Clean out the basement and when you're through with that, I'll find something else."

I nod. No surprise. She has obviously figured out that these days I like staying in my room, even though she doesn't know Risto is the reason why.

"What was this meeting, anyway?"

"It was a scientific conference, like Dad goes to."

"What kind of science?"

"Parapsychology."

"I didn't know that this was an interest of yours."

"You and Dad encourage me to be curious."

She does an almost-laugh, she's calming down.

"What did you learn? Did you see any ghosts?" She's being wry, yet getting dangerously close to the truth.

"Oh, sure," I say, like I'm also joking. "I see them all the time. They're around." Except Risto is not around. It's been almost three weeks and now time in my room is cut short to sleeping. "You know, like your muse. What's she like, anyway? Does she hang out in your studio?"

Mom takes a long breath. "She hangs out in my head, or maybe it's my heart. She's the fountain of ideas." But the picture I'm getting isn't a fountain. It's a woman. a Sofia Vergara-type, spilling out of her filmy flowing dress. Or more like Mom's old-movie hero, Sophia Loren. One way or another, that's her name. Sophia, a woman who's hyper-vivid and slinky, like an exaggeration of Mom.

The look on Mom's face has melted to nice. "I find that it's wonderful to have an inner guidance counselor. But a human one can sometimes help too." She moves over next to me, puts her arm around me. We sit for a while, not saying anything. When she gets up to leave, she takes my phone.

HOURS LATER, I finish my homework at the kitchen table. I can't even text Charlotte to see what she's doing, or let

Martin know what I think about him being a snitch. But he and I are going to talk, first chance I get. I know what he'll say: he was worried about me. Like that makes it okay that he ratted me out. If Martin could ever meet Risto, then he'd have to believe what's happened, and we could talk, things would be okay again between us again.

First I have to see Risto. As if that's likely.

An idea pops into my head. I could get a wig! One that looks like my old hair. Put it on and then stare into the mirror. Sounds ridiculous, but it could work. Scrying didn't work before, but maybe it would if I look like my old self. I'll do it tonight when I'm allowed in my room to go to bed. I'll stand there scrying until I melt through to him or at least to somewhere out there in his world—or until he shows up in front of me.

Where can I possibly find a wig now? Tonight. This very minute.

Google Google Google. Craigslist...eBay...wig stores... drama department...drama! Does Mom have a wig or two from back when she was in plays? It would have to be plain and brown. It's possible. She might.

I find her stretching a canvas in the middle of the living room. "Mom, do you have any old wigs?"

When her gaze turns slowly to me, I see the darling-you-need-to-talk-someone look again. She shakes her head no. "You're needing a costume? For a school project?" Then a hint of relief on her face: "You decided you don't like your haircut!"

I shake my head. "Just playing, you know, trying out

some ideas." I hate that I have to do these deceptions, with
her and almost everybody.

"Sorry I can't help you with that," Mom says. "I don't
have any wigs." Long meaningful pause. I wait. "I've also
been thinking since your recent trip whether I need to keep
track of where you go—online and otherwise. I understand
there are apps that do that these days."

Horrifying! "You would do that? Rob me of my privacy?"

"I'd rather not."

"You've always been so into everybody being an individual and doing their thing."

"As I said, I'd rather not."

The threat hangs in the air. I take a step back. "Okay, I get
the message: don't leave town."

Getting ready for bed, I'm seriously on edge from what
she said. I'll probably be jumpy forever now. When I get my
phone back, I'll permanently be wondering if I'm being
tracked.

Risto is who I need to make contact with. My phone
won't help me with that. And there's no wig handy. Behind
every thought I have is the big ache of him being gone. Like a
bad sunburn that goes deeper and deeper.

And where is Dad? He lives God-knows-where, in an
apartment I still haven't seen. Very wrong. Why haven't I
seen it? I'm going to call him on the landline in the hall. Set
something up. He'll be pleased I'm "taking initiative."

He answers his cell first ring. "Darcy!" He sounds happy,
as I knew he would.

"I was thinking," I say, "maybe we could go bowling

again this Saturday and then visit your new place." Then I remember: grounded. "No, make it next Saturday."

"Here's the problem, Darcy. I'm going to be out of town next weekend."

His tone seems off, too hurried. He's hiding something. "Where are you going, Dad?"

"Getting away for a little break. Thought I'd ride down toward the beach."

The beach. He's taking some woman to the beach. I won't let myself picture this.

"How about this Saturday?" he's saying. "We could—"

I stop him. "That won't work." My brain has gone fuzzy. I hear myself sounding squeaky-voiced and hang up quickly as possible, go back in my room.

Fallen back on the bed, I let my eyes follow along the ceiling cracks. He's never been a beach-weekend guy. Waves are for research, not recreation. Once again, I think: something weird is going on with Dad, with the split. I've had that feeling all along.

CHAPTER

SIXTEEN

Waiting for the printer in Dad's old study to print out some pictures. Now lying on the floor on the dusty-smelling Oriental rug in this space that has changed so much since Dad moved. My heart is exhausted just from looking around this room. All the framed pictures of Mom and me are gone, and nothing has been put in their place. The bookshelves have vacant spaces, like somebody with missing teeth. I used to lie in here on the floor and read while he worked. Why did I ever stop? This could get me upset, but I have to keep going, because what I'm doing is going to help with the Risto/hair problem. It's what Dad would call "a sound strategy." The wig strategy turned out to be expensive and none of them looked like me anyway. None of them were at all straggly.

Instead I'm printing out enlarged copies of school pictures of me: one with my old hair that I can wear as a mask to entice him into the room. I know it's juvenile, but I think it might get his attention enough to pause so we can talk. Then I can show him school pictures with my hair at different lengths at different years, how it gets shorter and then longer again. If thinking I'm no longer Darcy is the real reason he's disappeared, this ought to get him here again.

Back in my room, I hold the picture in front of my face as I stand at the mirror. This isn't going to work: I can't see the mirror. To do the scrying, you have to stare into the reflective surface, make a bridge. I cut two eyeholes, tiny ones, look again.

If I get caught doing this, I'll be hauled to a therapist whether I want to go or not. I'll be under constant watch. Or people will treat me the way some of the kids do with peculiar-neighbor Mr. Frederick.

Maybe ten minutes have passed. How long can I stand to stand here?

I stare deep deep deep into my eyes in the mirror, or the picture of my eyes with the little peepholes, looking for Risto to swirl into being, but I see only me. There I am with the photo of my non-edgy old hair, the way I was when Risto thought I was wonderful.

I look until I feel cross-eyed, which seems like over an hour. Letting the mask fall, I check the time: fourteen minutes. I don't think it's going to happen.

THE BASEMENT IS CLEANED UP, the five days of being grounded finished. I'm sitting in English, taking a partial interest— we've finished mythology, have moved on to folktales. After this class, I intend to talk to Martin, never mind that he hasn't answered my text. I need my allies, my friends. I can at least deal with my normal human life. I let my relationship with Risto interfere with my everyday life and friends, and I have to fix things.

So I'll find out what Martin told my mother and why—and what my father is doing that he's being so vague about. I'm going to dig up what's happening underneath everything else, what nobody is talking about.

A plan is starting to form. I'll need Martin to do the driving again. More important, I want him to be with me in this. Also, I want to know what's going on with him. I'm convinced that something's bothering him, and it's not just me. There's no concrete reason for me to be so sure about this, but I know him and I feel something churning around in him.

It's not until after fourth period that I see him, dropping coins into a drink machine to get his Gatorade. I pause for a moment, yards away, to decide how to make my approach. This is still new territory; he and I have never had a rift before. Makes me feel like I'm falling and falling through empty air.

At the machine, I come up beside him. We're elbow to elbow. He jerks his head back when he sees me, starts to say something, cuts himself off.

"Martin, we need to talk. I'm unhappy you told on me."

"I was worried about you. I still am."

"What did you do, call Mom when you knew I was out of the house?"

"It was an accident, Darcy. I was getting stuff at the

grocery for my mother and I ran into her. At the ice cream freezer."

"Exactly how did the subject of me come up?"

"What else would we talk about?

"You know what I mean."

"She asked me. She said, 'Does Darcy seem okay to you? Dealing with all the changes?' I said you were maybe developing some new interests."

"So you jumped right in and told her about the parapsychologists?"

"She got it out of me. She's good at that. I couldn't lie to her when it was maybe something she ought to know."

"*Ought* to know?"

"You did pass out at Jared's. I didn't say anything to her about that. You *are* different from how you used to be. I hear you've disappeared from social media entirely."

"You're different too, Martin. You never told on me before. I have this feeling that stuff is going on with you that you're not saying." He's backing away from me, his face closed down.

"Martin, wait!" He's my friend. I can't lose him. He keeps walking, doesn't look back. "Traitor," I mutter after him, not loud enough for him to hear. I rush blindly toward the girls' bathroom before I'm seriously crying.

POST-DINNER. Back in my room. Texted Martin. No answer. I'm trying to put my life back together and it's only getting pulled farther apart. Also—and this is big—I'm now quite worried about Martin. He doesn't seem like his usual self—

too moody and overly quiet, on the edge of irritable—and I can't believe it's all about me being interested in spooky stuff or chairing the prom committee.

He's never been somebody who talks a whole lot, and he doesn't always say the right thing when he does. But he's always been stand-up solid. He never would have walked away from a conversation the way he did today.

Watching my phone for a reply from Martin, I remember Great Hawk Wing's number. I've been hesitant to text him, even though he and I shared that moment at the convention, because he's older and too weird and I hardly know him and he could get the wrong idea. But I'm going to do it. Now.

"H-a-w-k..." Not sure how to word this. *Hawk I need 2 talk Will call Darcy*

Yes. That works.

Minutes pass. More minutes. He's the type who could have his phone off. He's probably studying. I don't know if he's a grad student or if I only thought he was.

I'm obsessing. This is so Charlotte. I'm stopping now. Probably I should get my thoughts organized about what exactly to say if he calls me.

Ringing! And it's his number.

"Oh hi, Hawk."

"Hey there." He sounds uneasy.

"Is this a bad time?" I say, although he called, not me, which proves he's not busy.

"Not too bad."

I fear he's thinking I'm crushing on him, which I'm not. "This is probably a bad time," I tell him. "So, bye. Talk to you later." Before he can say a word, I hang up.

Now I'm embarrassed. That was ridiculous. Silly! How can I be so anxious about a phone call? I got stage fright or something. Maybe this guy makes me nervous. Or maybe Mom and Martin are right and I'm not doing well at all.

Sitting on the brick wall that borders the school's breezeway. Kicking my foot at my backpack and waiting. It's late. Most everybody's gone. Football practice at this distance sounds like soft clapping. Whistle, yells, more clapping and slapping. Martin was supposed to be here twenty minutes ago. He said he'd come, but that was before our fight at the drink machine. I'm ready to leave without talking to him, but I can't. We have to get past our problems. I can't be Martin-less.

Finally, he comes loping up. "Editing some video took way long," he says, sitting down, leaving a big space between us. He turns sideways, puts his big feet in that open space of brick. The wall is barely wide enough for his shoes.

I jump right in. "Martin, let's do a day trip Saturday."

"You want to go on a day trip with a snitch?"

"I'm sorry. I was upset. I need your help and your company. And I can't stand this weirdness between us. So, if you're willing, here's how we can do this."

"What is how?" He's looking wary, resentful.

"'What is how?' That sounds so funny." I can't keep from laughing. "That's not the way you talk." I feel him getting pissed off. Of course he is, who wouldn't be, but I can't stop. Doubled over, I see the feet of kids passing. It wasn't that funny. Maybe I'm crying. Ballet flats pass, and big running shoes.

A voice floats back from one of the guys: "Party on, children..." Drama kids; no one else would say that.

Sitting up, I wipe my face, rub under my eyes at the mascara I know has run. Martin isn't looking at me, he's staring straight ahead, his face turned hard.

All at once, I'm exhausted. Completely fizzled.

"Martin, forget the thing with my mom. It's okay. And I'm sorry I got hysterical just now. I need you to help me. Dad's going away this weekend—I know this may sound ridiculous—I want us to follow him, find out what he's doing. It's something suspicious, I'm pretty sure. The one time I tried hard to get him to tell me went badly, really made him mad."

Martin's eyes roam all around my face. "So you think following him is going to go well, Darcy?" He does a weary, disgusted sigh. "You need me with you if you're going to do something this dumb."

SEVENTEEN

M artin and I are in his car by 7 o'clock Saturday morning. What I've gone through to make this happen is my most complex organizing ordeal ever:

1. Squeezing out of Dad what time he's leaving on his trip without raising suspicion.

2. Presenting an acceptable excuse to Mom without outright lying.

3. Dealing with Martin's second thoughts about going.

4. Googling tips on how to follow a car without being seen.

5. Asking myself—over and over—whether I really want to know what Dad's up to.

6. Pondering what to do if I get caught, what to say to Mom, also how to keep Martin going instead of doing a U-turn and taking us back home.

7. Important: making careful note of Dad's license plate number.

8. All the time feeling bad about things being not-good with Martin and about Risto being gone. Makes my chest hurt to think about.

But here we are. So far so good. We are parked at the corner nearest Dad's "room"—the place he is currently living, and what a scuzzy place it appears to be! No wonder he hasn't wanted me to come here. When I finally saw the outside two weeks ago, it was at night, so I didn't see the run-down look of the old house. He's kept saying he wants to see me on "familiar ground." Like a bowling alley?

"I don't know what he thinks he's doing," I say. "This is not how semi-famous professors who hold patents are supposed to live."

Martin takes a swig of coffee out of his thermos, wipes his mouth with the back of his wrist. "Divorce is expensive."

"There he is—" I duck down so I'm barely peeking over the dashboard. Dad throws his shaving kit into his car, across to the shotgun seat. Does that mean no one is going to be sitting there? He's not picking anyone up? "He's traveling light. He's going to wear the same clothes all weekend? Not if he's going to impress some woman."

Martin doesn't say anything. He's not bothering to hide. Dad's car is pulling out. He turns left, heading away from us.

"Okay, now. Go!"

He slowly reaches for the ignition, slowly turns the key. Dad is already nearly a block away. "Please hurry." We're rolling, turning onto the street, maybe three-fourths of a block away from the back of Dad's Prius. He makes a turn.

Moments pass; losing sight of him makes me tense. We turn. He's in front of us again, his license plate that starts DVR is easy to remember.

"You have a full tank of gas, right? I mean I'll pay you back, but we can't stop."

"Full tank," Martin says. Two syllable answer. He still disapproves of this adventure.

Onto the Beltline. Chasing Dad's car, changing lanes to keep him in view. We turn, heading out of town to the east. He hasn't picked anybody up.

"Maybe he has a girlfriend at the beach," I say to Martin, "and keeps extra clothes at her place. That could help explain his drab location in town. Except I don't think that's it. If it were, he'd seem happier."

He ignores my comment. If things were normal, he'd be helping me consider the possibilities. Like what kind of woman would Dad be seeing? I'm picturing someone earnest and quiet like him. I see her as tall and thin. Serious. Flat-chested. Martin says nothing.

He licks his lips, clears his throat. "Have you thought about what you're going to say if you get caught at this?"

"Maybe he'd think it's sweet that I'm following him?"

Martin rolls his eyes. He's right, Dad would not be happy.

We're one car behind him as he continues to head east. Definitely toward the beach. The Emerald Isle area. Long straight stretch of road ahead.

"So, Martin, what's going on with you? I mean, aside from stuff with me?"

He gives me another you-have-got-to-be-kidding-me look and turns on NPR. I rip open a giant box of Raisinets—

his favorite—and reach it toward him. No reaction. His face tells me he's through talking. If Risto were here, I'd be in utter bliss. As it is, I ache full-time. Risto has disappeared and Martin's so cold.

If Risto would listen to me for one minute, I could explain hair, that it grows and changes. I'm going to send him a message, psychically. Like a silent chant: Risto! Listen! Hair grows back!

Sending to Risto: I'm your Darcy, same as before!

This is serious. With my eyes closed, I can see the two lines of message, tumbling end over end into space.

Risto, Risto, hair grows back... I think it again and again and again, maybe a thousand times. It has to work.

...And I must have dozed a little, because we're starting to make turns, which is what woke me up. Looks like we're heading for the beach, the south end of the Outer Banks. So I slept for hours, emotionally tired, also hiding out from Martin's silence. Did I dream? Did Risto get my message?

I was right. The beach. We're coming into Emerald Isle, clouds deep over on the ocean side. I rouse myself and sit up and straighten out my rumpled top. Dad's ahead of us, slowing. He's obviously looking for something. If he has a girlfriend who lives here, he'd know which house.

Signaling a turn onto a road that leads into deep woods. "Hang back, Martin! Let him turn. Then we can cruise up there to see what the situation is."

Martin slows, but doesn't even look interested. I am literally on the edge of the car seat. Beach traffic—in February—is starting to pile up behind us. I don't care. "Look, there's a sign." It's serious-looking, stone, like the entrance to a subdivision. "The Dovecote. Doesn't sound like a beach cottage name."

We've passed the entrance where Dad turned. "So google it," he says. It's a relief to hear him speak. Here it is: Dovecote NC Emerald Isle. The site comes up, top of the list.

"Are you kidding me? Oh, jeez. Martin, pull over."

"Not here, I'll get stuck in the sand."

"The website says '...silent retreat...prayer retreat... Daily Offices from the Book of Common Prayer.' He drove all this way to pray? Since when does he pray? He doesn't pray! He would have to be a completely different person to do this, someone I don't know at all. A stranger. And what is he praying for—getting Mom back?" Martin is pulling off into a restaurant parking lot. The Crab Shack. "What are Daily Offices, anyway?"

"They're little prayer services, I think," he says when the car comes to a stop, "at particular times of day."

"He needs to pray several times a day and drive all this way to do it? He doesn't believe in praying. This is wrong. He's not that kind of person. He's rational, logical, evidence-based, a thinker, which is what he's encouraged me to be. And praying isn't going to fix their marriage, whatever's wrong with it."

"Could he be involved with a woman who works here?"

"How would I know? He tells me nothing. Everybody tells me nothing." I'm on the edge of crying, in the parking lot of the Crab Shack at the beach. The beach, which I've hardly noticed. I can't keep from crying. Why am I so upset by him wanting to be silent at the beach? Maybe that's all it is—a getaway. I picture him walking by himself in a jacket with the collar turned up, under the gray February sky. So sad!

Martin paws in my purse, hands me a Kleenex, then stares ahead, waiting. "What now?" he says when he sees I'm starting to recover.

"We have to go down that road to see what's there."

He blows out his breath, swears at the closed window on his other side. "We know what's there. You're risking getting caught. Is that what you want?"

"I have to find out more. I have to know why my Dad is acting like a different person: not taking me to his apartment, not answering my questions, letting our family fall apart. It's obvious to me that Mom didn't change. He did. Martin, what I'm doing, I'm trying to hold my life together. And I'm worried about my dad."

He wheels us out into traffic, back in the direction of the turn Dad took. He's going to do it, in spite of everything. He's still with me.

CHAPTER

EIGHTEEN

P arked in the sandy lot, Martin has his car seat tilted back, pretending to sleep. I've been slumped down out of sight and peeking out for twenty minutes, waiting for a safe time to get out. I have to know: is Dad here to do religious stuff or meet up with some woman or just read and walk on the beach?

He has every right to go to the beach in winter weather or date anyone, but I need to know if there's some big change, if my father isn't who he was.

The door to the big house opens. Crouching low, I can barely see out. Already this has happened three times, and it hasn't been him.

A guy—not Dad—comes out. He's probably twenty-five years old, sort of gorgeous in a ghostly blond way. How many guests are crammed into this place? Does every one of them have to parade by? The guy pauses at the top of the steps, looking back.

Dad appears behind him! Blond Guy trails down the stairs, followed by Dad looking like his usual over-concerned self. Are they together? My heart does a quiver. He made Mom feel untouchable. No, my gut would tell me if Dad were gay. The guy was probably already here, works here maybe. There's a Risto quality about him, though he's pale. He has a sort of shine.

I sink lower, onto the car floor. They're coming into view in the outside rearview mirror, passing twenty feet from where I'm scrunched down below the open car window. The other guy is talking about "the campus" and the sacristy here. Sacristy? Not a word I've heard before. They talk in a polite careful way, like they've just met. Now heading down the sandy road, back toward the highway. The sound of their voices gets smaller and disappears, leaving nothing but seagulls and the steady wind in the twisty oaks around the house.

"Martin?"

He opens his eyes.

"My dad and some guy left, walking. I'm going inside. I'm going to see what this place is and what goes on in there. Call me if you see or hear any sign of him coming back."

"What are you going to do if he does, jump out a window?"

"It's a big building. It has to have more than one door."

"What do I say if your father sees me?"

"Keep your head down and he won't."

Getting out, I slam the door loud like an unworried person, walk at a leisurely speed up the front steps. Above the scrubby beach trees, the wind has a sharp unfriendly edge. If I see anyone inside, I'll keep walking authoritatively, like I'm supposed to be here.

I enter into a big living room/kitchen with a tray of little cupcakes on the counter. How bad would it be if I ate one? If I took one to Martin, since we haven't stopped for lunch? I eat a couple—they're so small—with strawberry icing. Walk down a hall. Lots of windows in the little rooms I can see into, tiny spaces with single beds, a desk and chair in each. The ocean is out every window on one side of the building, the place full of a whisper and swish from the breaking waves. I could live here.

Is that what Dad's thinking about? Living here? Who could blame him? He'd have to quit his job, though, and see a lot less of me. It would be a long commute.

Beyond the foot of the stairs is a tiny chapel, the size of a walk-in closet. Two closets at most. It's pretty in here—full of sun and the sound of the ocean from the other side of the dunes. But you can't see the ocean, which is kind of fitting, since you can't see God. Or I can't, anyway.

The light from the church-type window is nice, and the whiteness of the sand outside. Risto would love all the crooked-trunk trees and the long beach. At least I think he would; I don't really know. Hardly anybody out there today. He and I could walk two miles probably and see almost no one, or sail along. I'd rather go for an ordinary walk on the beach with him, like people do with their boyfriends. I'm determined to make that possible, but first—

Was that a honk? Oh, no!

Rattle of a door opening on the other side of the house. Quick, close the chapel door! It doesn't lock. I drop down, sit with my back pressing it shut. I'm in hiding. If anybody tries to come in, I won't say anything. They'll think somebody's doing silent prayer.

My heart feels like I've sprinted. He's out there. Dad, with the guy. I hear them talking—can't understand. They're over near the bookshelves, on the other side of the room.

"...Thinking that I might not be able to discern..." Dad! His voice has moved closer to my door. "I wanted time," he says. Time for what? Discern what?

A mutter from the other guy: "...Hard for the partner of course."

The partner?! They're both moving near my door. The partner: that's Mom. Dad wanted time. Obviously this has to do with them separating. Mom was in a hurry. She didn't want to give him more time. She better not have been seeing Webb then.

Turning so my ear is pushed hard against the door, I can't make out any more. Then a footstep sounds like sandpaper against the floor inches away from me on the other side of the door, and the doorknob makes the slightest movement, the start of a rattle. No! You're not coming in here!

I press against the wood with all of my weight. He's going to find that this door is stuck. Nobody will be able to move it. Nobody!

"Curses!" whispers the voice—not Dad—as the door shakes. "It can't be locked."

Wham! The door bangs against my head and sweeps me aside. Standing over me is the young blond guy. I look past him. No sign of Dad.

"Holy cow!" the guy says.

I'm holding on to where my forehead hurts, which is already swelling under my fingers into a lump. Any second Dad could walk in behind him.

"Are you alone?" I ask.

"What?" He stares at me like I'm some kind of odd creature he's found on the beach. "Are you okay?"

"Fine." I keep my hand on my forehead to hide any damage. "You surprised me. I was having a quiet moment. Don't worry about it." Getting up, I'm dizzy. I manage to look past him into the other room. Empty. Dad already left. This could still work out.

"Are you here with your family?" the guy says.

"No! No, no family. I have to be going." I'm on my feet, slipping past him. Best not to run. "I'm visiting, checking the place out." A strategic thought: "What brings you here, by the way?"

"Me?" He's walking along with me. "Silent worship. For a few days. Needed to reconnect with my vocation."

We're past the library, down the hall. One room away from the door. "But you're not silent."

He seems annoyed. "There have been some interruptions."

"Sorry I disturbed you. You can be silent now." We're only a few feet from the exit. "Bye." And I'm out the door, closing it firmly behind me.

Starting down the steps, I see Martin's car. And—Dad, standing at the driver's side window. I *told* Martin to stay down. He's getting out, his back to me, standing up facing Dad.

Taking two steps back, out of sight, I sink down onto the step. Need one moment to pull myself together. But Martin could be saying stuff that makes this worse. Instantly I'm on my feet, down the stairs, rushing toward them.

"Dad!" as if I'm simply happy to see him, which I partly am. Martin turns, and he and Dad stare at me, looking horrified. Martin puts his hand to his forehead. I touch mine, the spot I kept hidden before, now wet. Look at my fingers: bloody.

"What—!" Dad is coming around the car toward me. "What happened? What have you done?"

CHAPTER

NINETEEN

artin's mom and mine have been called and
informed. The three of us—Dad, Martin, and
me—have settled into a booth at a fried fish
place. Lowish light. Dad's eyes look pouchy and tired. Martin
is mostly watching the surfer video over the bar. He thinks I
had this coming.

What is it about me riding to the beach that makes Dad
look so defeated? His expression—forlorn and bitter—makes
me almost wish I hadn't done it.

The waiter wants to know if we'd like something to
drink. Martin is looking uncomfortable. Everybody wants
only water to drink, as if we can't order anything frivolous
when everything is so serious. Martin and Dad get veggie
burgers, which reminds me that I left Martin's cupcake on a
chair in the little chapel. Nothing to do about that now. I
order fried oysters. We're at the beach and somebody around
here has to act like it.

Finished ordering, Dad gets ready to speak. Martin being here is cramping his style, but he could hardly ask him to go away, so I'll get only the watered-down version of whatever is coming. I know I'm in trouble. I don't care about that. In the big picture of where our lives are now, it's just not important.

"So Dad," I start, "what are you doing in this place anyway?"

"Over and over, I've said I wanted to talk about these things in my own time." He's right, he has said pretty much this same thing four or five times. He's shaking his head, looking bummed.

"You don't have to tell me. Forget it."

"Dr. Colvard," Martin says, "I think it'd be good if I left you guys. I'll go over to the ocean for a while."

"Stay where you are, Martin. You're already involved and Darcy counts on you."

Martin settles back in, looking unhappy.

"I'm serious," I say. "You don't have to tell me." I'm starting to get scared. "Are you sick, Dad?"

"I'm not sick. I am of sound mind, never more so."

"No, I mean, do you have cancer, something physical?"

"No, no diseases." He looks away. His face is arguing with itself. I wait. "What's happened, Darcy, is—" His whole face brightens. "I'm not sure how to word this. I suppose it's what some would call 'getting religion.' I came here to meditate and pray." His expression, I've never seen him look this way, like he's completely full of happiness, no pinched-up place between his eyebrows. I wish Mom could see.

But the look is already fading as he says, "I know I've

handled this badly, with your mother and you." I want him to stay the way he was a moment ago, all the tension and heaviness gone from him.

Twisting a straw round and round my finger, I'm trying to think and take all this in. Because he doesn't approve of religion. He's against it. Beside me, Martin's leg has gotten nervous.

"Dad, you never even made me go to Sunday school. You probably wouldn't have *let* me go. You don't believe in that stuff. There's no proof."

"This has been unexpected. I tried to fight it off."

"I don't understand what you mean."

"I came to feel the presence of God, to want a more spiritual kind of life. You could say I fell in love with God." Again, I see the expression of gladness take over his face, light his eyes. He looks beautiful. Happy and beautiful.

"So is this why you and Mom split? She didn't want you to love God?" All the radiance goes away again. I wish I hadn't asked.

"I wouldn't put it that way, nor would she. But something like that. I was going to tell you more about my belief, my conversion, when I'd fully made sense of it."

"How did this happen? Did you just wake up one morning being religious? Did you have a vision?"

"I was at the lab at the coast, out of sight of land on one of their vessels. The ocean was so smooth and calm, I felt like I could see the curve of the earth and feel the depth beneath us, all of it immensely large. And alive, Darcy. Alive! The fact that we were floating in the midst of it seemed like a miracle. A flood of joy washed over me, through me. My edges disappeared. And the thought popped into my head: 'It's all true."

"All of what?"

"All the religions. The ones at least that recognize we're connected to something divine."

"But you've been out on the ocean a million times."

"I can't tell you why that day was different. There's a lot I don't understand. Faith is supposed to make people kinder, more joyful. In my case it has mainly led to my disappointing your mom and all the distress the separation has caused you. I'm completely torn up about how this has turned out."

"But, Dad, lots of couples have two different religions. I know people whose parents are like that. They have Hannukah and Christmas or whatever. Or one is religious and the other isn't. I don't get why it has to be a big deal."

"Darcy, that's a matter I'm simply not comfortable explaining to you."

"Not comfortable?" I can't believe I'm hearing this. What would he not want to say to me? That he made Mom feel untouchable? That he literally stopped touching her?

"I'm truly sorry not to tell you more." He looks sorry, which is the only thing that keeps me from exploding.

"Okay." My voice feels weak and breathy, like I've just run for miles.

"Likely the time will come," he says. "But let's not make Martin any more uncomfortable than he already is. How about we have lunch?" His voice tries to get cheerful, but his eyes remain sad.

"Okay. I guess." I don't know what else to say. I've lost

my dad. He's changed. He changed months ago and I didn't see it. And he doesn't want to talk to me about it.

WE'RE JUST FINISHING our speedy, mostly quiet lunch, Dad asking Martin a few questions about his classes and track. Now I'm the one who's looking at the surfer video across the room—or down at my plate. It's late for lunch. There are only a few people here and they're mainly at the bar.

There! My eyes make a sudden stop. Two tables away— Risto! Sitting so he's facing me, poking at French fries. He looks up, sees me watching him and smiles. My efforts have paid off! He has to have heard me sending him messages on the road! He knows I'm upset and he's here. I get tears in my eyes. Dad looks where I'm looking. Can't tell if he sees Risto, in a brand-new just-unfolded T-shirt with a sailfish on it. Where does he get an ordinary human T-shirt? Maybe it happens automatically, like protective coloration. What doesn't look ordinary is the glow of his skin. Suntan doesn't do this. Also unusual: he's spearing fries with a knife.

We make eye contact again. Again, I send him the silent message, hard as I can: Risto, hair grows back. Risto, I'm still me. He smiles as if we'd never been apart, his fabulously beautiful sun-shining-on-water smile. He puts a hand up to his own dark hair that, I remember, smells like pine needles. He understands. He got my messages. He came to find me here and he understands about hair. I feel huge waterfalls of relief and happiness.

And now I know I can communicate. I have some power of my own. I can reach him if I think hard enough.

Then I remember: my face. I make sure my bangs are still covering the horrible scraped purple lump on my temple. Can't let him see it or he'll think I've changed again.

"That bump hurting you, Darcy?" Dad says.

"It's okay."

"You need to keep ice on it."

I lift my icy drink glass to my forehead, like I'm toasting Risto, look back in his direction. But he's gone.

Dad's watching me, carefully; he's worried about me. I'm the one who should worry about *him*. Religion is the last thing he ever wanted. Really, he always hated it. What he's always wanted is logical, rational science—plus Mom and me. He has lost so much. This God business had better start bringing him a lot more than flickers of happiness. Maybe the reason he was so against it for so long was that he was always fighting it off.

I need to understand Dad and Risto, what worlds they're in. They both seem to slip away so easily, but I can't lose either of them.

CHAPTER

TWENTY

S eems there's another price to pay for what my mother called "running off across the state for the *second* time." I've used up my reserve of parental tolerance. I'll never be trusted again. Almost two weeks since the beach trip and I have to ask permission to walk down the street. Also, Mom has made it plenty clear that I am going to the cookout with Webb that's been delayed twice already. She's using my guilty-busted-in-trouble situation to get something she wants.

More upsetting, though, is that Risto hasn't returned. I could live with being grounded forever if only I could count on seeing him, could understand who and what he is. But I'm worried that his appearance at the beach was some kind of good-bye. Definitely didn't seem like it then, but I've started to wonder because he hasn't been back for so long. It's not like I can run into him at school and get a feeling for what's going on. I think constantly about him. It can't be healthy to obsess over someone who is either lightyears away, or... Or what? A fantasy? I still get tiny twinges of doubt.

I thought he understood the hair message I sent him, but maybe his showing up had nothing to do with that. Maybe he just does what he wants! I have moments when I wonder if I could have invented this whole thing. Then I remind myself that Charlotte saw *something*, and Hawk heard the same sound I did at the convention—though it wasn't Risto —and Risto moved a glass across the room and my feet were red where he touched me and...and...

And I've been going to bed early every night to try some sort of telepathy to reach Risto and convince him to return. I've told Mom I'm catching up on sleep, but I'm sleeping in a slip dress just in case Risto should return—clothes that flow seem like the right thing with him.

Night One: he doesn't show. I woke up with a faint trace of make-up on the pillow.

Night Two: same story. Except I wake up every hour, thinking I'll find him sitting at the end of the bed. Every time, I lie awake for a while, sending out mental messages to Risto and worrying about Dad. At the coast, it seemed that he could hear me call him, but now I'm not so sure.

Night Three: frustration. Irritation. Throw the slip dress in the laundry hamper, then take it out, stuff it in the back of a drawer—can't have Mom asking questions about the radical change in my sleepwear...

Night Six: stay up late watching old *Seinfeld* episodes with Mom. Go to bed in extra-loose shorts and a tee.

Sometime in the middle of the night, something wakes

me. Before I can think, I see Risto! He's here! He's back! Standing in the middle of the room, he looks eager and in a hurry. Like he's trying to rush me with his eyes. Never mind the tee and shorts; doesn't matter.

"Risto! You're here! Don't go! I've been trying to communicate with you for so long."

"I received. Then I have come here upon two different days seeking for you and found only empty room full of light. Hasten, please. We have not many hours."

He was here and I missed him? Did he come during the day? Why didn't he find me at school or wherever? When I hop out of bed, he looks at what I'm wearing and smiles. The shorts are baggy, riding low. "This is clothing for sporting man. Comfortable garment for travel."

"Where are we going?"

"To see the world. Your message say you want to know more. We proceed to distant Earth location, romantic, full of loves to give to MyDarcy."

I am mad with excitement. Don't need to figure out or find out anything. I don't even care that he's misunderstood my messages—it was *his* world I wanted to know more about. Doesn't matter. He wants to give "loves" to me.

I reach for him and all at once we're moving. The floor is gone. I'm lying on air. Everything else has dropped away.

I'm rolling.

"Risto!" My stomach lurches. I'm going to get sick. Oh, please no. Sparkling cities swoop under me, disappear again. We're sailing like gliders cut loose from a plane, wafting on currents of air. The surface of the Earth slips past far below in the dim light.

We're coming out of night, into day. Round the world. I don't care where we go. I don't care how he's doing this or how any of it works; I don't tell myself it's impossible, because it's happening, it's better than fantastic, and it's *real*. And whatever he thinks is romantic is fine with me. I love drifting beside him, his shoulder close. His curly hair has the same billowy surface as some of the clouds. If he showed up with a brush cut, I guess I'd be upset too.

He's looking carefully below us. "We are nearing." All I see is clouds, cirrostratus, I think. But I don't think too hard about it, don't need the name right now. They look like a soft mat, like cotton you buy in a roll. If I let myself fall, I would sink deep into it, bounce back up again.

"The moment is here. Follow."

Fear seizes me. We're about to plunge. I'm in motion before I can think another sentence, flipping into a jackknife dive and zooming down, headfirst. Now entering the white cotton layer. Deep inside it is wet and gray. My face collects water like a windshield.

Then lighter up ahead. Warm air brushing over my cheeks. We're out of the clouds, into the low sky. I'm looking down on flat brown land, a wide muddy river. Not romantic.

"It is there," Risto says. "Observe this direction."

I see it! The Taj Mahal! White against the brown land, as if it's a ghost of a building, the dome so smooth I want to reach down and let my fingers slide over it. Sun glistening on white marble, gleaming on the long reflecting pool in front. The tall towers at the corners look fragile, like they're made out of sugar. So many bright green birds! "The real Taj Mahal!"

"It is most real." He drops onto the white terrace, as easy as touching the bottom of a pool. I do the same. Here we stand, about three feet away from an Indian woman in an orange silk sari so bright I taste citrus. I'm still in my stretched-out shorts and tee. "Uma," she keeps saying to her little girl, who is running all over the place.

They don't seem to see us. Invisible! What an amazing freedom. I tangle up my fingers in Risto's hair, kiss his neck. We have total privacy. He puts his arms around me, and swoosh, we are inside the Taj Mahal together, holding each other like we're slow dancing.

Packed in here with us is a crowd of tourists led by a guide talking about the inlay of flowers in the walls, the rare auspicious stones. The two lovers have been buried in this most glorious location—the Mughal emperor who had this whole Taj Mahal built as a tomb for his beloved wife. Travelers fan themselves with souvenir booklets. This floaty-looking white building is hot and dim inside, the air heavy with incense.

Two lovers buried here. My parents won't even be buried together now. That's weird. I run my fingers over the stone flowers. The spirits of the couple must be here too, invisible like Risto and me. The thought of it makes me reach for his hand. "Can you see them?"

He looks confused.

"The emperor and his wife."

"I cannot see these." His eyes smile like he's delighted I would think of such a thing.

We stay wrapped around each other in the midst of the tourists. It's so private and cozy that I hate to break the mood, but I have to. I promised myself and I need to know. "Risto, I need your help understanding."

"I am happy."

I think that means he'll try. "The thing is, I need to understand about the spirit world, how it works. I need to know how Dad could suddenly want such a totally spiritual life. You're a spirit, right?"

Risto pulls back from me. He's getting pale, the colors of him going thin and see-through. He's gone.

No!

I am on the other side of the world with no way to get home. Panting with fear, I search frantically in every direction.

"Risto!" I yell. He doesn't reappear. No one looks in my direction. No one seems to see or hear me. "Come back, Risto. Please!" He can't leave me here!

The air still feels hot where he was. I slide my back down the nearest wall until I'm sitting, flip-flops and running shoes passing me. Ten minutes go by. I'm sobbing. Doesn't he know what a terrible thing he's done?

Twenty minutes, if human time counts. I wipe my face on my T-shirt hem and start to think about how I could get home. Could I get myself to an airport and sneak onto a plane? It should be possible if no one can see me. But if I can float myself to an airport, then I ought to be able to float myself home.

Through the crowd, a pair of feet is coming straight toward me, long tan feet in hippie sandals, dusty. I look up and see Risto. It's him. In different clothes, wearing an Indian kurta. My throat feels too tight to speak because I'm so angry and at the same time so relieved. I need to get home, though, before he pulls some trick like this again.

"When you disappeared, I thought I'd lost you," I say. "I thought you'd abandoned me here."

"You cannot lose. You are safe."

My chest floods with joy at hearing him say this, though I know he may be talking only about this trip.

"I have come with some answer for you," he says.

"What answer did you get? About my Dad."

"For you, MyDarcy." The sound of my name in his voice makes me want to cry again. He hands me a small gift-wrapped box tied with ribbon that looks like it's made of fast-running water. Touching it gives me the faintest shock.

"What is it?"

"I have not examined the within."

"I will open." I'm talking like him. His inner language gizmo needs an upgrade. Coming up from my slumped position, I pull the box open, watery ribbon still clinging to the outer surfaces. Inside, a picture of Risto. But he's transparent. The trees behind him in the photo are visible through him. There's our creek, the greenery has that hyper-electric look.

"Spirit," he says.

"Yes?"

"You ask me what is spirit."

I turn it to face him.

He seizes the paper, studies it closely, top to bottom, side to side. "I do not know this entity."

"Entity? That guy is you, Risto."

He laughs as if I'm being silly, hands the picture back to

me. Again, the faint shock from the ribbon. I look again, and the image of him has grown brighter, almost solid.

"You don't recognize yourself at all?" I'm remembering the day years ago when we showed Charlotte's cat BangBang his reflection in a mirror. He sniffed and nosed at the glass and flicked his tail in the air and walked away. I can't believe Risto hasn't seen himself. No mirrors? He knows how to come out of a mirror. "Risto, you haven't seen yourself reflected in water at least?"

"I enter into water very much," he says. He looks like he's being accused of something, or laughed at.

I give up, for the moment anyway. "It's okay, don't worry about it." He looks unhappy. I don't blame him. A guy with something like superpowers — a guy who can levitate and take me with him! —ought to also have the fundamentals. No wonder he doesn't like being asked questions. What else doesn't he know? I think he knows even less about where he comes from than he does about life here. Here?! I'm in India, I forgot. I'm sitting on the floor inside the hot Taj Mahal, feet and ankles — brown, white, badly sunburned — shuffling past.

The box in my hand starts to blur and Risto's face...

I'm lying in my bed at home in my room. Risto's gone, no India or incense or crowd of tourists. In my hand is a cardboard box, ordinary, with no watery ribbon.

WEBB'S BACKYARD HAS A POOL—THE night lights have come on —and a patio with those big warm heater-columns that outdoor cafes use in winter. Very showy. A grill the size of a car behind a big colonial house. He's tending the meat with a long fork, and—the absolute worst—wearing sandals. He thinks *he's* in India? He thinks it's August? I do not want to see his bare naked feet.

"I'm sorry Tony couldn't be here," he says over his shoulder. "I know he'd like to be. I expected him this weekend... His mother had different plans." He knows better than to face me with such a lie. Tony does not want to be here. He's probably upstairs with the shades pulled down and his earbuds in.

Mom smiles encouragingly from her lounge chair. She's wearing her starchy white button-down untucked over skinny jeans and ankle boots and her bright green cashmere sweater: casually elegant. I'm slumped on the picnic table bench in my oldest sweatshirt, which is all Webb and his pool deserve. Now I have to say something in response to his Tony lie.

"I see Tony around," I say. "Don't really know him."

"He's not a big talker. Got a good mind, though."

"Right." It's the best I can do. I refuse to discuss Tony's mind.

"Darcy, give me a hand here," Webb says. "Hold this plate for me." I get up and take the plate, hold it for him to flop the sizzling meat onto; it's easier than conversation. I can't be expected to do both.

"Gail," he says to Mom, "we're about ready, if you'd like to get the wine and salad."

Mom heads into the house, where she seems to be very much at home, as if she's been here a thousand times. I'm alone with him. I put the plate on the table, go over to a holly tree at the edge of the patio, study one of its leaves. I really am somewhat interested—it's a blue holly. Where I'm standing, to his side, he can see I'm busy avoiding him.

"You a gardener?" he says.

"Not really, my—" I almost said my Dad is, or was. Can't think fast enough to finish the sentence.

"Oh, yes, your dad's the landscape guy. No need to tiptoe."

Surprise: didn't expect straightforward from Webb. I don't like it, could be dangerous. Dad says he has only my houseplant growing in his apartment, which is disturbing. He's given up everything except, so far, his job and me.

"Okay to say whatever comes to mind, Darcy."

"When did you get divorced?"

Quick glance from him, slight smile. "Four years ago. Tony had turned twelve." He keeps busy with the corn cobs that are wrapped in tin foil.

"Does your ex live in town?"

"No. She's a couple of hours away, in Greensboro."

So Tony does a lot of riding back and forth. "You and my mother are getting serious?"

Dishes thunk down on the table ten feet behind me. "Darcy!" Mom, of course. Perfect timing as ever. I don't care if she hears this. I want her to. She says, "You wait until I ask a friend of yours such a question." She's trying to act jokey.

"He told me to say anything I want to."

"Webb, you have no idea what you've unleashed."

He smiles at me. "I'm not worried. In answer to your question: we're taking it slow. Not rushing into anything. We're enjoying the moment." Since Mom's here, and getting more rattled by the second, I'm not going to blurt out what I think about that, which is: doesn't look slow to me.

By the time we sit down at the table, I'm feeling pretty much on top of things. We don't usually do steak at home; we're more of a fish-pasta-soy household. Or were. The smoky grilled meat smells better than tofu ever did.

Webb steers conversation to applying to colleges and whether I like one of "Tony's teachers" and what we think about him putting in some tile mosaic somewhere in the pool area. They don't kiss goodnight in front of me or touch at all, although the air feels full of what they're not doing. I never once call him Webb like he wants me to or any name whatsoever. But I have to admit, Mom looks happy and I can't argue with that.

CHAPTER

TWENTY-ONE

"Help me understand," Mrs. Hartsell, my math teacher, says. We're the only ones in this big hollow-sounding classroom after school. "The errors you've made don't make sense." She holds up my paper full of angry red marks. "Here you seem to have a grasp of the concept. In the next problem, you've lost it completely."

My stomach is already feeling queasy. Not much hope of even a B in pre-calc, and I can't let my grades go. The bright-future-factor is the main thing I've always had going for me, the upside to being a leaf nerd.

"Lost it?" I say, after what was apparently too long a pause. Mrs. Hartsell makes a stern face, as if she thinks I'm making a stupid joke. She has bushy blond hair and hip glasses and a lot of eyeliner. "Lost the mathematical concept, Darcy. I think you know what I mean."

"I wasn't being..." Can't say smart-ass. What *is* the word? She's already moved on.

"I'm not sure what's needed here to turn this situation around." She's wanting me to come up with something, like: Oh, I'm going to get focused, Mrs. Hartsell. But I can't focus when half my life is up in the air, literally, and the other half smashed to pieces on the ground.

"We could set you up with a student tutor."

Tutor? I don't need that. Dad can answer any math questions I have. Although he's not exactly handy at the moment.

"I don't know." I hear myself sounding weary. The thought of math drills makes me tired. Hartsell sends out a don't-cross-me glare and flips through a worn notebook.

"I need to check, but I think I can hook you up with Tony Llewellyn." My mouth drops open. Can I never escape these people? She's going to "hook me up?" No, she will not.

"Not the ideal choice," I say. "I mean, temperamentally. It won't work."

"He's an excellent student, as I'm sure you've noticed in class. Able to reduce a problem to its simplest terms." I am too stunned to speak. I want to tell her: No! No! No! My voice is paralyzed. I'm drowning in dismay. That sullen hostile son of Webb... This has to be a conspiracy.

"I'll speak to him."

"No. He'll say no." My voice box is turned on again.

"I don't know why you think that."

"We don't like each other." This woman must be thick in the head. How can she insist? For all she knows, he has gotten me pregnant three times.

"I see." She flips through her papers. "There are other students who could help you."

"My dad can help me." I start to get up. "If I need any help." In the process, I'll figure out some way to help Dad, which is much more important.

"Fine," she says. "I will not press this—if your grades improve."

DAD DRAWS numbers and equations and graphs like they're designs for little houses, tiny neat constructions. Sheets of them are strewn all over the table at his so-called apartment. Finally, I'm seeing the inside of his sad little place. More than ever I know he badly needs help. It's not a real apartment, it's a studio. No wonder he calls it a room. That's what it is, with a kitchenette in one corner and a minute bathroom walled off in another corner and on the one shelf a couple of pictures of me.

"You understand what I'm saying, Darcy?" He's holding a page in front of me, graphing rational functions. My life is irrational, and so is Dad's. The plant I gave him is the only sign of life here. At least it looks like he's watered it.

"Run through it again, please." I promise myself to follow what he's doing this time. Don't want to seem dumb in front of brainiac Dad. But why does he have a picture of a blissed-out nun, a photo of a marble sculpture of her, thumbtacked to his wall? This is too weird.

"Are you paying attention, Darcy? Do you want my help?"

"I do. Seriously. Sorry." He goes back to tapping the

super-sharp point of his pencil on the paper in front of me, walking through the steps again. "Dad, what is that picture?"

"That's Saint Teresa."

I wait for an explanation, but it doesn't come. "Why do you have her on your wall?"

"She inspires me." He leans back in his chair. "I find her encouraging."

"Dad! A saint?"

"I told you, Darcy. I've unexpectedly developed a passionate certainty—that's the only way I can describe it— about God."

"You never said passionate. Not once. And passion is supposed to be fun and alive, not depressed the way you are." I'm going to lose him big-time. This God thing is going to get him. It's going to take him away to some monastery or ashram or meditation guru. That's what he wants. That's why he's living in this bare drab cell and eating bad food. That's what he's being so secretive about. "I don't understand, Dad. God wants you to live like this, with hardly any furniture?" He says nothing, lips pressed together. "What do you believe, anyway?"

"I wish I could clearly say—I only know that there's a tremendous presence. The invisible source of everything."

I picture him studying waves in his lab. "Like the ocean, but you can't see it." He half-nods, which means I don't have it right at all.

When people get religious they're supposed to be happy. He isn't. I feel sad for him, for me, and for Mom. "Forget I asked about the nun, Dad. Let's do my homework."

. . .

CAN'T GET to sleep and it's not because I'm waiting for Risto. For once, I don't feel like flying away with him. I'm not in the best-ever mood. This bedspread is too heavy. The sheet by itself isn't enough. Dad has a saint on his wall. Does this mean he wants to be one? I picture him in a long black skirt with a pious look on his face. Creepy! Or a martyr—there my imagination stops.

Maybe he's lying awake expecting a nun to show up in the moonlight to take him somewhere. The Taj Mahal? Or Heaven, which is where a nun might go. You might not make it back. You might not want to.

The way he's talking—and acting—it's completely possible he'll decide to lock himself up in a monastery where the monks live in silence, going around with their heads bowed and hoods hiding their faces. Half my family would be gone, disappeared. Because I would hardly ever see him. He'd be a different person. He is already, and there's nothing I can do about it. What am I supposed to think? This is my *father.*

TWENTY-TWO

S tanding at the front of the decorating committee, I take a deep breath to speak and see the faces of the others get suddenly too attentive, a little wary. My Risto thoughts, my Dad worries, for once slide to the side.

"I have an announcement to make." I hate myself for doing this. I'm a loyal person, not a quitter, but it's already March and ridiculously warm outside, only two-and-a-fraction months from prom, and we don't have a theme, which is unbelievable. Everything anybody suggested has fizzled. Something has to be done and I'm too distracted to command a decorating platoon. I need to focus on my personal relationships.

Say it fast: "As of now,"—they're all staring at me, my mouth feels dry and stuck together—"I resign. From this chairman job. Also from this committee. I'm dropping out."

A rustle of movement. Instant exchange of knowing glances, back and forth across the group. Some seem delighted: mainly the two girls who split the most-popular-kid voting block, allowing me to win. "I know this might seem like a not-good thing to do, and I'm sorry, but I think it's for the best." That phrase—"for the best"—is how adults dump obligations, break vows, hurt people's lives.

Martin, who knew this was coming and didn't try to talk me out of it, is looking at the floor. Mrs. Kellum, our faculty advisor, is stern-faced. I have added to her workload. "So I'm going to sit down and you can elect someone else." Within minutes, Layna, who came in second after me, has the job. She shakes her hair back behind her shoulders, steps to the front of the room, all full of authority and the rightness of being Queen. Where does anybody get that kind of confidence? The "I Rule Socially" kind. I'll never understand. My effort to try being normal has now made me seem weirder than I ever was before. Which is fine, but I hate being a quitter.

When I sit down, my face is hot and I can't look at anybody. I made the right decision for the committee and prom, as well as for me, but it still makes me feel shitty. I'm not coming to these meetings anymore, even as an ordinary member. I'm too embarrassed.

Hawk and I both need somebody, an Earth human ally. It's not like either of us has lots of friends to talk to about the Risto world. I don't, anyway. And I'll never feel safe online ever again, not with Mom threatening to follow me. Finding searches about connecting with spirits would just upset them. Neither parent needs me to be more trouble right now.

This time, I won't hang up on Hawk. I'll be brave—assuming he answers. I could ask him about the box I brought back from the Taj Mahal....

He picks up on the second ring. "Hawk! This is Darcy, from the convention." Half second of silence. "You know, the parapsychology meeting."

"Sure, Darcy. I remember you. Of course." We're both acting friendly and cheerful, like our earlier quasi-conversation didn't happen.

"I was thinking that—you know, if you have a moment—we could talk about what we both heard, the banging and crashing sounds in the lobby that nobody else seemed to hear? What was that? Do you know what causes it? The main thing: do you, like, have any friends of an unearthly nature who show up out of the blue?"

Pause. Sounds like maybe he's swallowing coffee. "That describes all my friends."

"Ha-ha. You know what I mean: a spirit person, who shows up sometimes when you hear a crashing sound."

"I have no such friend. That noise, in my view, signals a breaching of the barrier. Between one realm and another. Between the physical and the astral."

"Astral," I say. Astral, like astronomy and astrology. Stars. I google it once again, hoping to find something new. And find again how it's a zone of existence where the energy that makes up everything is higher frequency, less dense and lighter than the ordinary physical... The plane that's the nearest neighbor to ordinary Earth life. The lightness fits since Risto and I are able to fly. So my life right now is half-astral. Life split in half, like my family is. Half-assedtral. I want to explode with laughter, but manage to hold it back.

"Do you go across the barrier yourself, Hawk?" I imagine seeing him in the crowd at the Taj Mahal, traveling with some magical girl, a fairy princess in a tutu.

"No," he says carefully. "Do you?"

"Sometimes. I'd like to be able to do it whenever I want to."

"No doubt you would." He's talking in a formal way I don't remember from our last conversation. "Sometimes I'll see something like running shapes," he says, "except they're transparent, colorless. Mostly a thickening of air—the best way I can describe it—vaguely in the form of a person."

I'm excited and disappointed. He knows less than I do. But he has at least seen outlines of spirit people, and more than just one.

"They move fast. It's hard to catch a glimpse. Once, though, I swear, I felt as if they had come toward me and run through me."

When I hear that, my skin prickles like it's happening to me.

"It felt like being a window screen, letting in a breeze. It sharpened my senses somehow as they passed through."

"I have a visitor sometimes," I tell him. "A guy. He shows up pretty often. We go places." Maybe Risto and I would look like wind to Hawk, who can see, but only a little. Maybe I'm seeing only a little more than he is. Are there invisible beings in this room all around me now? The thought makes me want to run down the stairs and out the front door.

"Where do you and the guy go, Darcy?"

"Different places: a party, a restaurant..." Seems like too much to say the Taj Mahal.

"Regular nightlife. You go out clubbing?"

I don't like his snarky tone. Silence lingers.

He says, "How old are you, by the way?"

"Old enough to have an intelligent conversation."

"Older than your years."

"Right."

"Do you know what you do that gets you across the barrier to your friend each time?" Now he's taking me seriously.

"That's exactly what I want to learn. How to do that on purpose whenever I want to. Mostly, he comes to me. There's the cracking sound—sometimes, not always—and pretty soon afterward, he appears."

"You saw him at the conference?"

"No. That wasn't him. It didn't sound like him."

"Wow, that's pretty specific."

"It's a feeling as much as the sound. I would know..."

"Sounds as if you have some feelings for this friend."

Do I want to answer this? It's a private matter. "I'm seriously in love with him."

It came out of my mouth before I'd decided what to say.

Quiet from Hawk's end. Then: "This all seems pretty advanced. Your explorations, I mean."

"I don't know how it works or where he comes from. I sort of tiptoe, because I'm afraid of asking too much and messing it up."

"I know that feeling right here on Earth." Hawk's little chuckle sounds sad. A picture of how he seemed flashes through my mind: jumpy—uncomfortable, but pretending not to be. Do spirits pick out the most anxious humans? I don't want to think so. In fact, I'm certain that's not true for Risto. He'd already known my "spirit voice like a whisper in the trees" since way before that day. It's true that the first time I got near him—and could see him—I was rattled to pieces by my parents, but he'd long been nearby.

"Is it possible you're dreaming this, Darcy?" His tone is hostile now.

"I resent that. You're someone who should know better. What are you, anyway? A grad student, or do you have a job?"

"I work in cheeses at Whole Foods. And I'm writing a screenplay."

"About the wind people?"

"Sort of. That and some other stuff."

"Are you making it up, or is it all real?"

"The wind people part is real."

"So tell me how to see these wind creatures, Hawk."

"I wish I could. I don't know any more about the mechanisms than you do. We're both hopeless."

"I can't give up and call it hopeless. For you, it seems like it's an interesting experience, but for me, it's my relationship."

"Lucky you," he says in a sarcastic tone and tells me he's signing off. And he's gone.

I put the phone down slowly. I said the wrong thing and upset him. Didn't mean to. Maybe he's going through a break-up. Or maybe he's a disturbed kind of guy. Anyway, he and I seem to be over, which might be a good thing. But I'm going to have to figure out everything by myself.

Two minutes later, my phone rings. It's Hawk. "Just one piece of advice," he says. "You should be careful who you tell about your astral boyfriend." I don't like his tone of voice, it's not friendly. "This stuff gets out," he says. "It can really mess you up. People think you're sick."

When I hang up, I'm thinking: guess I'm not the only one who wonders about this guy. And: am I like him? How much am I like him?

CHARLOTTE IS the one who tells me the latest development. "You haven't been online," she says as we're standing at the edge of hall traffic. "That's how you don't know what's happening. People are getting really mean about this."

My first thought is Hawk. He posted what I told him? No! I can't make my mouth work well enough to ask.

"...about you quitting prom comm," Charlotte says. "You had to know somebody was going to say something."

"I expected there'd be a few texts between committee members."

"More than texting. It's all over the Internet. That you're 'a prom-killer.' "

"Are you joking? Who gets cyber-bullied about quitting a committee? That's silly."

Charlotte looks away. "They're saying you're too flakey and spaced-out to even be on a committee. People are pissed that you won't stay around as a member to help."

My mind is dizzy from batting back and forth. Internet

bullying can ruin people's lives. Last year a ninth grader switched to home-schooling because of what some guys were saying about her online. She didn't want to see anybody.

"Darcy, I'm pretty sure it'll stop soon. I mean, it's about a committee. Not very juicy. But I just thought you should know."

"I wouldn't be any help if I went to those meetings. That ought to be obvious to everybody by now." The prom people and their friends all hate me. I somehow destroyed my connection with Hawk. More and more, I seem to be turning into our lonely neighbor, sad Mr. Frederick. And people don't even know about the truly spacey half of my life—yet.

CHAPTER

TWENTY-THREE

M y Earth life is emptying out. Nobody and nothing is the way it used to be. Plus, now I'm a joke online. This afternoon I tried again with Hawk, texted him that the Navajo believed wind people breathed life into creation. His response: *DC*. Meaning: Don't care. Don't call. Disconnect. What did I do that was so bad?

It's 3:12 a.m. when Risto skids into my room, feet first and leaning backward, as if it's hard to stop and he needs to make sure he doesn't hit the wall. Maybe he thinks he's late. In a way, he is. I haven't heard from him in—well, I've decided to stop counting the days. It feels too desperate and clingy. But it's not like he can text. Anyway, I forget all the details when he ambles the last couple of steps over to my bed and lies down. I feel the whole length of him beside me. We don't say anything; we wrap our arms around each other and hold on. His neck feels so warm, I feel his heartbeat there. His hair smells like wind on a rainy day, as if it's full of damp leaves.

My plan for when he next appeared was to talk, to listen to him until I understood whatever I needed to for us to be together in my familiar world. But I can't bring myself to interrupt this moment for any reason. Right now, our two worlds *are* together. And we know each other so well without conversation. We have since almost the beginning. When our hearts talk to each other, not a lot of English is needed.

He kisses my eyebrow, touches my ear with his tongue and his breath, slides down to the base of my throat, my collarbone.

I hook a leg around one of his legs, pressing against him. So much better than flying. Or finding out facts. Or anything. We go on and on like this, rolling around, kissing, wrapped together, for hours.

WHEN I WAKE UP, Mom is calling from the foot of the stairs. "Are you up, Darcy? It's late." From here, I can smell the mug of coffee she's holding. My eyes are still asleep.

Risto is gone. I didn't find out anything. Mad at myself. Last night, though, was definitely what Charlotte means by "getting hot." I thought I already knew, but I didn't. It was *amazing*. Why do we ever do anything else? I don't care if I miss school. I need to lie here and remember.

"Darcy!" Mom's sounding urgent.

"I'm up." I let my eyes close, for a second. He kissed my

eyelids. I can still feel it. My pillow has that leaf smell from his hair.

"I don't hear you getting ready, Darcy."

Get ready for school. Do it.

I turn on my side. I can afford to slack off, my grades are good enough. I've never obsessed about my rank in class. Even Dad said it was the wrong thing to focus on. These days, I can't imagine anything more trivial. My brain is starting to wake up. Might as well roll out...

Figure out clothes...

Throw myself together...

Say good morning to parent...my single-mother in-house parent...

Grab energy bar...

Out the door...

As I enter the school hall, I focus my brain, stroll into my first class—on time—as if I've never rushed to do anything. I'm at a terrific new place in my life. Radiant, like a bride is supposed to be on her wedding day. Heat and light all around me. Smiling at everybody. Being this way is how I'm dealing with anyone cyber-trashing me. A couple of guys, glancing at me, look startled and it's not because of what somebody's posting. One whips around, catches himself and looks away. Oh, jeez: it was Tony.

Ha! He's embarrassed. He knows I saw that look. I caught him off-guard, threw Mr. Chill off his private zip-line.

Leaning back in my seat, I feel immensely pleased and completely un-ruffle-able, powerful, generous even. I don't know why I troubled myself for a second about cyber-lies or anybody's messed-up attitude toward me.

I feel so good after last night with Risto that I practically get a grip on calc. Two nights ago, I got a text from a fairly cute boy I hardly know—Jacob Adams—wanting me to ride with him and his friends to the East Chapel Hill game. I wasn't in the mood, was scheduled to hang with Dad anyway and he needs me. Cool, though, that this guy asked me. It's all because of my confidence from Risto, his choosing me because of hearing my truest voice.

LATE AFTERNOON and Charlotte is on the phone with me, both of us tapping at our keyboards, googling "astral lover." This is one term I haven't searched. Risto is so hot and physical, yet he's a spirit. After our last get-together, I need to understand. I tried "astral boyfriend" and that just took me to a video game. In the meantime, Charlotte can't believe that I haven't looked at a word of the crap about me online. And she thinks I've been ridiculously inhibited in my Risto research by worries of being tracked on Google.

All I have to do, she says, is erase my history on any computer I use and don't leave my devices unattended. If either of my parents should *succeed* in tracking me, he or she will see that I've researched tracking apps and know exactly what they're up to.

But she doesn't know my Dad's magical skills with computers.

"Astral lover" produces 2,220 results, not many by Google standards, but finding any at all is reassuring, shows me again that I'm not the only one. "Listen to this, Charlotte.

'Your lover could be anyone or anything from an elf to a ghost to a deity.'"

"No elves," Charlotte says. "I want Risto's twin."

"Don't say that." I shouldn't worry, but Bink did ask her to prom and not me.

An elf, a ghost, or a god. Risto is none of those. Maybe the reason I didn't look for books before is because I subconsciously knew they wouldn't apply to him. "Charlotte, here's one that says you can develop a lasting relationship with an astral lover..." A *lasting* relationship. So it's possible! If this book is a reliable source, then I've just made a major discovery. Of course I want us to last, in his world and mine.

I read on: "'Meld chakras with divine beings in the ultimate sexual encounter.'"

"Come and meld with me, my pretty one," Charlotte says in a seductive voice.

The comments are the strangest part. Accusations of black magic. Warnings of danger... Risto is not dangerous or demonic. He's the furthest thing from bad. I'm not sure I want to read any of these books. I have to, though. I need to know more about this chakra melding. Plus, I can't be narrow-minded. In our family—my *former* family—we are open to new ideas. We think and explore. In a way, that's what Dad's doing now, so I should cut him some slack. I would if he seemed happy.

LUNCH IN THE STUDENT UNION: the crew I'm talking with has eaten and we're sitting around in the cheeseburger-smelling air talking about an app to tell you where your love interest

PEGGY PAYNE

is currently located. "Do I want to know?" Sydney is saying. I desperately wish it would work for Risto, but this phone obsession is so retro, I pay no attention; I let the talk go over my head, which is what I'd do with this group anyway. Whenever I find myself clustered with two or more social superstar kids, I become an observer. I'm a fringe member of this bunch, but I can't do their brand of banter.

One of my identified cyberbullies, Diego, straddles a backwards chair at the far end of the table, pretending he doesn't notice me. You'd think he and the guys he hangs out with would have better things to do. I hear they've moved on to new victims, but people are still giving me judgmental looks. I don't care. If he wants to think I'm spacey, I'll give him something to post.

"Pretty soon," I comment to no one in particular, "we're not going to need phones. We'll send a hologram-type version of ourselves to wherever we want to talk to someone. Like a ghost messenger."

"Until then," Diego says, "I'll stick with my cell."

"Fine, but I'm playing around with way more radical stuff."

I get a couple of sparks of interest and maybe one eye roll. Taking a sip of my drink, I lock my gaze on Diego. He looks a little like Risto, dark eyes and hair. But Diego has no lights on in him.

"Radical how?" he says, tilting his head back, patting the red razor burn under his chin. "You're hooking up with a hologram?"

I do a non-committal shrug.

"I could handle some electrifying outer space relations,"

178

he says. Like Bink, he's always reminding everybody of his hotness. But his eyes don't do what Risto's do. Risto's look all the way inside me, make me feel like I've snuck a sip of Dad's ancient left-behind Scotch. The thought of Risto makes me feel a surge of reckless power.

"Do say more," Sydney says. She has a wry way of saying things, but she seems sincerely interested.

What difference would it make if I did say more? Labelers already tag me as off-center. I don't want to be a total misfit, though. Where is Martin when I'm sliding into stupid? I give myself two seconds to, as the parents say, "think twice." Then: "I'm in a relationship that's on a different level."

"What level is that?" Diego says. "Middle school?"

I give him the supercilious glance he deserves while a couple of people are yucking it up over his attempt at wit.

Cindy, a girl I hardly know, says, "Relationship with who?"

I've already said way too much. But I so want to tell about Risto, to bring him into my Earth life. Hawk would tell me not to. But he was just trying to scare me.

The little box up on the wall does its electronic click and in the next instant, the bell rings.

Relief floods my chest.

"Got to hurry," I say over the scuffle and talk as they start throwing together their stuff. They've already dropped the subject. Permanently forgotten it, I hope. I'm literally saved by the bell—at least from saying any more than I already have.

TWENTY-FOUR

inner with Dad at his disturbing apartment. He's cooking everything in one pot, some kind of stew, stirring and stirring whatever's in there, while I chop up a salad. The kitchenette corner has none of his fancy tools: no coffee equipment, nothing to puree with. At least he dresses the same: khakis and a sweatshirt over a tee, his leisure uniform. The lonely little pepper grinder seems like the only remnant of his old life.

"Standing over that pot, you look like one of the witches in *Macbeth*, Dad. 'Double bubble toil and trouble.'" I've been keeping the conversation light, though that is about to change.

That gets a fake heh-heh. He's preoccupied.

Sitting at the table whacking at the radishes, I start the planned conversation before I lose my nerve. "Dad." The words pause so long in my throat that he looks at me. "Dad, it's time for a total report."

His whole body does some kind of shifting motion. Maybe this is what a gush of adrenaline looks like from the outside. I knew he was hiding things.

"Does that mean I'm about to learn some news from you?" he says. He's looking wary, getting ready to dodge me again.

"No, I want news from you."

"What do you want to know?"

"What's the whole situation with you, Dad? You believe in God—I get it. Though you're not sure what God is. That doesn't explain all the changes."

"You mean your mother and me?"

"Yes, and you act zoned-out, like you've given up somehow. Being that way doesn't seem to bother you." A new idea flashes across my brain. "Dad, are you turning into a stoner?" The same thing Mom asked me. "Is this religious stuff coming from weed?"

Maybe Dad knows about wind people.

He almost smiles, shakes his head. "No, honey. No mind-altering substances."

"Why don't you act alive then? Are you depressed, is that it? You live in this bare room like you don't care where you are and you go off to church at the beach in winter. You don't seem to do anything other than work or take me somewhere." What I can't say: *Mom said you wouldn't touch her.*

He's nervous, not looking at me, scraping at the sides of the pot with that spoon. "You don't pay attention to what you eat," I say. "Everything is so simple and plain." I'm sweaty under my arms. I halfway wish I hadn't started this.

He turns the burner down, puts the lid on the pot, and

takes a seat with me at the table. Leaning back in his chair, he searches the ceiling, as if he's going to find something there.

My stomach does a tiny sick-ish drop.

The way he's ruffling his hair shows how uncomfortable he is. Him and me both. "Your mother said the same thing. She felt I was withdrawing into an 'inner world', that I was letting my spiritual experience take over my life. And hers."

"You weren't dragging her to church or anything. Although, I know what she means about withdrawing. Seems like the old normal you has vanished, like we were all riding along and you fell out of the car."

"She said she was tired of living with a monk."

A monk. It's like he has shot me in the gut. I say it out loud. "A monk?" But he doesn't have to explain. I get it: no sex, no nothing. Again I see Dad in robes like a dress. Then beefy Webb, his big bare feet... I have to make my mind stop.

He rubs his temples with thumb and middle finger. "I shouldn't have repeated that."

"Dad, are you going to actually *be* a monk?" My worst fear—and it's already gone further than I thought. This explains everything: why there haven't been women around, why Mom instantly took up with a guy who is definitely *not* monastic. "Dad, answer me. Please." My voice has a pitiful little squeak to it. "Are you considering it?"

"I don't know what I'm thinking, Darcy. I need time. I need guidance from God. What I've come to know—about who and what we all are. It's larger than anything I ever imagined. I feel moments of joy like I never imagined possible and then, more often, I see I've ruined everything that ever mattered. That's why I wanted your mother to give me more time. And why I haven't been more direct with you."

"Direct? More like mute." He's withdrawing from me, from our life. Panic and fury are filling my head. "Are you kidding me? You! A scientist! An atheist! A person with a wife and a kid—you can't withdraw from the world! No wonder you didn't want to talk about it. It's not rigorous. It's fucked up!"

I practically knock the chair over getting to the picture of the blissed-out nun. It rips when I pull it off the wall. I try to throw it to the floor in front of him, but it's too light, and it drifts like a dead leaf.

His face is stricken. "Darcy—" The wounded way he says my name hurts to hear. My anger is draining away and I feel empty and bad. I fall back into my chair.

"Dad, how can you of all people be suddenly living in some imaginary spiritual world?"

How can *I* of all people ask such a question? But Risto isn't imaginary.

Does Dad have proof the way I do?

"I thought you might ask that a while back," he says, "about the differences of faith, mine and your mother's, that I mentioned the day we told you."

"I never heard anything about religion that day. I wasn't completely listening. Because..." I don't know how to say it.

"Because it was too much to take in at once," he says. "What I'm experiencing is real, Darcy. As real as anything that ever happened in my lab."

"So what is it? What exactly is it like? I really want to

know."

"It's difficult to do it justice in words. You sat with me once in a sanctuary."

"I was hanging out with you. I figured you were thinking about your research. Not praying. Is that what you were doing? Talking to God?"

"Yes. And to one particular saint."

"The one I tore?" Practically the only thing he has here and I had to go and tear it up.

"No. A different one. Saint Brendan."

"I never heard of him."

"Brendan the Mariner. Given my area of research, I'd run across his name."

"Patron saint of wave motion scientists?"

He smiles. My normal sarcasm seems to reassure him. "Patron saint of mariners." He takes a deep breath, as if he's getting up his nerve. There's more? This scares me. "I began to have a sense he was nearby."

My mind is starting to feel soft at the edges. "Dad, do you see him? Do you go places with him?" Does Dad have a Risto? No wonder he's distant and different! His life is cut in half and he's losing the Earth part. "Why isn't *his* picture on your wall?"

"The pictures of him aren't real, just stylized icons, usually with a dour expressions, which isn't how I imagine him. I don't see him. I have a sense of him, his presence, in the places I go. On campus. Here in the apartment—"

"He's here now?"

"I'm not feeling his presence now. I'm focused on you."

"Oh, Dad. I get it. You were too focused on Brendan

instead of on Mom.”

“That’s a big part of it.”

“Did she know about him? Or did she think you were thinking about some girlfriend?”

“She’d have preferred a girlfriend.” He winces at what he said, pushes back from the table. “You want a snack or something? Dinner’s not ready for twenty minutes.”

Now he’s up rummaging in the fridge. Dad doing nervous eating. This is new. I don’t like it. Enough of this conversation. “Sure. A snack. Anything.”

WE’RE SITTING on the floor in my room, Risto and I. He shows up pretty often these days, and I usually get a sense a few hours ahead of time that he's coming. Maybe we’re both learning how to manage the situation better.

I mention that my Dad’s hanging out with Saint Brendan —then instant, huge change! The room around us vanishes. We’re no longer there. A fraction of a second later, we’re hovering high above water. We dive toward it so fast the surface seems to explode toward me, my mouth and eyes and ears full of roaring air.

We plunge in—I expect to be killed, but the water slows us and slows us. We bob back up, now rising and falling with big fat swells. We’re so far out that I can barely see the land on the horizon when the water lifts me.

“Island of the mountain,” Risto says when I squint and look that way. The sun is ferocious, hitting off the surface all around us.

“What island? Where are we?” We’re drifting, the water

moving us inches closer together, then inches farther apart.

"Island is Levanta in Sea of Phoenicia."

"There's still a Phoenicia?"

He laughs as if I'm joking. "You brought us to this sea, MyDarcy. You have said this name Brendan."

"But Brendan was Irish. I looked him up. He wasn't here, even in the legends." When he wasn't sailing the Atlantic, he lived in a monastery, which made me instantly hate him. He is *not* going to take my father away.

"I cannot know more," Risto says, looking happy as ever. We both wear fabric that flows and floats around us, pale green like sea lettuce, feels like it's not even there. This is the first time my clothes have changed like magic. The brown of his skin shows through. I look so wan and pale beside him, he's almost golden.

I ask about Brendan and I wind up here. Risto isn't going to be able to tell me anything in the usual way. That was pretty clear at the Taj Mahal. But at least he brought us to salt water. I know he did this, not me. He knows more than he knows he knows. It's a step forward.

He dives under, rolling like a swimmer doing a racing turn, his back shining through the cloth for a moment in the sun. I let myself sink to cool my face. We play like two porpoises. For hours, or minutes, or days, I can't tell. Am I waiting for Brendan to show up here? If not, what?

Suddenly, we're drifting in early spring air, just above my house, as if we'd been swimming in sky all along. Changes come so fast, I struggle to catch up and see where I am. Risto points over the top of the roof to the sycamore tree. "There is where I discovered you, MyDarcy."

Now I get it: he's telling me about himself and his world —and Brendan— by showing me places. I have to super-concentrate in order not to miss anything.

Next instant, we're on the ground, standing beside the tree trunk. The patchy bark is giving off heat, feels like sunburn against the palm of my hand. "Risto, this tree is hot."

"The tree is a conductor. She brings me to you."

"Trees are conductors?"

"Some are."

I always knew it: trees are the answers, trees are special.

He gazes up into the branches. He loves our tree. The leaves have a trembly motion, stirring in every direction, though there is no breeze. The air is weirdly still.

"Teer-ta," he says, patting the smooth trunk. At least that is what it sounds like.

"Is that a name? Or a word in your language?" I find I don't want to say it aloud.

"Teerta is a somewhere that is conducting between realms."

Relief floods me with gratitude. Again, he has answered a direct question in words. Carefully, I ask another. "Then how did you get to that party and the restaurant at the beach?"

He smiles. "For me, you are now conductor. Like a tree."

"Perfect." I'm like a tree. This is better than I could have imagined.

"We are standing on the same location as your world," he says.

"I thought we were already back to my world."

"No, soon we are bursting through to there."

"Bursting makes the banging sound? Crossing into another realm?"

I think he nods, but so slight that it's hard to tell. He seems to be concentrating. This place looks like my regular home, but now I see it's not. The window of my room has a peculiar shine, a look of wavering motion. What if I see myself in there: a dead-eyed zombie version? Fear ripples in my stomach.

"Risto, let's go back to my world now. Together. How do we do it? Do we climb up the tree? Or fly?" I'm not ready to be without him, but I'm exhausted. So tired I can't believe it. Only a little while ago, we were swimming far out at sea in big wide waves. Going where he goes uses up all the juice in my batteries. He seems exhausted too, maybe from thinking hard enough to answer questions in words.

He laughs at my questions, a tired sound. "Only step to the side inside your mind."

I feel that jolt again. And I'm in my backyard—alone—standing near the fence, with ordinary breezes and distant traffic and leaves that blow only in the direction of the wind. I get it now: we each need to recharge in our own world. Crossing either way is draining for both of us. Seems like he needs to spend time where he comes from, as much as a couple of weeks, to build up the energy to come back here. Today he showed me and told me more than any time before. The part about the tree made sense, but the Sea of Phoenicia? I'm pretty sure it doesn't exist. Maybe there's no way for him to get across clearly how his world works. I couldn't give a simple explanation of life on Earth.

CHAPTER

TWENTY-FIVE

S aturday morning, and I'm thunking up the bare wood stairs to Mom's studio to see what she's gotten going while I've been flying around the world. I've neglected her, which is bad for both of us. I feel like the parts of my divided life are plants, miles away from each other, and I need to water and check on each one or they'll die.

Smells like she's using that little soldering iron. She could probably draw Risto without seeing him if I described him feature by feature, like one of those police artists who asks you to pick out which nose and which chin. She had a big-deal show not long before Dad moved out, sold a lot. Mom could paint me a perfect picture of Risto. The one he gave me at the Taj, when I got it back here, was only a scrap of paper in an ordinary box.

"There you are," Mom says as I round the corner into her sight. She sounds truly surprised.

"Here I am." I drop down onto my traditional place on

the scruffy sofa. The paint-and-welding burned smell makes me sad. I've stayed away from here, and I shouldn't have. This is where Mom's soul lives; Dad always said so.

But I need to be in my room. She would understand if I could tell her. "What are you working on, Mom?" I now know it wasn't fair of me to think she was to blame for the split. Dad's new passion didn't include her. It's more like she was abandoned.

She holds up a silver, popcorn-sized item. I have to lean forward and squint to see it. "An elephant! She's so cute. Beautiful." I roll the little creature around in my hand. I love this; it's no effort to find nice things to say. "Is it going to be jewelry?"

"Not sure yet. I'm cranking out the tiny animals. I'll figure out at some point what to do with them."

"I've never seen you make anything small before." That's putting it mildly. Across from me leans a stack of canvases about a quarter-acre each. The subject of these is color, as she likes to say about this style of her work.

"I hadn't planned on it. One day I started playing with making a model to cast. I find I like the intensity that comes with the compact size."

"Did your muse tell you to switch to these?"

"Could be. There was a definite pull."

"Does she have a name or anything? "

"My muse? No name." She gives me a quick glance, her hands barely pausing at the tiny block she's scratching and chipping. "Just a sense of someone steering me one way and another. A sort of non-verbal GPS."

I look behind her, as if I'll see the slinky husky-voiced

woman I imagined. Instead, on a low shelf is a tray of little silver figures.

"Are all those elephants, Mom?"

"Nope. Have a look."

"Mom, there are dozens! You made all these? They're wonderful!"

"Thanks, Darcy." Her voice sounds grateful in a too-quiet way. I glance over at her, only for a second. It stabs me with sadness that she's so happy we're having this conversation. I hate guilty, I hate sad.

Picking up the little elephant again, I say, "These would make great birthday presents, Mom." Risto would love these little animals. I could bring him up here and show him.

"Take a couple, if you want. Charlotte might like—I don't know, which one do you think?"

"This leopard, if that's what it is." Charlotte's still a bit miffed with me for not telling her more about my secret life.

"Perfect," Mom says.

Which one for Risto? A bird would be good, a big one. "What's a bird that's large and super masculine?"

Mom gives me an inquiring glance. "California condor. They have something like a seven foot wingspan. You have someone in mind to give this to?"

"Not really." My heart does a little fear flip. It would be so nice if I could tell her. And it would help to explain anything off about my behavior.

"I'll make you one."

"Thanks." The thought of her doing this makes me happy. Though I may have to figure out how to explain what I did with it. I can always be coy and plead teenage privacy.

PEGGY PAYNE

Maybe having a silver bird from me will always make him think of me.

"Mom, do you ever worry that your muse will go away?"

"Often. Whenever I'm not working. I have to at least sketch something on a napkin to feel like I'm making contact. When I'm at work and I know she's backing me up —that's when I forget myself enough to feel almost fearless."

"That's so cool you have a way to reach her. But you pretty much always seem fearless." She smiles, in a way that says, *It's not true, but thank you.* I get up to go, but I pause at the top of the stairs.

Mom is already deep in her work again. But behind her: a woman, the shape of her vague, as if she's in the distance.

The colors—fire-yellow dress, long red hair—shine as though through a soft fog. The flowing clothes, wavy hair— all of her is in gentle motion. Can't tell exactly where she's looking, but she seems to be keeping watch over the room.

The air clears. She's nowhere in sight, but I sense her still watching. She didn't feel real like Risto is real. I almost could have imagined her.

Best not to mention it. I give Mom a wave as I start down the stairs.

LATE IN THE DAY, I go outside and sit by the tree, where the astral half of my life and the broken bits of my Earth life meet. This is the gate between worlds—and the barrier. It can be very frustrating, but I love our tree. I want it to make the two worlds join, mine and Risto's.

I think of the tree by name, Teer-Ta, as Risto called it. I

googled the way it sounds and came up with: "Do you mean *tirtha*?" It comes from Sanskrit. Means a place to ford a stream, a crossing. Like he said, a bridge between realms. But why our backyard tree? It'd be easier to go to Sanskrit school in India than to get Risto to explain. Though he did tell me the word Teer-ta; that's progress.

Looking up, I ask the tree out loud, "Tree, how did you get to be a door?" I keep my voice low, practically a whisper. Imagine I hear a rustling above, a little louder than before. I stare up there until I have seen every leaf. Nothing out of the ordinary.

Leaning against the trunk, I position myself so the tree can feel my heart thumping in my back, but again, nothing happens.

"Tree, you're extremely important," I tell it out loud. "I wish you would answer some questions, tell me how to put the parts of my life together, so Risto can be with me like he's living in a house two blocks away." There are people who say they can hear trees talking. But that's different from trying to interview one. In mythology, oak tree leaves rustling together were supposed to be the voice of Zeus. Druids got advice from trees. How did I happen to have a *tirtha* in my yard? Or did Risto make it into a portal?

An ant is crawling up my arm; its little body segments look hard and shiny. Bringing me a message from Risto? Or from the tree? It's possible. Nothing could be any more exotic than what has already happened. It kills me to have to keep it so secret.

. . .

AT HOME IN MY ROOM, I finally download one of the books I found, *Perfect Love: Find Intimacy on the Astral Plane*.

Looking at the title, I think: I could have written this myself. But I'm happy there's someone else who did. I don't want to be the only one having this experience. That could make me doubt myself. No, that's not true. I think I'd figure that there were others, but they're all keeping it secret the way I am.

I do a search for chakra melding, which is what grabbed my attention when I first found the book. Page 117, here it is. "...sooner or later you will desire an astral love experience." I already have that. Every time I see him.

The description sounds almost technical, like describing a yoga position or an abs exercise. "One by one, the lower chakras begin to open... The high-level being moves closer until your bodies are first touching..."

I don't believe in chakras. Little whirly energy things in me that I can't see or feel? No way. Except a year ago, I wouldn't have believed Risto existed.

This melding that's supposedly "the ultimate sexual encounter"... it sounds more like two shadows blending together.

I'd rather keep doing what we're doing—which is the ultimate making out.

TWENTY-SIX

T his whole house is jammed with partiers; the floors are sticky. Jared's folks are out of town again. I never meant to come back here. But Risto showed up at the last party in this room, so how could I not come? Someone is breathing on my hair behind me. Is it him?

No, it's Tony Llewellyn.

"You're kidding," I say right in his face. He hangs a little over me, because he is so tall and because he is so drunk or stoned or something.

His arm falls slowly to his side. His brain seems to be moving slo-mo too. "Heard you ate steak. In my yard. With my Dad."

"I did. You weren't there."

"Wasn't invited."

Not what I expected. Tony Llewellyn playing the pitiful card. Or speaking at all. "You wanted to be there?" He makes me mad, he always has, because he's so smart and cool-looking and could be wonderful if he wanted to, but no, he'd rather be a surly bad guy with zero potential.

He shrugs his shoulders in an inebriated, exaggerated way. "Didn't know about it. So I couldn't. Want to." He laughs. Another first. Though he doesn't seem amused. He's ridiculously drunk.

I may as well make the most of this opportunity. "Do you think it's serious? My mom and your dad?"

"Serious," he says, tipping his head back in a theatrical way. He could lose his balance and fall over.

"Well, *do* you?"

"I have no idea. You?"

"I have no idea either."

"Doesn't matter beans to me. I'm not around that place too often."

"Do you know when they started seeing each other?"

"Can't help you there."

Does that mean he doesn't know or won't say? I still have a squirmy feeling about how long it's been going on. I could ask Mom, but I don't want her to think I've suspected her if it turns out there's no reason to.

"How come you're here?" Tony says.

"What kind of question is that?"

"Doesn't seem like your kind of thing."

"Having a conversation doesn't seem like your kind of thing. I do go to parties."

Now he's pissed off. It shows in how his eyebrows flatten out. "Marshmallow roasts. And other prudish entertainments."

"I beg your pardon." He's grinning as if he's said something clever and sophisticated, looking all around like he expects to be applauded.

I'm not putting up with this. I slip away. Ducking under Henry's arm, passing in front of him and two girls, I'm safely three people away from Tony's obnoxiousness. Glancing back for a second, I can see him hunting around for what happened to me. He won't find me.

He doesn't care about the future of our parents, so the conversation is finished.

RISTO DOESN'T SHOW up at the party, but as soon as I flip on the light in my bedroom at home, my heart jumps. A woman —who is sitting on the bed—stands. She has a shining look to her, the way Risto does. This is not an ordinary person.

"Who are you? Are you a friend of Risto's?" She's the right age to be his mother, wears a long blue skirt and a shawl around her shoulders. Like a pioneer woman. All my muscles tense. Blue skirting, pioneer dress: she's the one who stared at Risto that night in the restaurant.

"Hello, Miss Darcy." Her tone is not friendly.

My skin ripples with fear.

"Who said you could come in here? Why are you here?"

"I'm stopping over for a visit. With you." She's short and plumpish—stout, he called her— hair in a knot on the top of her head. She's probably forty-five or fifty by Earth stan-dards. Has she been watching us? Surely Risto would have noticed.

"Okay, please sit down." I force myself to speak with great politeness. I drop into my desk chair. "Is everything okay with Risto? Why are you here without him? Why were you watching him, anyway?"

"You have too many questions. I've come to help you with your learning."

"Risto helps me." He's told me hardly anything but I want to defend him.

"He's a young'un, a know-nothing fledgling, about such matters as crossing to your world. He can't yet answer questions easily. It's like shining a lantern straight into his eyes." She's right, my badgering only confuses him. I appreciate even more all the effort he's made in his recent answers. "You can answer my questions?" Hope surges up in me. Her coming here could be the greatest thing.

"I'll tell you this. He was never once alive in terrestrial, in Earth life. He's schooling for it now, making his preparation to live a human life."

A human life? My heart does a joyous bounce at the thought. We can be together any time, even out in public. My life won't be half hidden. Tears jump up in my eyes. This is huge. "He's going to be a regular human?" I want to hug this woman, who acts as if none of this is any big deal.

She's looking around my room, which I've kept straighter since Risto started coming around. "Very fancy, this place. Fine as cream gravy. Like no life I ever lived." Her voice has a western twang as well as a breathy sound—now I realize Risto's does too. He has no accent, though, which probably means he sounds like me.

"He'll be born," she says. "If one set of parents doesn't bring him on, another will."

"He'll be the same? The way he is now?"

She shrugs. "In his soul."

He would change then. He would have human problems that could change him, make him guarded. Awful thought: "Does this mean he'll start off life as a baby?"

"That's how it's done."

No! It would be a disaster. I wouldn't recognize him or know where he was. I'd be so much older. He'd be as lost as if I'd never met him. "Does this happen soon? Will we have any warning? Who decides?" Is this woman here to ruin everything? I can't tell if she's on our side or not.

She laughs, searches in her purse, pulls out a grungy-looking little book. "You'll find your ABCs here, about spirit worlds, including this one." She's holding it close and turning it over in her hands like she's telling it good-bye. A little hardback the size of an old-fashioned address book.

"A good start for you here," she says. The book seems to be hand-stitched and ancient. "And you ask who decides? Think of an apple ripening on a tree. It's a law of nature. The tree lets it go when it's ready." She is starting to turn ashen, her skin and hair, her long blue skirt. She's fading.

I reach to take the book before it's too late. Her hands are already like a draft of cooler air, now a hard gust of wind and I lose my balance, slam down hard across the arm of my desk chair, roll off to the floor.

My side! It hurts so bad.

Oh my God! I can't speak, it's so painful to breathe.

The little book! Where is it...?

There—slid under my desk.

Can't grab it now. My side and back are killing me. I have the book, almost in reach, but the woman is gone.

CHAPTER

TWENTY-SEVEN

An unforgettable night: the emergency guys putting me on a stretcher—killer painful—sliding me into the back of the ambulance like a slice of pizza going into the oven. Mom thought my back might be broken, told me not to move on my own. Her extreme worrying about me has gotten hyper-amped lately, and will probably now only get worse.

No broken back. One cracked rib. We're on the way home. "I stumbled," I tell her for about the twentieth time. "I fell over the chair. I wasn't paying attention." And I got hit by an unearthly blast of wind. Risto's leaving doesn't do that, but I think he is especially gentle. All I can think about now is getting to the book under my desk, if it hasn't vanished like Risto's picture in the little box.

"You need to start looking where you're going, Darcy. This kind of thing happens to people who walk around in a cloud."

This and a whole lot more, I want to say. She would understand, because of her muse and channeling her art. Although, I now realize that she doesn't talk much about that unless Dad or I ask. Still, it would be disturbing if strange other-world stuff was happening to your kid. Parents don't like their children to lose touch with "reality."

"It hurts to breathe, Mom." How am I going to scramble around on the floor to reach the book? I'll do it no matter how much it hurts.

Getting up the stairs is so painful I want to rest and recover, but I have to find the book. Slowly and carefully, I lower myself to the floor. Keeping my back stiff, I lie down and reach with one arm under my desk. Nothing. Only bare floor. It hurts to grope around, and my hand comes out dirty with dust. I can't possibly get up to get a flashlight, or yell for Mom to find the book for me. Reaching again: I don't think it's here. The woman took it back with her! I push my arm underneath all the way to my shoulder. This shirt is going to be one-armed filthy.

Something brushes at the tip of my middle finger. I feel an edge, at an angle from the wall. This has to be it. Got it, two stiff fingers closed on it like scissors. Pull...pull... Carefully, I'm sliding out, what? A ratty old book. The right size and color, yet so much more beat-up looking than when she handed it to me. The edges of the yellowed paper look torn instead of cut. Maybe being on Earth in the air ages things fast.

I make myself calm and open it.

First page: blank.

Second: yes...! Doodles. With a light pencil, someone has

covered most of the page with meaningless squiggles. Is this an alphabet? I'll figure it out. This could tell me everything I need! If I turn the book sideways? The marks don't run side to side or up and down. It's a swarm of little marks, lots of them like fat commas that have heft and volume, and some exclamation points and something that looks like a pi symbol. The pi-thing gives me hope, because it's almost recognizable. Light spider-track lines connect the clearer images. Some of the other ones are faint, as if they're farther away, which makes the set of marks seem three-dimensional.

Next page: same thing. Filling all the pages after that until the middle of the book—the rest is empty.

I need a decoder method, like holding invisible writing over heat to make it show up, shining a light on the marks and maybe they'll look different....

Flashlight in top desk drawer. I fight my way to standing, darting from the pain every time it starts to stab me.

The flashlight comes on, but the scribbles look the same. Something else to make it readable. Darkness? Could it show up legible in the dark? I hold the open book inside my closet out of reach of the crack of light. No good!

This is discouraging. All I have in the way of solid evidence of Risto and "the other side" are this book of squiggles, some twigs, and the box that briefly had Risto's picture in it that turned into cardboard when I got it home. It's like somebody's playing a game, trying to confuse me.

Not Risto. Not on purpose anyway. The woman was right about him. He's young, which accounts for his wonderful bear-cub goofy sweetness. Earth boys aren't like that. They think they have to act cool.

That woman had to know I could never read this writing. I toss the book in with my bras and shove the drawer shut, which causes me to shriek, it hurts my side so bad.

She's back two nights later. The same woman. I can barely see her, though she's starting to get some edges and color. Same frumpy outfit and sturdy button-up shoes. I'm ready for her, the little book in my hand.

"I've been trying to reach you," I say before she's even completely solid. "I need help."

She finishes arriving before she starts to answer: "What is it you're in such a hurry to know?" She settles herself in my desk chair, picks up a ballpoint pen and turns it as if she hasn't seen one before.

"You gave me this book, but I can't read it. Would you read it to me? And what is your name?"

She looks at the book in my hand as if she hasn't seen that before, either. "Philomena."

It's a name I've heard somewhere. Old-fashioned, like Prudence or Charity. I don't want to say it. She's too old for a first name. "So, please, will you read me what's in this book? Philomena." I manage to get it out, for emphasis.

"Don't be trying to read it in the schoolbook way, Miss Darcy. What happens—you soak up the meanings of it with your mind." Her voice is the opposite of ethereal; even with the breathiness, she sounds earthly, like she's plowed corn-fields and milked cows.

"My mind has not soaked up any of it and I've stared and stared at these pages." She looks at me like I'm stupid or refusing to understand. Still, she's come back, so she must want to help me.

"Is this some kind of astral language?" I ask.

"Universal language."

"Humans are part of the universe and we can't read this language. So it's not universal." Logic is on my side for once.

She looks tired. "Did you used to be human?" I ask her.

She nods. "A right smart number of humans."

"Have all of you been named Philomena?"

"Only the one. A difficult life."

"The way you are now: is this who you were last time, when you died?" She would have been young to die: though she seems older, worn, as if she got up at 4 a. m. to bake biscuits.

"I was just what you see."

"Did you have some easy lives?"

"Doesn't every life have a hardship or few?"

I won't argue with that. "How do I go about soaking up what I need to know from this book you gave me?"

"Fix your thinking there when you start to sleep, and when you're doing chores."

"Does that mean stare at one of the pages? While I'm unloading the dishwasher?" Sudden thought: "Is this some kind of test, like an obstacle course?" I wondered this once before, with Risto. "Am I supposed to prove myself somehow before I get my questions answered?"

"Yes."

"How? What do I do?"

"Do what's needed to unlatch the gate into what's sitting

right before you—and by that I mean the workings of the Almighty."

"I'm supposed to figure out how to do that?"

"When you take hold of meaning, it's no big starburst, child. It's remembering a bit of ourselves that's been mislaid for a while."

She's gone. Not a fade-out. Instantly, maddeningly gone.

TWENTY-EIGHT

P assing the doorway where my former prom comm is hard at work, I pick up speed, which jars my injured rib, making me gasp and scrunch up my face. I turn my head toward the other wall. Can't let them see me sneaking past looking anguished.

They're much better off with their new leadership. They are so lucky to have lost me. Still, I dodge them when I can. I don't like the quitter feeling that gets stirred up when I see them. And, for a change, I don't want people trash-talking about me being odd. Usually I want to be unique, but not now with everything that's going on, I don't like it. I am not nuts or irresponsible. I am a reasonable, normal, almost-popular person having an unusual experience in life—including trying to grasp what Philomena says is the Almighty. It's hard to keep something like that from show-ing. When I passed Diego yesterday, he made noises like the

Darth Vader theme. The guys he was with grinned in a taunting manner.

On the other hand, this morning, coming into the first floor hall, I got some nods from guys who don't usually speak. Instead they jerk their heads and make a slight noise if they even deign to acknowledge you. Is this because of my increased joy? Maybe being the target of a cyber-attack plus the "pass-out" episode at Jared's is making me spicier. I'm somewhat ignoring school and its inhabitants, but maybe being zoned-out and non-eager gives me hall cred.

Now I'm practically the only person out here on the front sidewalk after school who isn't actively texting. Instead, underneath every other thought I have, I'm trying to figure out how I'm supposed to change to be able to read the gibberish book and know how Risto and I can be together like a normal boyfriend and girlfriend. Also, I have to watch where I'm going so no one bumps my broken rib and causes me to scream.

Mom has a key to Dad's apartment. She off-handedly mentioned it when I saw the separate keyring. What is this about? Are they having non-Darcy communication?

"Your father's," she said.

"He gave you a key?"

"Yes."

"I'm the one who should have a key."

"Here you are." She puts it in my hand.

But that isn't the point. He'd give me a key if I would ask

him. What I want to know is why *she* would have his key in her possession.

"What are you two up to?" I say.

"Up to? We are not *up* to anything. There is no change in our situation, if that's what you mean." A flash of sympathy shows in her eyes when it occurs to her I might be hoping for that. "Honey, I'm so sorry we've disappointed you, that we've let you down so severely." She adds, as if it didn't matter: "Someone other than him needs to have a key to his place."

"Disappointed." What a surprising word to use about having your family smashed to bits. Is disappointed what I am? "It's okay, Mom. I know you got blindsided too. By Dad's God stuff." Could Dad tell me how I have to be to understand Risto's world? I file the thought for later. To Mom: "That probably wasn't what you signed up for."

"I had no problem with him believing in God. It's his increasing self-denial and silence that's troubling."

Not just self-denial. Denial of her, too. "I completely agree, Mom. Great that he's found religion, but I'm scared by how he's changed." Is this no-touch monk life the kind of altering Philomena was suggesting I do? I won't do it.

Mom looks out the window, her face doing some kind of restrained wrestle; it's the what-or-how-much-do-I-say expression. She has to know that Dad hasn't given up on her, however much he's into St. Brendan, however much he's given up on everything else. After all, he could have given the key to one of the lab guys he sees every day.

"The God stuff wasn't what he signed up for, either," Mom says. "A hyper-rational man like him, a guy who loved his earthly pleasures. We've all been blindsided. I have to remember that."

TONY LLEWELLYN GRABBED my elbow as I walked into class an hour ago, said he wants me to meet him after next period, near the closest water fountain. Maybe he wants to apologize for our conversation at Jared's?

Chilling thought: he might have news, something he overheard or his father told him. Maybe Webb and Mom are talking about living together? Or—no, they *can't* get married. No. No. No. Mom's still married to Dad. Maybe Mom is pregnant? She's young enough. She *has* been eating a lot lately and acting moody. Oh, God.

All around me people are packing up their stuff to leave.

Another class to sit through before this Tony conversation. Omigod...

HERE IS what I experience simply by pausing in the stairwell, then walking down the hall before I find Tony:

1. Text from Mom: *you left the bathroom downstairs a total disaster and what is this black stuff on the white tile?* (Return text: *stepped on mascara sorry will fix*)
2. Text from Dad: *Get together this week? Apologies for acting mysterious. Don't want to have secrets.* Poor Dad, so precise he takes the time to capitalize and punctuate.

3. Martin passes with a bunch of guys, gives me a strange look and says, "You look sick."
4. See myself in the mirrored backing of the trophy case. I *do* look sick—too pale. It's probably the lack of sleep.

Tony's up ahead, leaning against the wall, looking surly as usual. My face feels blank. Not sure what expression is right for this moment.

He makes a slight move to push off from the wall when he sees me coming, but not hard enough to stand up completely. He doesn't speak. Neither do I. I should have given thought to how to handle this. If he were an adult, he'd say, Thanks for taking the time to meet with me. But he is not an adult.

"So, what's up?" I say, since someone has to speak.

He clears his throat. "I had this idea."

Pause.

Longer pause.

He bobs his head like he's hearing music, stares around at everything except me.

"What idea?"

He starts to form a word. Clears his throat again instead. I'm getting curious.

"See, I think we could do a number on our parents if we went to prom. I mean, together." He stares off down the hall.

Total body shock. Tony Llewellyn?! He hates me. He hates everyone, *especially* me.

"Are you serious?" Only Risto and flying around the

universe are more surprising than this. (And my father believing in stuff that's invisible.)

He licks his lips, tries for a tough-guy half-smile. "Yeah," he says, head still bobbing to the imaginary music. "Or are you already like, going with somebody or something?"

I can't think fast enough to—

"It's a cool idea, doing this, you have to admit."

I can't speak.

"Seriously," he says. "It's drastically cool." He's starting to relax like I've already said yes—which I haven't.

"I need to think," I say finally. "This has ramifications. It's caught me by surprise."

"The parents need to think twice about *their* ramifications."

That much is true. Doesn't mean I should spend a whole big-deal dressed-up event not-dancing with Tony Llewellyn. He'll wander off somewhere for the whole night, leaving me looking abandoned.

"What do you have to think about?" he says. I would never have expected him to be so persistent.

"It seems kind of mean."

"Mean?" He shrugs. The bell rings. Hall traffic has almost cleared out. "Okay. You think. Let me know."

TWENTY-NINE

C harlotte and I are walking back from Campus Mart, eating snackies: nachos and Hohos. "What does Martin think?" she says. "About this whole Tony thing."

"Haven't told him yet. I'm going to. Soon. I guess. I think he's been avoiding me."

We walk half a block in silence.

"Tony's too wild for you. But this is a one-time special situation. You should go."

I cut her a sharp look. "I can handle wild. You underestimate me."

"The main reason I think you should go with Tony is that it'll give you so much social capital."

"Social *capital*?"

"You know what I mean."

"I suppose. Perceived hotness, the magic powers that go with it..."

Charlotte cuts a glance at me. The whole idea of magic powers brings front row center my relationship with Risto and the actual supernatural. Way more vital than who's-cool-at-school, or who gets the most likes on social media.

"Anyway," she says. "You have a negative attitude about Tony, but he's smart, and also hot in an outsider kind of way. He's quiet, is all."

She's licking the salt off of a nacho chip.

"Don't do that. It's not cool."

"The salt is the good part. If I only eat the salt, there are no calories and no carbs."

"Seriously, it's disgusting, Charlotte."

"You are *so* judgmental, Darcy! Tony is bad. I'm disgusting. Who else is on your bad list? No, who's on your *good* list. The ghost-guy? Is he why you've been so distant from everybody?"

"I'm not distant. I'm talking about an intimate topic in this very conversation."

"Not the most intimate topic on your mind. I've heard almost nothing about ghost-guy. I mean, I only found out about him by accident! And he was barely a half-second flicker of light, which, in my opinion, is not enough to be proof of anything. And poor Martin—who knows *nothing*—thinks he's lost his best friend."

Whether she believes her own eyes is up to her. What hurts is what she says about Martin. But I know him well enough to know that he has something else he's hiding, too. I can almost see it—but I can't insist he tell me.

I'm scared to tell Charlotte more about Risto. If I do, I'll wind up slipping when I'm talking to somebody else. Or she will. All I want—I would just like to be able to mention him to whoever I'm talking to and say "we" and have people know that someone wonderful loves me. Why do I have to solve a puzzle, alter my personality, *and* figure out how Philomena wants me to be to find out whether or not that's possible?

"Anyway," Charlotte says. "You can think about it all you want to, but you're going to go with Tony. I know you are."

CHARLOTTE WAS RIGHT. I'm going to prom with Tony, though I don't fully understand why. To make Mom and Webb think twice? Because I think this will do great things for my social standing? Because nobody like him has paid attention to me before? Because he's a mystery and super-smart? Or because his black hair—if he washes it—will look good with a tuxedo? Or to prove I'm not scared of him?

Maybe it's all of the above.

Telling him, I kept it short but not sweet. He nodded in reverse, throwing his head back in the way that means: *got it, no need to say more.* We headed in different directions for class. I have erased from my memory the "ha-ha-I-win" look in his eyes.

Martin has to be informed, since he no doubt assumes I'm going to prom with him and his crew, so I sit and wait for him at our meeting place on the school's low breezeway wall. I don't look forward to this. He knows how I feel about Tony, and he knows the situation with Webb. He will think I'm being, in Martin-speak, "untrue to myself and seriously a jerk to Mom". And maybe he's right. He already thinks I've been a jerk to him. I've been "distracted...preoccupied," and I've refused to explain.

I don't know why he's still talking to me. I dread this worse than I did telling Tony.

Here he comes, with his leg-slinging walk. Blank-faced. Trying to look non-judgmental, or "like-I-care".

He drops down beside me. Slings his backpack off his shoulder, then sits silent, looking ahead with his elbows on his tall angular knees.

A pang of sadness. "Miss you lately," I say.

"Wonder whose fault that is."

"I hate when you're sarcastic."

"I hate when you're nearly unconscious, a walking dead person. You never did any of this before."

He's worried about me, underneath his hostile facade. "I'm okay, Martin."

"You're so *not*-okay it's freaky."

"Freaky? Who says freaky? That doesn't sound like you. Where are you getting this?"

"Everybody is talking about it. 'Freaky Darcy'."

"Everybody." That's sobering. "Martin, I'm going to prom with Tony Llewellyn."

He whips his face around to look at me. His eyes are cold.

"Darcy?" He shakes his head, can't seem to decide which outraged thing to say first. Keeps on shaking his head. "Darcy, that is seriously messed up."

Once again, I remember what some people think: that Martin has a secret obsession with me. Wrong. If that were true, he'd make a move. He's not shy.

"What's so messed up about it?" Like I don't know. But

it's right to give him a chance to blast me with his views—better than this long-term seething.

"He's doing this to take a shot at his father," Martin says.

I feel some heat rising, making me sit up straight. "He's using me? That's what you're saying?"

"Exactly."

"There's no other possible reason a person would want to go with me?" It's why Tony asked me, but Martin doesn't have to automatically assume that.

"I'm saying obviously that's what *Tony's* doing."

"I don't know why it's so obvious."

"Because he doesn't go to prom. He's asocial."

"Nobody is completely a loner."

"He is. Plus he has that gambling stuff going on. Seriously big-time. It's criminal but he calls it his 'start-up.' I heard it began when he was in bed for weeks after a wreck a couple of years ago."

"Why didn't I ever hear about that?"

"It was summer. Happened wherever it is his mother lives. It wasn't his fault and he was angry, probably wanted to break some laws. Anyway, taking bets, developing a system, was something to do."

"I don't see what that has to do with prom."

"He's not your type, Darcy. " He gives me an I-rest-my-case look, as if he's convinced me to tell Tony I've changed my mind.

I haven't. "Anyway," I say. "What difference does it make if I go with him?" Question to myself: Would a person who's able to read the little book go to the prom with Tony or not? How am I supposed to know?

"You're right," Martin says, hoisting his backpack onto his shoulder. "It doesn't matter at all." He gives a little wave with the hand hanging nearest me, not bothering to lift his arm. In two seconds, he's halfway down the breezeway. And then he's gone.

Mom says she's okay with my upcoming prom date. I guess I believe her. I guess I'm relieved. It was Tony, not me, trying to disturb the parents. She and I are sitting in her studio talking while she stays busy poking semiprecious gems into melty soft metal. It stinks and it looks dangerous.

"I see no reason why not," she says again. But if she and Webb were to live together, Tony and I would be living together part-time. Do I have to point this out?

"Of course, I'm surprised," she says. "Since you've said you don't like him. However, I know we all sometimes try to talk ourselves into or out of being interested in someone. For whatever reason."

I am not "interested" in Tony.

"Your father tried valiantly to talk himself out of this religious thing of his, to at least keep it from taking him over, driving him into a different kind of life. No luck with that."

"He did?" I wait to see if she's going to reveal more. Then I steel myself. "So was his religious thing the whole reason you guys split?"

"I suppose there are always a lot of reasons, some we're not even conscious of."

My hope of getting information drops fast.

"Religion was the major problem," she says. "No, that's

not true. It was the way his new beliefs affected his behavior. You saw how he'd become so withdrawn. Though that was probably more his inner conflict than the faith itself." She hesitates. "Monks aren't supposed to be married."

"Monks?" My stomach again does a horrible drop. Will this threat of a monastery hang over us forever? Or crash down on our heads when he moves into one of those places? This is what Dad said: she was tired of living with a monk.

"He hasn't signed up with an order. Not that I've heard. But he's already become an ascetic of sorts." Her face gets a stiff, holding-back-anger look.

Ascetic, which means—and my mind runs through it again: no fun, no pleasures, all self-denial and doing without. Poverty. Chastity. No sex. Like, no sex *ever*. Crap! I was right. It's now completely confirmed. How could he have gotten like that? My dad, who is so good-looking and his students fall in love with him.

If I move, I might throw up.

"Not life-affirming," Mom says, "in my opinion."

"He can't be like that. Not him." My voice sounds high-pitched, pathetic. "Religion shouldn't make you get withdrawn and ascetic. It's not healthy. It's terribly wrong for him."

Mom's seething look has softened into sadness, embarrassed like she's said too much. Which she has.

Dad turning into a monk! This is why I was forced to see Webb eating waffles in our kitchen, a mistake she hasn't repeated.

She falls into silence, and so do I. What she's told me

confirms what I've mostly tried to hide from myself for a couple of months. Knowing for sure is radically, disturbingly worse.

THIRTY

O ut a side door and onto the sidewalk, kids flowing in every direction or stopped in clumps, school buses pulling away.

A few minutes ago, Tony passed me in the hall and ignored me almost as much as usual. I tried sending Risto a mental "hi" last night, but I had no sense that I had reached him. I've been a little less confident about sending messages lately, since I don't know who might show up.

I've got that end-of-school-day feeling of fatigue and relief after almost seven hours of having to be outgoing and focused. The drums from marching band practice sound like they're rolling down the sidewalk toward me. I feel the hollow beat in my lungs.

"Hi, guys," I say to Tiffany and Kumar passing, and Kumar's sidekick, Curtis.

Two-syllable "hi" from her. The other two did the cool-guy lift-of-the-chin greeting. It looks silly on Curtis. Nobody should try to act cooler than they are.

I'm in a bad mood. Didn't know it until now. I have a deadline for getting a grip on the universe and I don't know when that deadline is. Risto could be born at any moment. And for all I know, there's nothing useful in that little book, anyway.

My fingers trail along the bushes in front of the school, rifling through the Nandina leaves. Papery. Some kinds of leaves have such a distinct feel...

An idea! My backyard tree! If the tree can bring Risto to me, then maybe it can take me to him. Maybe the change needed is for me to be more assertive and active and strong. I'll figure out how the tree can be a conductor for me. Maybe I already know; possibly some info from Philomena's book has already soaked in. She did say that it would be as if I always knew.

SITTING against the tree doesn't work. Standing in front of it and staring at it doesn't work. Nothing happens, no matter what I visualize, no matter what kind of chant I do under my breath. The tree does not propel me anywhere. Maybe there is nothing about this in Philomena's book.

Thinking about what to do has kept me lying awake most of the night. It's still an hour before the alarm goes off. The light through the window is a pale lemonade color.

Possibly I was holding back because I'm scared. The tree feels too strong, like it might take me too far and I could never get back.

I'm not scared. I refuse to be scared.

Pulling the covers over my head, I close my eyes and envision a spirit tree on the other side, an astral tree, sister to the one in the yard, fluid energy running through the trunks in a smooth green stream from one to the other and back, the two of them working together, conducting Risto to my very patio. The spirit tree looks different, the branches thicker without so many twigs, the leaves bigger and glossy, a breeze rustles through... A wind touches me, lifts me...

The wind feels thick, solid almost. A little damp. Suddenly I'm passing through night and clouds, but there's no moon. It's so dark, the lemonade light from my room long gone. I could get freaked out, but I won't let myself. Wispy strands I can't see run across the sides of my face, like ghostly seaweed. I'm traveling fast. It's dark ahead, dark below.

Stay calm. The spirit tree is pulling me. I have no idea where I'm going. This trip may be a terrible mistake, but I'm not stopping. I'm keeping on.

Bang: light! All at once! Like a monster camera flash and the crashing sound when Risto arrives. I'm out of where I was, floating in bright light. All in one second. My eyes are adjusting—down below a little island, translucent turquoise ocean glittering all around. So bright! If I squint, I can stand it. This could be the little island where Risto and I swam. Coming closer, closer... This time I'm going to hit land. Fast. Head-first. Terror rushes through my whole body. My insides loosen and turn to liquid. I'm going to crash and die.

I want to go home!

I *wham* into a chair. Back home, in the reading chair by

my bedroom window. Sprawled as if I were flung here from outside, my hurt rib suddenly aching again.

I'm back. I didn't get wherever I was going. I lost my nerve. But I got close, and I did it all on my own! I could try it again, but I'm exhausted. I feel myself drifting off to sleep...

THE NEXT DAY, the classroom feels too quiet. I glance around in a furtive way. A few people are looking at me, Martin especially, shaking his head like I'm hopeless. Mrs. Hartsell is waiting. I wasn't doing any astral travel. I was sitting here feeling discouraged, because of how I lost my nerve last night.

"I'm sorry. Would you repeat the question?"

"I asked you to come to the front and sketch a diagram that gives some idea of the concept of the fourth dimension. Will you do that, please?"

At least I was right; she was asking me a question. Fourth dimension? Did I miss something? This is math class. Homework was about shapes rotating. She never said anything about the fourth dimension.

"I'm sorry, I can't just now." Which is what Mom says when she's not going to do something, ever: Not just now, thank you.

"I see." Mrs. Hartsell hesitates, maybe thinking I'm having some problem like an anxiety melt-down or blood on the back of my skirt. "All right then."

Tony watches me; I see him out of the corner of my eye. He is halfway smiling, if you could call that look a smile. I settle back into my seat while Mrs. Hartsell selects Tony to do what I have refused to. She always calls on him. He's a math-head.

Tony draws something like a cube inside a cube, tosses the stylus aside, and goes back to his seat. Smug, even though his little sketch shows nothing about the amazingness of the universe. Risto probably knows everything about the fourth dimension and the fifth and the sixth, whether he can explain it or not. Philomena knows more. I could blow this class completely out of the water with *real* other-dimension experiences that Mrs. Hartsell and Tony never imagined.

How did the fourth dimension get discussed? That's something I could be interested in.

I LET myself into Dad's apartment with my new personal key. I need him to tell me about this fourth dimension business—and whether calculus could teach me anything about navigating the other realms. If so, it could be worth some serious study.

His two o'clock class should have finished by now; he'll be here soon. I go looking for something to eat.

Open one cabinet, open the other—this is so pitiful. A box of oatmeal. Peanut butter. Stale crackers. A guy like him should *not* be subsisting this way. He was a foodie. I eat a couple of spoonfuls of peanut butter out of the jar and put it back on the shelf. Don't want to cut into his supplies. Anyway, I'm not here to eat or deal with his diet.

When the door starts to open, I instantly call out to him —"Dad!"—so he won't think I'm a robber.

"Darcy! You're here. Best surprise I could have."

Who ever knows what to say to something like that? I give him a hug. He smells tired, which on him is like hot road tar in summer, like bicycle tires. Otherwise he's the same as ever, thin as usual, but not wasting away.

"I need some help with something."

"Sure. What's up?" We sit down at his little bare table.

"What does the fourth dimension have to do with calculus? Does math really have some kind of clues in it about other realms?"

"Realms? You mean the parallel universe theory?" He sits back in his chair.

"That sounds right," I say. It truly does. A universe running parallel to this one. Risto's realm right on top of us, and we're mostly not seeing it. "Are scientists doing studies about this?" It wasn't on the menu at the paranormal conference, at least not that I recognized.

"There are various ideas. Well, you know about string theory, right? The idea that the particles of the universe contain minute filaments that vibrate through maybe ten or so other dimensions that we don't see."

"I've heard the term," I say, though I never before paid any attention, and it doesn't make sense now.

"The theory was, of course, developed mathematically. More through differential geometry than calculus." He starts to reach for a piece of paper, then stops himself. He knows I don't want him to start into a sheet of equations. "Why do you ask?" He looks proud of me.

"The fourth dimension was mentioned in class."

"Fascinating. I'll bet that perked up interest."

I take a semi-deep breath, feel my heart do an actual flitter. "Dad, do you think your friend St. Brendan might be living in one of these other dimensions?"

"No, honey, I don't. It's highly likely that these other dimensions—if they exist—are minute."

"But math somewhat supports the idea that they're real?"

"You could say that, yes."

"That's huge! Why hasn't this been in the news? It's much better than ancient raindrop tracks on Mars."

He laughs. "It's a theory, Darcy."

"The theory is right, Dad. Brendan exists. You've convinced me of that much."

"*I've* convinced you?"

"Completely. I mean, look how you've changed your entire life because of God and St. Brendan, who are both invisible. You wouldn't do that if they weren't real."

Now I lay me down to not-sleep, wearing a loose goddess-y dress I found at a thrift shop last week. When I pictured myself swishing through the air, I didn't like the image of jeans and clunky boots. I need to be light and floating as a cloud. That'll help me focus on the spirit tree—and whatever might help from Philomena's illegible manual of spirit worlds.

Focus—that's what I need to do. Maybe that's all I need to do, be a more focused person. Can't force this to happen, though. Struggling to lift off from the Earth plane is like trying to talk yourself into going to sleep. The effort only gets in the way. I'll aim my attention at my destination and then relax.

Just lie here. Don't think.

Am I going to sleep? I don't want to.

Go blank.

Blank blank blank. Gray blank, silver blank, white screen...

My legs feel jumpy like I'm nervous. Rib hurts like a toothache.

Picture the tree. It's tall, green. Downstairs toilet flushes. I roll over on my side, start again: imagine myself climbing the tree, reaching up for the next branch. It's easy, I'm hardly trying. Another branch, and another. Climb higher. Up ahead, a nice perch where I can sit and look out, see for miles.

Hand slips. Lurch out of balance. Scramble to catch—

I'm falling. crashing through leaves.

Where are the branches? I'm falling through air, spinning like a winged sycamore seed, dropping...

And I'm landing, knees bent, arms flailing to keep my balance. My side isn't hurting, not even the slightest twinge, even with all this motion.

Amazing! I'm here, I've come to a stop beside an enormous tree at the top of a steep hill.

The tree is just as I thought it would be, like a cross between a magnolia and a fig. I rub my cheek against a leaf, which feels as warm as a person's skin. I don't know how I managed a fall without banging into branches. Putting a foot out, I test the ground ahead of me. It's solid. I don't have to hold on to the tree. I want to, though. While I watch, a landscape opens up around me. Mist has cleared in every direction. In the distance is the shine of water.

I see a traffic of people passing, circling this one steep hill, this one tree, all of them swirled together in a million colors and kinds of clothes. Everything and everyone is flowing past, sharply visible for seconds, then melting back into a river of color: camels and horses and a guy in a terrycloth bathrobe and, there, three girls in antique bathing suits and a kid doing flips on parallel bars and the huge face of a man gritting his teeth like he has a headache, and a million flittering little birds, all flowing together: every kind of living thing. Drooling babies, a long-tail monkey, fish that flash light, every size of dog. Eden, if there was one, must have come spinning out of this place, a big garden flung like a Frisbee and scattering everywhere.

This has to be the center of the universe. A tree in the center of the spiraling river. Of course. I always knew it.

If I let go of the branch and slip into this parade, will I get lost, never be able to go home? But I have to do it, it's irresistible. From where I hover in clear bright air, I head toward the stream of traffic. As soon as I touch the edge, I'm pulled in.

All at once, the sound comes on: voices, laughing, animals clopping and braying, rumbling machinery, creaking furniture. Music! Sounds Hawaiian, like Abba and ukuleles. Plus the smells, my God! A llama-ish creature is nudging me from behind. Musty reek like dirty carpet.

A mishmash of shapes and motion and color, faces coming in and out of focus. A man with bushy eyebrows is close to my face, then he blurs away. A fat lady carrying a cooler and a beach chair. Here's the ocean—in an instant, gone. Spirits in tunics like Risto—the never-born?—and a few who seem a mish-mash of human history: the man in a World War I helmet and earbuds, the one on an old-fashioned tall-wheeled bicycle wearing Nike trainers. At first I think no one is talking with anyone and then I feel the constant hum of communication; everyone is talking with everyone. Though I can't understand them.

Yet all the time, I'm floating in the same parade, the Gulf Stream of Everything, going round and round in an endless twisting limitless circle and all of it feels good. As if I'm made of light, I'm everywhere at once and anything is possible.

I need to remember: anything is possible.

CHAPTER

THIRTY-ONE

Weight sinks the nearest corner of my bed. Not Risto. It's Philomena. Again. Looks the same as before: hefty, making me think of aprons and dish towels. I want to like her, but I don't think she wants me to. She's irritable, yet she keeps coming back.

"I found the spirit tree," I tell her. She nods.

"It was crowded. There were too many spirit people there for me to find anybody. No hope of seeing Risto." I don't even attempt to tell her how amazing it felt. I don't have the words for it. And she knows.

"Of course not. But you did right well to get yourself there. Not many do." She says it a bit grudgingly, but still she says it.

Hearing that, I feel a warm rush of pride. My shoulders relax for the first time with her. "I don't know how I did it. Not really."

"Untether," she says. "Be loose as sand, light as the ashes of the hearth, in mind and in muscle."

"I guess I did that, then. But wait a minute—is this the thing I was supposed to do so I could read the book?"

She says nothing.

"It is, isn't it?"

She sees what I'm thinking on my face. "It has to be relearned," she says, "many times every day."

"But this means I now know whatever is in that book. It's soaked in!"

Again, she is silent.

I still have so many questions, though, so I can't have absorbed it all. But now I remember: she said the book would give me only ABCs, a beginning.

"Philomena, tell me, please. Can we stay together, Risto and me?"

"There are plenty of affairs between born and unborn," she says. "Mostly brief, people don't realize. And too, the spirits of the living meet outside their bodies. But they forget it happened, or think it was a dream. You with your boy are aware."

She hasn't answered my question.

"He sensed you from far away, your clear-seeing, your heart both gentle and venturesome. It could happen because you are one who lives close to the boundary of the realms. It's your nature to be this way. When you two met, you chose, and he chose again."

"You mean we fell in love."

"You got a good start on it."

"Was this somehow planned, him and me? Were we meant to be?" Trying yet again: "Are we meant to stay together?"

She says nothing.

"I mean, like arranged by God's plan. Or predestined by nature, like an apple ripening, the way you said Risto would get ready to be born."

"No, it was how you fit to each other, and the force of both your desires that caused it."

She's fading. Last chance: "Philomena, can our desires keep us together?"

I'm losing sight of her. She says, "If you find," then trails off in words that sound foreign or mumbled in sleep: "*oraham lasparay...*"

And she's gone.

SIXTH PERIOD, I made a list of questions about him, about him and me, practical stuff we need to know to be able to operate in my world and his. The main thing is, what do I have to find? What is *oraham lasparay?* I mentally sent Philomena my questions, and I also made this list for myself, for the next time I manage to slip into that loose-as-sand entranced state when I know things I don't know I know. I'm pretty sure I can get myself to the spirit-tree world again, but I haven't done it and I'm not sure why. I guess it scares me, that I might get lost and never come back. I'd risk it and go anyway if it was important, but there are no answers in simply being there sight-seeing like a tourist.

That night, as soon as I walk into my bedroom, I see her. "I'll take you to him," Philomena says. "Let him show you answers to your thousand questions. He needs the practice."

Take me to Risto? This hits me like lightning. I feel it in my hair. "You can? You can do that?"

"You need much schooling on how to keep company with a being like him, and I am not planning to spend eternity doing it." She's going to help me so she can be rid of me? Check me off her homework assignments? I don't get why she's bothering to help me at all. But I'm not going to question and give her the chance to change her mind.

"I'm ready," I say. "Let's go."

Traveling with Philomena is dramatically different than with Risto. More like being in a bubble elevator, less like being a soaring bird. I have no sense of the air around me, but I do have an odd sensation in my stomach.

We arrive quickly. Here is my spirit tree, just below. But, as we drift to the ground, I see that the spiraling river of life looks different today.

"Philomena, who are all these people?"

"Others like him."

"I don't see anyone else like him." What's in front of me is a melty stream of faces and figures, but none of them look like they've ever lived on Earth. Nobody wearing a bathrobe or a coat or a tie. Nobody with clear edges.

"Very unborn creatures," Philomena says.

Adrenaline bursts inside me. Then Risto is more advanced, more defined. "Is Risto already scheduled to be born on a particular day?" Please, no. This is exactly what I don't want: Risto disappearing into the form of someone's baby. He would be gone for the rest of our lives!

"No given day," she says. "Not today."

"How do you know?" My revved-up bloodstream has not settled down.

She looks at me in a way I can only describe as condescending. "I know. It's my nature."

"Which is what, exactly? What is your nature? Why are you doing whatever it is you're doing with me?"

"I'm here to help you. Though you are a sassy slip of a girl. You always were."

"You said you were taking me to Risto." I'm human. I get to be impatient and unreasonable. As a spirit, she ought to be a little more angelic.

"I will bring the boy along shortly," she says. "When I have his location." She's not doing anything, must be waiting for the info to pop up in her mind. Then I hear again in my head, what she said about me being sassy: you always were.

"Philomena, did you know me before I was born? Did you help me get ready to become human?" As soon as I ask it, it hits me hard: I'm helping Risto get ready to be born. Which is what I don't want to happen.

She lets the silence stretch, watches the whispering stream of spirits coursing by us on either side, floating up to us where we stand. She's not going to tell me, but I'm pretty sure I'm right.

"You were one of mine," she says at last. "A right troublesome one, following me around annoying me as I worked the kitchen garden, always wanting to know."

"If I was so much trouble, why are you helping me? It's not like you were ever my actual parent. Why were you staring at Risto in the restaurant that night?"

"I had to know he was grown enough to be large-hearted, not one to do you mischief. And strong-natured. You're like me, ever paying close attention, wanting no nonsense. You're like me. That ought to answer both your questions well enough: why I bother with you, why I wanted to make sure of him."

Sudden upward lurch in my stomach, like from an elevator going down.

"Darcy!"

"Risto!" It's his voice, but I don't see him.

I'm suddenly somewhere different. Where? In a tree. Yes, I'm sitting in the sycamore tree, at home in my backyard, on the lowest branch, where the trunk divides. One running shoe is dangling loose, about to fall off of my foot. No Philomena anywhere.

"Risto, where are you?" My eyes are searching madly. The ground below, the neighboring trees, the top of the fence, the alley...

"I am here."

"Where?" I'm keeping my voice under control. There's no reason to get angry. "Wave your arms, Risto. Do something so I can see you."

"Here. Stay in the place where you sit. I am approaching to you." Then he's seated beside me. I feel his warmth all down my side, but his weight doesn't dip the branch at all.

"Where were you? Were you invisible?"

"Perhaps invisible. If so, an accident."

It's like he's still got his learner's permit or his training wheels. So what? I'm so glad to see him that my happiness is almost unbearable. I wrap around him as much as I possibly can while sitting in a tree. "Let's go to my room, so we don't have to balance up here—"

Before I can say more, we are in my room. In daylight, which has only happened a couple of times.

We're eyes-to-eyes lying on our sides on my bed. My fingers play with the wisp of chest hair that shows at the top of his shirt.

"Philomena helped me find you," I say. "Or you to find me. She's the one who watched you at the fish restaurant. "

"You know this? She has visited to you?"

"A couple of times and explained about spirits learning to be born. She likes you."

"I know her only from the distance," he says. "The way all spirits know all. Not more close than this."

Oh, no! I forgot! I was so excited I didn't ask her in person about the words I couldn't understand, whatever I'm supposed to find. *Orham lasparay?* I already googled about a million different spellings. Nothing!

"She is friendly?" Risto says.

"Not very. But she cares about me, in a grumpy way. She hides it, acts like I'm some kind of duty or assignment."

"Assignment. We all have. It is part of our nature."

My insides seize on this. Am I an assignment? That would be awful. "What is your assignment, Risto?"

"Acquire education."

"In what?"

"Earth human."

I'm glad I talked with Philomena, or I never would have understood this answer. "That's why you're with me? I'm giving you an education?" I want to be his girlfriend, not his teacher or his tour guide. Even though he's learning from me, I don't want that to be the main reason.

He takes his time answering.

"I come to Earth plane to find the education," he says slowly, almost like he's building strength. He brings the full warmness of his eyes back to me. "I come to you, MyDarcy," he says, "because I have great love feeling for you."

He loves me. He said it out loud.

"Risto, I—"

But his expression has clouded, so quickly. He looks troubled and doubtful. I dread his answer, or non-answer, but I have to ask, "What is it, Risto?"

"My Darcy, I bring this question to you. Do you have love feeling? For me, Risto?

He's worried? How could he possibly be? "Risto, I have the love feeling for you, so much it makes me dizzy. You are My Risto. I am Your Darcy. Completely. Forever."

As soon as I say "forever," I'm flooded with anxiety all over again. Because I don't even know what it is I'm supposed to find, and he could be born at any moment.

"Risto, what is your education for?" Maybe Philomena had it wrong somehow.

"So when it is I am born that I am not empty blank who is only confusion."

Born! There it is again. A ball of fear falls open in my

stomach, because maybe he's learning too fast, and I'm part of the reason. "Risto, when is it you are being born?" Maybe he knows more about himself than Philomena could. "How long can you be the way you are now?"

He laughs. "How could I possibly know this?" With one finger, he pushes a strand of hair away from my face. His eyes are full of his great love feeling. My adrenaline dies down.

"I want you to stay the way you are, Risto. With me."

"Plus intensely more knowledgeable, I think." He smiles. He's already better at communication, at answering questions.

"You might be educated enough now. I'd hate for you to lose your..." Trying to think of a nice word for dopiness. The main thing, though: if he learns too fast, I'll lose him. I can't stand to think of him being born, disappearing into some distant human life. I'll be staring at every baby I see and wondering if it's him. There has to be a way around this. Fast. "Risto, how old are you?"

"Age of existence in river current? English has no—"

"The age you are now. With me."

Long pause. In my head I hear ten of us singing "Happy Birthday" to Martin at a table outside Goodberry's, everybody loud and happy, as if a birthday is a good thing.

"I cannot know," he says.

The day of Risto's birth. Is that the end of us?

"Give me some idea how long we have, how long this education takes. Weeks? Centuries? In human time."

He looks embarrassed. "I have not understood yet human time."

It could be five minutes from now for all that either of us

knows. How do I possibly cope with the constant threat of him vanishing? Humans do have the threat of the other person dying, but who thinks about that? Nobody my age. Anyway, he loves me. We love each other. That's what's important.

CHAPTER

THIRTY-TWO

P hone blurps its little text signal. Charlotte wants to go look at dresses for prom. Now. She'll be here in ten minutes.

I let the phone drop onto my pile of desk papers. Looking for a dress, I'll pretend Risto will see it. Of course he will. I'll make sure he does, somehow.

Car honks outside. That wasn't ten minutes. Charlotte's friend Katrina has her license and she speeds. Banging at the front door.

"Coming, coming!" Down the stairs, I slam the door behind me while I'm still pulling on my jean jacket. "Are you guys in some kind of hurry?"

Charlotte's already down the front steps, heading back to the car. Katrina is *not* my completely favorite person. She makes me feel socially backward. If she starts acting superior, I'll remind myself that her off-and-on boyfriend asked two other girls I know to sext him nude selfies.

"I'm not making any decisions today," I say as we both fall into the car, me in the back. I need to take the pressure off myself, not make this a huge deal.

"How can you know that already?" Katrina says. I see her eyes in the rearview mirror, looking back at me.

"I make up my mind slowly," I say, looking out the side window at the houses streaking past. That isn't totally true, but it gives me something to say—since I'm certainly not going to discuss my actual prom conflicts.

"Darcy doesn't make up her mind in front of others," Charlotte says.

That was a jab—though it's true. I kick the back of Charlotte's seat. "Correct. I like to have my mind clear."

Katrina pulls her beach-streaked hair up off her neck, then lets it drop. She has all the right mannerisms. I don't do mannerisms. They're juvenile.

"You know what you're looking for, Darcy?" Katrina says. The car smells like cigarettes.

"Something ethereal," I say. Charlotte gives me a meaningful look. Unlike Katrina, she knows what the word means. "You know, filmy."

"Angelic," Katrina says.

"Ha ha." She's so sure that I'm a one-hundred percent prude.

"Darcy has a secret life," Charlotte says. "You'd be knocked out in awe, Katrina." I could get alarmed at what she's saying, but at least she's defending me and my sense of adventure.

"Really?" Katrina's watching me in the rearview again. I

gaze mysteriously out the window. "Like who you're going to prom with? Not a secret."

I say nothing, but continue to smile enigmatically as we stream past the cars parked along the curb. Each car is like one syllable of my inner chant: *or-a-ham las-par-ay*.

"Well," Katrina says, "I hope they have lots of filmy stuff in your colors."

By the time we get to the store, I'm sure of my Earth-life coolness. I walk into the place feeling sublime, as if Katrina, with her perfectly tan midriff, is one of my entourage. I'm the one the clerk looks to when she says, "What can I help you find?"

But Katrina answers, "Cheap fabulous formals," and the clerk-girl laughs. Everybody who works here has long hair and black clothes and smiles most of the time.

I've never worn a long dress in my life. This is a check-it-out mission. No money or plastic at the moment.

Charlotte pulls out a pale green sheath. "Perfect," I tell her. "You found it on the first try. You are going to look fantastic in that."

"I hope it's long enough," she says. She always has being tall to deal with.

"Oh my God," Katrina says. "Charlotte, what do you think?" She holds a long glittering gold dress in front of her, pulling it to her waist, turning it this way and that. Charlotte says something I don't hear, because I am completely stunned.

This dress is ethereal, not drifty fabric like I'd imagined, but better. It looks as if it's made out of pure light. This is my dress. In an instant, I find my size, whip it out, step in front

242

of the mirror. Picture Risto behind me. He has on a dinner jacket, white against his tan. No, he's in black, to go with his shiny dark eyes and hair.

Katrina stares at me. "So like, you're going to get the same dress as I am?"

I've just violated the first law of shopping. But this isn't an ordinary mall run. I'm dealing with an unusual situation. The way she's standing looks seriously angry.

"There are do's and don'ts to shopping, Darcy! You do know that?"

"Whoa, Katrina, take it easy," Charlotte says. "You don't know what it looks like on, *or* what it costs."

"It's ethereal," I say. But there's no way I can make this right with Katrina.

The smiling girl comes back. "Have we found something to try on?"

"We have," I say. In this case, "we" is precisely the right word. I don't blame Katrina for hating me.

The clerk looks at the two identical dresses. "Matching! What a great idea!"

Suddenly, I feel awful. I've made a mess of dress shopping. Worse, I'm stressing over what to wear to a school dance with a boy I don't like who doesn't like me.

I put the dress back on the rack. Risto is who I want to look good for. How can that work? Is he going to see me at home in the dress and be wowed and dazzled, then disappear while I ride off with Tony? It's not going to work.

Katrina hasn't said anything. She still grips the dress against her.

"I don't want to go to prom," I say to Charlotte. "What

was I thinking?" What if Risto feels wounded, or gets mad, or thinks I like Tony?

What if I tell both Tony and the groups of friends that I'm not going with them and Risto doesn't show up that night and there I am, sitting by myself in my room when it's too late to make any other plans, feeling pathetic and stupid, like nobody in the world—or anywhere else—cares about me?

"You try it on," I say to Katrina. She's looking at me like I've confirmed every bad thing she's thought about me, cool gorgeous Charlotte's weirdo sidekick. Katrina matches the other side of Charlotte, the party side. "Seriously, go try it on. I'm not in a prom dress mood. I'm rethinking everything. I'll be on the bench out front."

I wave vaguely in that direction. I feel like somebody kicked me and my whole body is sagging. I don't wait for them to say anything before I turn and walk out the door.

Outside, I don't get far. Slumped against the store window, I want to slide to the pavement like somebody who's been shot. It's hit me: going to prom with anybody but Risto is the official public start of a fake life. So much important stuff—like relationships, for one major thing—will be fake and pretend so long as my Risto life is happening in secret.

Horrible! I can't do it. I won't.

IN THE MORNING, I feel even worse. Can't get out of bed. Can't face any of the things that happen in a regular day. All these months—the whole school year—everything I've done in my Earth life is a lie. Or at least *partly* a lie. The thought makes me too tired to sit up.

I can't go to school today and say hi to people on the sidewalk and in the hall.

"Darcy, are you up?" Mom, of course.

"I don't feel good." Can't make my voice loud enough for her to hear. Her footsteps are coming up the stairs.

"Darcy," she says as she comes into my room. "You're still in bed." There's actual shock in her voice.

"I can't go."

She puts her hand on my forehead to see if I have a fever. "You feel all right."

"I feel bad." I stop myself from saying I'm sick. I'm not going to add one more lie to the mountain of others.

Mom sits down beside me, her hand on my back. "What hurts?"

"Everything." And that's true. I feel vague hurt everywhere.

"Is anything wrong?"

"Nothing new."

I know she's deciding this is divorce-related. And in a way, I guess it is. If the shock of the news hadn't flung me out of my body, I might never have found Risto. I turn my face into the pillow. This is how my whole life will be, as long as Risto is a secret. Lies and lies to people I love.

THIRTY-THREE

M om did let me stay home yesterday. I lay there all day, sleeping and thinking. I kept turning over and over in my head the last words Philomena said: that I have to find something—and then the foreign-sounding: *oraham lasparay*. I tried all day and night to reach her. No sign of her. She did make pretty clear she's finished answering my questions.

Worse possibility: she's told me all she knows, or that she's conscious of knowing. When she said those last gibberish words, she sounded half asleep, or like she was being loose as sand. Today I went to school and still felt hopeless, like most of my life is never going to be any good.

This afternoon Charlotte and I are sitting in the kitchen at her house, eating the cookies her mother makes from cake mix.

"When I looked at those dresses with my own eyes, and the whole idea of prom became real, I knew I couldn't go with Tony," I say. "It would have been a Fake Prom. Fraudulent, like a lot of the rest of my Earth life is getting to be."

Charlotte makes a half-listening sound, eating a cookie slowly, swinging her leg against the metal rung of the counter stool. She's preoccupied because Bink spent all of lunch today talking to Sunitra.

If I had total courage I would go public, tell Tony I'm seriously with someone now, therefore can't go. I don't care if—

Wait! I have an idea.

My breathing stops. This could work.

"Charlotte, Risto has to go to prom with me."

She jumps to attention. "Oh my God, Darcy."

"The public-ness of it would get him completely into my world so I don't have to keep him secret. I have to make it happen."

Charlotte looks doubtful.

"I think he can do it. If he can be visible for me, he can do it for others. The waiter in that restaurant saw him, treated him like a regular guy. You saw him. What's so different about a dance? We could figure out what to say about where he's from, like he's an exchange student. He *is* a foreign student."

"Oh, Darcy, I love this!" Charlotte is instantly wired, racing in circles while sitting still. This is something she can be part of. "Will he go along with it?" She's this excited even though she still has doubts Risto's real, even though I haven't used my "superpowers" to keep tabs on Bink. Maybe my invisible other world has made her feel left out. Warm feeling for her washes through me.

247

"I'm sure he'll come if he possibly can," I say. "You and I can work it out from this end."

"Tell him he has to! It would be the most amazing prom in history, even if no one knew it but us."

I picture him with me, out in the world—*my* world—for a perfect night. Happiness rushes through me, my mind turning flips. I am so excited—and scared. This will either be the answer to everything or an unforgettable, life-wrecking disaster.

BY THE TIME HE ARRIVES, it's three-ridiculous-a.m. The room is dark except for the clock light.

"Risto, you're here," I say as he slides under the covers beside me. I stifle the word "late." He's not late. We had no set time, but it's been ten days, long enough for him to build up his energy again. I sensed he'd be here tonight, and I have not slept for one second.

I'm going to jump right into the subject, before I'm completely overwhelmed because of his breath on my neck and his overall deliciousness. I ask him to reach over and turn on the lamp.

"Risto?" My voice already has a too-high pleading sound. I start again at a lower octave, "Risto, there's something I want us to do that I know will be great for us." I tell him he will learn an enormous amount about being a person by attending this very special event, and we can have so much fun.

He doesn't seem to be listening. He runs the tip of his finger over one of my eyebrows, which makes the bottom of my feet tingle. I imagine us slow dancing, holding onto each other, swaying.

Lasparay. The syllables pop into my head for the millionth time. The other big question I need to ask—though I doubt he has any idea—is about the mystery words: *oraham lasparay.*

I say it out loud. Risto frowns. Not promising.

"Do you have any idea what it means?"

He shakes his head. "I am speaking English language," he says. "Your pronouncing this words is not enough to awaken other language."

"I don't know any more."

"You come to feast at my home," he says.

My breathing stops dead. He's inviting me home with him! Prom gave him the idea? Or was it the nonsense syllables?

"Yes, of course, I'd love to." A thought strikes. "You mean, out there in the ocean?"

He laughs, loud enough that I'm sure Mom will wake up and hear. "No, this part is location dry with fire."

I picture us in the circle around a campfire. "Others will be there? The kind who are like you?"

"Like me." He doesn't call them people.

"I am so excited. What should I wear—you know, so I'll fit in?" What about my hair that he seemed so bothered about. Do I mention it? It's longer, not as fierce-looking, but still....

"Wear feast dress," he says, sounding baffled that I would have to ask.

I know the one. Floor-length and every inch of it

throwing out light. Perfect. Back to that store. I can tell the smiling girl in black that it's for a feast in another realm. She'll say, "Oh, so cool," in spite of whatever she's thinking. She'll say, "Aren't you lucky?", which I definitely am.

NEXT MORNING, math class. No one has said the word "dimension" in the thirty-two minutes so far, and I've been listening for it. We didn't decide about prom last night, but that's okay. He's taking me to his world, which is equally important.

Tony texted, but I haven't texted back. All he wanted was to tell me he's driving and we'll probably be going with some guy I don't know and his girlfriend. He's looking over at me off and on, with his resentful heavy-eyebrow glare.

I should go ahead and break the date after this class, so he can get somebody else. That would be only fair, since it's getting late already; prom is only a few weeks away. But I don't want to do this in person. I'll text him tonight, then we can never speak or look at each other again, the way it was before.

But I still don't know if Risto will go.

The room is quiet. We're all scratching away at solving a problem. Supposedly.

I am, too. Mine's just a different problem.

When the bell rings, I race out the door, down the hall. Dodging anybody in my way, picking up speed.

And—how did he do this?—Tony's in front of me! Walking backwards and facing me with a taunting look on his face.

"Changed your mind? About going?" He's still traveling backwards with big galloping steps. I have to hurry to keep up with him. "You're not talking." He's smiling, smirking. That's how much he cares whether I go or not.

"I can't talk now. I have things on my mind."

"Are you thinking about not going? Yes or no."

"Am I thinking about it?"

"Obviously you are. So we'll call that a yes. What's wrong: you're scared of our parents? Or me?" He laughs in his mean way, which helps me avoid feeling bad about bailing on him.

"I have to go to class." Ahead is the corner where we diverge. Unless he follows me. He doesn't.

"Think hard," he calls out to me as he walks away. "Remember it's easier to go than to tell me no."

That stops me in my tracks. Two guys pile up against my back and make irritated sounds as they go around me. What he's saying sounds threatening. He thinks he can scare me?

I picture being at the dance with Risto and across the room Tony is there with some odd marginal person who is the perfect match for him.

"I'm not going with you," I yell back at him. He is long gone.

THIRTY-FOUR

S itting in the dark, trying to stay calm. I'm wearing the dress. And eye make-up for evening: heavy mascara, luminous pale-gold eye shadow. I'm going to Risto's home feast. I'm so excited I can barely breathe. Underneath, of course, I'm still thinking the mystery words, like some kind of endless chant. The mystery thing Philomena says I should find—I'm more likely to uncover it at his home than mine. Maybe if I stay loose as sand....

Anyway, we're going! He'll be here soon.

In study hall this afternoon, I suddenly knew that tonight is the night. I sensed it, like Risto's heart was talking to mine. We're in so much better contact these days, better than I would have believed was possible. And I can picture how he'll look. He'll have on his usual long shirt but decorated with gold braid, an elegant band winding through his curls. We'll arrive at the feast in an instant—no long flights doing childish tricks, no swoopyloopy flying. I close my eyes, try to relax—which doesn't work.

I give up and open my eyes, and here he is: Risto, sitting beside me, warm-eyed and beautiful, dressed pretty much like I thought. He says, "You have on your most brilliant clothings." He smells like an otherworldly aftershave. Salty and lemony and sweet. Makes me think of night breeze at the beach.

He reaches for both my hands. We rise in the air together. It's like we're slow-dancing and at the same time moving upward. The ceiling dissolves. The treetops fall away in slow-motion as we rise and rise until I'm light-headed, my whole body airy. I'm a feather, nothing more, a feather in a gold dress.

Is it the altitude that makes my head feel so light?

...Fast drop. All at once, we are at the flattened top of a little mountain on an island, big fires roaring, as crowded as the State Fair, full of shining people, everything luminous in the firelight, and moonlight hitting white on the ocean in a complete circle all around us.

"Risto. Are we here? Is this where you live?"

He only smiles.

"Risto?"

Again, he says nothing. An explanation pops into my head: "Risto, do you speak English here?"

He doesn't answer. Scares me that he can't hear me.

But then, what a sight!

The crowd passing—I hear no English or any other Earth language, though they seem to be communicating out loud. Sounds like a combo of music and water. I'm not sure that the sounds are even coming out of their mouths. I can't tell where any of it's coming from. Maybe their eyes? Doesn't sound like Philomena's words. I'm not even sure these *are* words. And it's impossible to tell whether Risto is saying anything.

The clothes are from different times and kinds of life, some a mix of lives, it seems. I reach out to touch a passing bit of flowing fabric hanging off of a man's dark-skinned shoulder. It feels alive, like Risto's tunic. Some of the people seem more like bright shadows, made of some smooth calm substance that has no details. Maybe this crowd is both the Earth-born and the never-born.

Risto watches this other-world street fair. He looks so happy, doesn't seem impatient. Though now that I think about it, he has never seemed impatient about anything, never worried that we wouldn't meet again.

I try once more to speak, but it's not necessary, because I'm here, finally, at Risto's place with him. His home. His mountaintop. Of course it's foreign and exotic, which is probably what it's like for him every time he comes to see me.

I keep expecting the passing people to speak to him, for them to recognize each other. Instead, it's as if they've all already greeted, everything is already said. Too bad I'm not in on the conversation. My dress, though, is right. As good as a human could come up with. It shines almost like some of theirs.

We're in motion now, Risto and I—together. Sort of walking, more like gliding on one of those airport moving sidewalks. Can't talk, but he sure can walk: the thought makes me laugh out loud, and the sound comes out like bubbles. If it weren't for the fires and the ocean below, I might think we were underwater or drifting in something like water. I have a feeling the spirit tree is somewhere near, but if so, it's invisible.

Risto steers us closer to one of the huge bonfires. The whole flat mountaintop, in flickering firelight, has the feel of a giant festival. Men and women and kids are drinking out of big metal goblets.

Here and there smaller circles of people separate themselves out, maybe a dozen or twenty in each. From every circle comes a musical sound, like a bell ringing, each cluster ringing a different bell note. So lovely! I've never heard such music.

Risto puts a drink in my hand. The metal is so cold, I think my hand may freeze to it. When I try to take a sip, a mist of bubbles goes up my nose. Tastes like liquid sun would—if it were smoking-cold. Is this going to make me drunk or not know what's happening? I mustn't miss anything.

Risto smiles, looking around us happily. He seems to be his usual self, not drunk at all. So I drink it. Like Alice in Wonderland, I drink it, though I don't shrink or turn into a giant the way she did. I feel pretty much the same.

"MyDarcy," Risto says. "Are you desirous of feasting?"

I can hear and understand him. What changed? Is this because of the drink? Staring down into the faintly gold liquid, all I see is my wavering reflection. How has he never recognized his own reflection in liquid or metal? He's talking about dinner. He wants roasted red mullet.

I have to interrupt."Risto, all of a sudden I can hear you talking. Before, there was only burbling and brushing sounds. And the beautiful bell music."

"When are you not hearing? I have been saying to you of so many wondrous things." He frowns. "Perhaps I hear so many speak spirit language I momentarily forget MyDarcy language."

"Did you tell me about the circles of people singing like bells?" I think I'm now speaking spirit language. Though it feels so familiar and natural, I can't be sure. It probably came from hearing it around me, not from the drink.

"I did not say of these. You do not know?"

"I don't."

He looks surprised. "A circle forms. Like a flower it comes. Each spirit entity is one petal. The blossom appears and sings, then disappears. And after, each of the circle stays friend forever, these individuals all in good harmony."

The thought of spirit blooms drifts down inside me, makes a sweet hum in my heart. I want to meet his circle, be part of it, sit in the midst of that music.

"Risto, where is your circle?"

"I cannot say when there is such blossom again for me." He laughs as if I'm silly.

"Can all the spirits make one giant circle of harmony? Can that happen?" Every one would be in tune with all the others. Life on Earth would be bliss.

"It is to come," he says. "So slow you cannot see the motion happen, it comes."

Could such a thing ever be true? "In my lifetime, Risto?"

The thought makes joy spill out inside my chest, my shoulders feel warm inside.

He gives me a brief glance, as if he dreads my reaction, shakes his head no. "Very not," he says. He means eons, millions of years probably, so slow, but moving in the right direction. So all will be well eventually. Risto knows about something as huge as this, yet now he's having to learn about stuff as ridiculous as telling time and haircuts.

"Risto, what did you tell me when I couldn't understand you?"

"Only I say this night is so beautiful and gleaming and how I love the water and the mountain. The tall fire before us extravagant and full of heat. These things I declare. In addition, your nice dress and your hair so lovely more long."

Long? I put a hand up to touch it, and he's right. It hangs loose at my shoulders, not spiky at all.

"How—? This never happened before, Risto, on any of our trips."

This is why he was worried about my hair when Charlotte first cut it. There are no edgy hairdos here, on men or women. Apparently he didn't know this automatic change would happen on arrival among so many spirits. What else has changed?

"Risto, am I going to be able to get back home?" I'm a little nervous about asking, because wanting to go home is what sent me crashing back to my bedroom once before.

"You are home at this present time." He seems to think he's being reassuring. But then he adds, "You can go everywhere. It is completely true."

"I can land exactly in my room?"

"Yes, it is always so. When I first came to you, fire flew down to the base of the tree. To come back to. To mark the ready portal. You have seen this."

So that's what the big falling spark was.

"You are here at the feast of my family," he says, as if my uneasiness has insulted him.

"Your family?" I haven't seen anyone greet him or recognize him. "Which ones are your family?" Now I remember: he has no parents.

"All," he says, a bit huffily.

"All? I thought I was going to meet your most special people." Maybe those from his circles. "Introduce me, Risto. To some of them, any of them. I want to meet Brendan. That's who I need to meet." I feel like I'm standing with him on a tiny island in a river, a beautiful roiling people-river, rolling on past us on both sides, with no one knowing we're here.

He gives me a puzzled look. "You are knowing."

"Knowing what?"

"All."

I'm starting to get irritated. "What about my grandmother? Can I see her?"

"Not ready. She is too young."

Too young, he says. She was not young when she died last year. Maybe I need more of the bubbly drink. It did help. "Risto, what was in that drink?"

"All of the seas. Every salted water together."

"It didn't taste salty."

He looks weary of our conversation, like I can't understand what he is trying to tell me.

"I am wanting meal of roast fish," he says.

"Okay," I say. "Roast fish." I give up trying to find out anything more. Maybe there will be peace on earth in ten million years, but what about him and me? How could I have imagined it was possible for the two of us to be together in any close-to-normal way? Risto and I will eat fish and drink all the oceans and then I'll wake up in my bed. This does not bode well for prom, or for what Philomena called the force of our desires. Only looking around at the amazing-ness of everything keeps me from crying.

CHAPTER

THIRTY-FIVE

Seventh period, the day after the night on the island, almost time to for final bell. I'm walking into home-room. Phone buzzes. I step back into the hall.

"Mom, what's up?"

"You may have already heard."

"Heard what?"

"It's Tony, honey. He's in serious trouble. Knowing how rumors travel, I thought you should know the facts imme-diately."

"What trouble?" Better if I don't say that I knew.

"He was arrested, charged with running a gambling business online."

He got caught. Probably thought he was too smart to get caught. "But Mom"—hard to know what to say, whether to sound surprised—"that doesn't seem so serious to me, not like assault or breaking into a house. It's not like he was fixing games or anything."

"It's serious. He had a large, sophisticated operation taking big-money bets on college basketball," Mom said. "ACC games, Duke and Carolina, the national championship —and drafting money out of the bettors' bank accounts. He'd developed a code to make it look like users were buying expensive cruises online. And it was based here, where it's illegal."

But the one text I saw looked so simple. "This sounds huge. Is Webb upset?"

"Furious and disappointed. He let Tony sit in jail overnight before he posted bail. The police were at their house yesterday afternoon. For a start, he's suspended from school."

I picture Tony skulking out between two cops. "But that's ridiculous. It's like arresting somebody for drinking a beer at seventeen."

"It's the law, Darcy."

People think there's a law of gravity. I know better. "I feel a little sorry for him." Just because he's rude doesn't mean he should be banished, or that I want him to be. I'd feel sorry for anybody who's being ripped out of their normal life for hardly any reason.

"I thought you might."

"Gotta go, Mom. The bell just rang."

But I can't go to homeroom. I feel bad. Girls' bathroom ahead.

The door squeaks shut on the hall noise, which is dying down anyway. The room is empty and hollow-feeling; everybody has cleared out. Smells like wet paper towels. Straight into the farthest cubicle, taking a seat on the toilet, I put my face in my hands. I'm going to stay here all afternoon.

Math-head Tony locked in a jail cell. So he's broken some law about gambling. So what? It may be illegal, but it's not *wrong*. He's hostile and surly, but I'm pretty sure he's not evil. I mean, who was getting hurt? I lean against the side of the cubicle because my hands feel too hot on my face. It's like him to have figured out a code.

Footsteps. I see feet walk in, pause at the mirror. Scuffy black ankle boots. Don't recognize them. She's talking to herself, under her breath, sounds exasperated. She's cutting a class, like me. Shuffle-clop-clop-clop-door-squeak-murmur-murmur. She's gone.

Nobody should be thrown out of school unless they're proven guilty of something that matters. I hope he gets acquitted and sues the school.

I can't stand for somebody as smart as Tony, even if they're hostile and obnoxious, to go off to some juvenile-delinquent cinderblock detention place. People's lives shouldn't be turned upside down and broken into pieces. Life on Earth is all wrong. It's as confusing as Risto's home place.

Mom and I are making a salad for supper. She's upset about the Tony situation, especially because Webb is so wrecked.

To me, she says, "You need to stay completely out of it. Don't text or email anything remotely related to sports or gambling or money. I mean, *nothing*."

"You think I'm involved in this?"

Her face switches from concerned to alarmed, like it now occurs to her that I might have bet on UNC basketball.

"Mom, you have got to be kidding. I don't like sports. I've only gone to games for social reasons." She still has that guarded look. "Mom, I have *never* bet on any ballgames. Or helped him run his gambling business."

She nods. "Good. Don't."

I limit my response to a flamboyant sigh over the fact that she'd suspect me. "But what's going to happen to Tony?"

"I don't know. He has so much potential. Or he did. This will put him out of the running for so many good things." She hesitates, looks around at me, her knife paused mid-tomato. "And, of course, he can't go to the dance with you."

"Not important." I feel a little bad that I'm hugely relieved.

She gives me a second look to see if I'm faking.

"Oh? You have a replacement lined up?"

"I do have another possibility. It may or may not work out." She nods, restraining herself from asking more.

It's going to work out. It has to. More than ever, I want Risto here. I want his company in whatever I do, whatever is going on.

RISTO and I sit in the backyard leaning against the trunk of the tree, which is a little risky. If Mom were to suddenly come home, it could be an awkward moment. If we didn't hear her in time, she might catch Risto vanishing before her very eyes. But we're getting more daring.

He seems unconcerned that I lost patience with him at his home feast, which is good because now we're facing all kinds of complications.

"You never told me before that there's a time limit to how long you can be here. Where does this rule come from?" I'm surprised and at the same time I'd suspected something like this was true. It makes sense of a lot of his behavior.

"It is no rule. To be here requires my great spending of strength. This is the true reason."

"I remember: Earth is fatiguing. But I've never noticed you getting tired. It's not like you're going to turn into a pumpkin."

"Pumpkin? Large orange vegetable?" He looks startled. "I can never become this thing."

I'm not in the mood to explain the Cinderella fairytale. He has agreed to go to prom—as I knew he would. But the time limit could be a serious problem. *One* of the serious problems.

Much worse, a curfew could obviously affect a lot more than prom. How can he ever be part of my Earth life if he could melt away at any second whenever he's tired?

I'm trying to remember how long his visits have lasted. I don't know, because I don't think we're always operating on a human scale. "Risto, how much time is possible? Why can I stay a long while on some magic mountain you came from, yet you can't spend a few hours at my school gym?" When I hear myself say it that way, the answer becomes clear. "You don't want to. Right? That's it, isn't it?"

"I desire it so much, your schoolgym. Because it is your

strong wish. I can stay until my understanding is fatigued. What is schoolgym?"

"Gymnasium, Risto. At my high school."

He seems taken aback. "Where the lifting weights reside?"

His confusion would be funny if I weren't so disturbed.

"Yes, but it will be decorated. Very nicely. They take the weights out, put up lights and sparkly stuff." When I remember the sparkle he's used to, the thought of glitter seems pretty feeble. "Is it possible for you to stay here longer than usual for a special occasion? To not try to understand too much. Or to save up energy in advance?"

Please let this be possible. Otherwise it limits everything he and I do on Earth.

"I cannot say this. Longer than what is possible is not possible."

There's no argument against that. I sit in silence. He can be with me that night for maybe a few hours—guessing from previous experience—although he doesn't know exactly how long an hour is. If he fades away, I'll be left standing alone.

Transportation is another problem—how to look like we need it. "Risto, can you drive a car?"

"There is no need."

"There *is* need. It's not a good time to fly." I have to be my ordinary physical body self at the dance, and he *has* to seem like a regular guy. Not one hint of anything else.

THIRTY-SIX

I n the mailbox on the front porch, a letter. A hand-addressed in-an-envelope-with-a-stamp letter to me with T Llewellyn on the return address. Tony—the capital letters look big and architectural. Guess I know what this says. Do I read it this second or act civilized and take it inside? I'm already tearing it open. It's on his father's business stationery and he has drawn wings on the logo of the car. Unfriendly dark comic-book kind of wings.

Darcy, is how he starts. No "Dear" or anything like that. *I guess you heard. Of course you had to, since everybody did. Can't go to prom. Obviously. Sorry. Bad idea anyway. I don't do that kind of stuff. So we're both off the hook.*

He at least could have said it nicely. In spite of myself, I feel a pang. His writing is clear and easy to read, as if he carefully drew the letters instead of hurriedly printing. *I'm waiting to find out what comes next. Already I'm in a cage. No phone or driving or electronics or ESPN or sports stats. I'm washing windows, pruning bushes, shit like that. And I can't leave the yard. Like house arrest. I have to keep up with assignments from classes I'm not allowed 2 go 2. This is to make me law-abiding. Also shooting baskets. Thousands of baskets.*

This is a real letter—it's long—goes on for a whole page and over on the back. He wants somebody to talk to. Who would have thought that possible that he'd ever for one moment choose me?

Your mom has been nice, the one time I saw her. She said there shouldn't be laws against what I did—or excuse me, what I'm accused of. She's ok.

Fear strikes my heart. All Mom did was say a few nice things to him, and suddenly Tony isn't entirely against her and his father being together! On the other hand, he never should have been against it; he'd be lucky to get her as a stepmother. But I need his opposition.

The last line: *Don't know where I'm going to land—prison, military school, four-dimensional space? Anyway, no prom.*

He signs it with a big T. He didn't say: please write. This amount of communication is already such a shock that it wouldn't have surprised me if he had.

Slumping down on the floor of the porch, I lean my back against the front door and look at it again. A handwritten letter. He could go to prison, disappear into "juvenile detention." So wrong!

I'm used to having Tony around to not like. I won't feel right if that changes.

· · ·

I'm sitting at my personal bedroom desk, writing back to Tony. The poor guy deserves some kind of response to his pathetic letter. He *did* put a return address on it. Humiliating for him that he has to resort to letter writing—so retro, so primitive—to people who are practically strangers.

I start to say "Dear", decide against it. That's for thank-you notes to relatives. Instead I write a capital T followed by a long dash, and: *You're right, prom was a weird idea anyway. But I'm sorry you're locked up.*

If Tony knew what I've learned from Risto about travel, none of this would be a huge problem for him. He could go anywhere. Including school.

At least you're allowed to go outside, I write. This is starting to sound like a child wrote it. His note had some flair, like: "prison, military school, four-dimensional space."

I could tell him a few things about going off to a far-away dimension. I'm shocked that my eyes are blurry with tears. Because half my life is hidden in a distant place nobody can find? Or do I feel sorry for a guy whose life is about to get buried? With a piece of scrap paper, I wipe my eyes and drippy nose; I can*not* drop tears onto a sympathy letter to Junior Felon Llewellyn. I would seem even more sad and ridiculous than I am. I finish the awkward letter and seal it so I don't have to think about it anymore.

Martin and I are going to have a conversation, the first in days. Many, *many* days, if I'm completely honest. He's sitting at a table in the mostly empty cafeteria. What I can see of him looks like his usual skinny, track-running self. He studiously doesn't look up, keeps going at his keyboard, though he knows I'm approaching. Can't get a clever greeting to come to mind, so I say nothing as I drop into the chair across from him. Awkward. Finally, he raises his head to look at me.

"Darcy." Flat tone, but not his pissiest.

"Looks like you're hard at work."

He pauses his tap-tapping on his keyboard. "Catching up on some stuff." He closes his laptop. "I called this meeting. So here's what's up."

"Okay, what?"

"I figured you aren't going to prom with Tony—"

"Right. I'm not."

"So I thought you might be wondering about going along with me and whoever."

"Well, I—"

"But I can't do that, so I should let you know."

"Oh?"

"Right. Seemed like I shouldn't be letting you count on it."

"I see." He's this mad at me.

"I'm already going with somebody."

"The regulars."

"One person."

"Like a date."

He says nothing. My heart is doing a weird shimmy.

"Who, Martin?"

"Jimmy Kingston." He looks straight at me, which he hasn't been doing until now.

My mouth is open, but not starting to say anything. Jimmy? Kingston?

"On the track team with you," I say, as if the surprising fact is his sport, and not that Jimmy Kingston is a boy. "Like a date." Of course like a date; that's exactly what he means. I am suddenly so happy for Martin that I feel full of warm liquid from my tear ducts all the way down to my feet. I fall across the table, hugging him as best I can.

"Oh, Martin, I am so seriously happy for you." He sort of shrugs me off, but in a friendly way. "This is the greatest thing. You're going to dance together? You and Jimmy?"

"Darcy, please, I don't dance. You know that. And Jimmy doesn't dance either."

"You'll wear a tuxedo? Both of you? Two tuxedos, I mean."

"Yes, one for each of us."

"You'll look fantastic, like two Neil Patrick Harrises."

"I'm struggling to decide how to react to that," he says with his wry look.

"It's a compliment, obviously. You're both the lean distance-runner type."

"Anyway..." His "anyway" means he feels he's said enough. Long silence while we stare around the cafeteria that smells like yellow cake.

Do I apologize? I'm still keeping my secret, still holding out on him, so I can't just come clean.

"Martin, I'll explain when I can."

He nods, as if he knew this all along, as if I have as long as I need.

"Martin, why now? Why Jimmy now—or at least going

MY LIFE ON EARTH AND ELSEWHERE

out in public with him now?"

"You were busy elsewhere," he says, doing the wide-eyed fake-innocent look he does when he's joking. "What else was I supposed to do?"

So my secret helped him come out? I'd like to think so. Maybe I played some part in it. At least his having had a secret these recent days means I wasn't the only one not saying everything. Most important: he's still my Martin. And both of us have somebody to be in love with.

CHAPTER

THIRTY-SEVEN

Twenty-one more minutes in the school day. Then the bell—when everybody will go into motion, shuffling and scuffling out into the hall, filling up the sidewalks like they're concrete riverbeds heading in every direction.

Charlotte is signaling me across the room, mouthing: *Meet... me...at...my...locker*. I nod. I have somewhat neglected her since the awful shopping trip, though not as much as I have Martin who's had no idea about Risto. I wonder what she's up to now.

She gets to her locker about ten steps before me. "So is Risto going to show up and go with you?" She keeps her attention on fiddling with her combination lock.

"He says he will, but there are unbelievable complications to figure out."

"Can he land on your porch and knock on the door? Would that work? Or would his hand go through the door?"

"Don't be ridiculous. He's perfectly capable of knocking on a door. I mean, he doesn't walk through me or fall through the floor."

"Well, excuse me for not knowing how to act around ghosts."

"He's not a ghost."

"Whatever he is then."

She still can't completely believe he's real.

"He's a guy," I say, "who hasn't been human yet."

As the hall crowd thins, the rectangle of light from the stairwell looks like a melodramatic book cover, doorway into danger. The thought of him being born clangs around in my head.

"So, he's like a soul wearing a body? Is that body his permanently? Or is it possible he could show up as an old lady? Or a third grader?"

"It's his body until he's born, whenever that is. After that, I don't know. But I do know how he looks now matches who he is. So it's his soul-body." I sort of made this up on the spot, but only because I know it's true. More and more I know things without having to ask.

"Okay, good. No third graders. Now, here's a plan. Ask him to come to the front door. You be there to let him in. You can ride with Bink and me. We'll come pick you up."

"I'll have on my long dress," I say, "and will have introduced him to my mother. How can it possibly work? It'll be a disaster."

"What's the worst that could happen?"

"Me walking around the living room in a formal dress

looking like I'm talking to myself because the parents don't see him. Me being sent to some psychiatric hospital."

"Your folks wouldn't do that to you."

"What would you do if your kid got dressed up and went to a dance with an imaginary guy?"

Charlotte twists her mouth around to her you-have-a-point expression.

"Right. It's what any parent would do. I'd be in the same sad shape Tony is now. Pretty much in jail."

PROPPED on one elbow in bed beside me, Risto looks sleepy-eyed and, in a lazy way, confused. He's been visiting more and more often and for longer lengths of time, which gives me hope about his energy and what's possible."Still I do not know what is prom," he says. His silver vest lies open over his bare chest.

"I told you, Risto. We talked before. It's a dance. A fiesta. I want you to go there with me. It's extremely important to me. You said you would."

"Let us go in this present instant, MyDarcy. I will be strong and stay the longest time. You have told me also about importance of schoolgym. We will have all of these things."

"Prom is the name of the fiesta that's *in* the school gym, Risto. It's all one thing." What zings into my heart is his saying that we will have all of these things. It's all possible, everything, not only flying to other countries, but also games and parties and meeting my people, and he's telling me so.

He starts to climb out of bed. "Let us proceed to prom at schoolgym," he says, ready to send us into flight.

I pull him back down beside me, letting my hand linger along his bare arm. "No, *mi amore*, it isn't happening this minute. It's two weeks from now. It's once a year."

He still doesn't understand time. How do you plan anything with someone who doesn't know what a day is? Why did I just call him *mi amore*? What Dad used to call Mom. Throwing in another language: not a good idea. His language machinery could switch to Italian. Also, it didn't work with Mom and Dad.

"Risto, darkness will come at my home eleven times. On the eleventh night, the eleventh darkness, there will be the fiesta. You need to wear a formal black suit, a tuxedo, or whatever you want to wear that's dressy."

"Wear?" He looks down at himself. His clothes, which are ever-changing, always seem to be a part of his skin. Does he understand the concept of "wearing?"

"You wear ordinary human clothes sometimes, Risto. That night we went to a restaurant and ate fish, and you wore a red sweater." I emphasize the word wore. "When you showed up at the beach..." I'm remembering that that was at a seafood place. Maybe there's something magic about fish, about eating fish.

"Yes," he says, "it is simple to accomplish."

"It is?"

"Yes."

"So you can wear a black suit?"

"If there are so many others wearing."

So maybe his clothes change like a chameleon's skin to

match what's around him? Possibly his silver vest is a super-natural version of my faded blue tee? If he comes to my house, there won't be so many others wearing tuxedos. There won't be *any*.

"Risto—"

He stops me, waving his hand as if he's erasing something written on the air. "You are gravely full of concerns," he says. "It is so sad misfortune."

"You're right. I'm getting caught up in silly details. Here's what I want so much: that you be with me in my regular life sometimes, especially when it's for something important. I go to your special places, your sacred mountain and out there in the ocean and wherever—"

"All places are excellent," he says. "I will come to your sacred mountain."

Is he making fun of me? We're talking about prom—which is important, especially for him and me—but it's no sacred mountain. It's not Jerusalem or the spirit tree. But I won't argue. He's saying once again that he'll come.

HARD TO BELIEVE this is happening. As if nothing has ever changed, Mom and Dad and I are having dinner together at our old favorite pizza place, Napoli. The three of us. Unbelievable. Makes me jumpy. I thought it would take graduation or me in a car wreck to bring this about.

The occasion is a complete mystery to me. "So how does this get to be family night?" I say after the waiter has left with our order.

They look at each other, deciding who's going to answer

that. They both make sentence-starting sounds at the same time. They both stop.

"I can already see this isn't about you two getting back together. You'd have planned your presentation."

Mom jumps in, "Honey, I hope we didn't give you the wrong idea."

"No, I have no illusions."

Dad winces at my saying that. I would have no illusions even if they *were* to get back together. The whole business would feel patched together and temporary and collapsible.

"Anyway, I'd still like to know what the occasion is for this get-together."

"The occasion," Dad says, "is that enough time has passed that we can comfortably do this, and I thought it might be nice for you."

"You don't have any news to announce that requires your showing a united front?"

"No news," Mom says. "Just pizza. Both of us catching up on things going on with you. So you don't always have to say everything twice."

There it is: the hidden agenda, catching up with me: what is Darcy up to? Probably I've been acting strange in ways I don't even notice.

Mom says, "You'll be going with Martin and friends to the dance?"

"Well...." I'm thinking, I'm madly thinking! Should have had my answer ready. The pizza platters slide between us on the table top, giving me extra time. I stare at white cheese and crust like I could read some answer there. "Maybe another friend."

"Oh?" from Mom. Dad has paused in his shaking red pepper flakes to give me an interested glance. No one asks. They wait.

"He's a good guy. We haven't worked out all the details." My heartbeat is going like a fire truck. My underarms have broken out in sweat.

"He's the same year as you," Dad says, "in school?"

"It's somewhat tentative," I say.

"His year in school is tentative?" Dad says. He has a nice look on his face. He doesn't mean it to be mean.

"My plans."

Dad says, "Of course I'm coming to the house that night to take a picture of you all dolled up. I'm sure not going to miss that."

Even discussing this is already the dumbest thing I've ever done. Mom says, "What's his name? He does go to your school, right?"

"I may ride with some friends and see him there."

"Either way," Dad says, "I want to see you all decked out in a prom dress. This is a first." He means what he's saying; he's also saying it to have something to say that isn't an intrusive question like: Where does he live? Does he carry a gun? The kind of questions Charlotte's mother would ask but that my parents feel are wrong to judge anybody by.

Risto doesn't do any of the things parents usually worry about. The real situation—zipping around the universe, being invisible in the Taj Mahal—is so much more huge and wild and unpredictable than they could possibly imagine.

I agree to pose for prom pictures and manage to change the subject.

THIRTY-EIGHT

H ow can this be? Pushing myself up into a sitting
position, I see I'm on the feast island again, still
in my gold dress. I seem to have taken a nap on
this sunny hillside. It's morning here now. When Risto
sees I'm awake, he smiles, takes my hand. I feel like I've been
asleep for weeks. Did I never leave here? Was my Earth life a
dream, or was I in two places? Did I leave and come back?
Looking around, waking up, I feel so light. In spite of my
sleepiness, I feel made of very soft breezes, of nothing more
solid than air. And everything I see seems almost to hover in
air, though feet touch ground in the usual way.

"Does anything here have weight?" I say to Risto. "How
do we keep from floating?

"Words have weight," he says. "And thoughts. When
they are put aside together, hidden in the mind's storage
place, then we fly away." He smiles. "Perhaps to the Taj
Mahal."

"I was full of thoughts when we flew there."

"But I helped some for you to have more lightness. My heart spoke to yours, saying: let these wordful thoughts be kept safe for later."

"That works?"

He laughs. "Of course. It is always so."

I won't argue. I have after all gotten myself light enough to float. And I didn't know how I was doing it. At the feast also, things seemed to shimmer or float, but somehow I thought it was the flickering bonfire light that was the cause.

The sun feels so good here too. So toasty-warm but without harshness. I think I'm drifting again...

It's voices that wake me, Risto and some guy sitting close to us who looks like he spent last night on a fishing pier. Weathered as an old tree stump, bright blue eyes and a beard that needs trimming and shaping. He has a silvery-gold aura around his head, like a cloud of ashes but finer and faintly phosphorescent.

My mind is clearing. What is the old guy saying?

"Fervent..." He repeats it. Sounds more like fair-vent.

Risto touches my arm. "You have said your need to meet this spirit being."

"Hello, Darcy," the man says. His eyes are ocean blue.

"You know my name."

"I do. I am Brendan."

Brendan? My dad's saint? Can this be? Risto did it: he found the guy. Except for the silver light that fades up closer, he looks like a regular old man, wrinkled, with out-of-control eyebrows. I launch the question carefully: "Are you..."

"I am. The friend of your *da*, Perry Colvard."

"My father. In Raleigh, North Carolina. You seriously are?" All it took was my asking and now he's in front of me?

He smiles in a crinkly-eyed way. I seize Risto's hand to thank him and jump in: "Brendan, I have something important to ask you."

I wait. He waits. I go ahead: "Did you cause my father to start acting like a monk? Are you the reason my parents split?" I'm ready to be very angry, no matter how warm and nice this guy seems.

Instantly I can see I'm onto something, because Brendan sucks in a long breath and turns his gaze away from me, looking off into the distance over the water. The faint silvery-gold light near his head is a bit like the gold tips Charlotte put on my bleached-out hair—maybe another reason Risto was freaked by it.

"This is a great and complicated matter," he says. "Your *da* is a hard case, hungering yet holding to the old way. All his calling then darting away—a pure struggler, is your man. I keep him company is all."

"*His* calling, you say? *He* was the one doing the calling? I thought a call was supposed to come from God to the person, not the other way."

"It goes both ways. Like any good talk."

"What was my dad asking for? A way to get away from me and Mom?"

"Never that."

"He *has* gotten away. I see him a couple of times a week."

"If you ask, will he not come more?"

"How do I have time? Already we have too many activities. I want him to be in another room in the house while I do my own stuff."

"He stays in a room not far away," Brendan says.

"You think that's the same?"

He lets out a long sigh. "I know it is not."

My throat feels lumpy and tight. Now it's me looking out over the ocean that's so bright yet doesn't hurt my eyes. "I need to know: What is Dad's calling? What is he going to do?"

"I tell you all I know. My job... I keep an eye for the lives of mariners. Your *da* is a waterman in his laboratories. I feel the turbulence in him, and so I sail at his side. I know no other than this."

He does his crusty-old-charmer smile again. His hands look hard and red, like he has handled nets in cold weather. Are we stuck forever with the bodies we have on Earth? Am I always going to have this no-volume hair? More important: "Brendan, do you know what *oraham lasparay* means?"

"I fear not, lass."

I hadn't really expected him to know, but still the disappointment makes my shoulders heavy.

"Come to the water's edge," he says, and in an instant, we're at the foot of the mountain on the narrow strip of beach, looking out across water like two normal people. Only the two of us—Risto is suddenly nowhere near.

"Your friend waits for you up the hill. We're not a trouble to him just now."

When I glance back at where we came from, all I see is a small conical mountain with one tree at the summit. A trail to the top winds around it—a rising spiral—and tourists are walking that path, up and down, ordinary humans who don't melt at the edges or shine. Instead they seem to trudge, to be so dense and heavy.

We stand ankle-deep in water that's warm, riffling. The sand is white and coarse, like the sea salt Dad used to use for cooking.

"Are we back on Earth, Brendan? We must be if I can see those tourists."

He's staring into the distance like some oil-painting of a sailor. "I bring you here," he says, "only to show how you can make a meeting place."

I wait.

"Between the worlds. Here on the strand at the very edge, we bring the realms together."

This is sounding good. I dig my feet down deeper into the sand.

"Here at the shores of the realms," Brendan says, "you can meet your Risto. Also souls of those in the human life."

This is so exciting that I'm scared to breathe. Oh, God, let this be true. "I want to try it out. Show me how. Dad would love to see you in person. How do I get him here?"

"It is an easy matter. Gaze down the length of the beach, the distant point of it."

I look to the right, where he's looking. The shiny line of water-meets-sand stretches as far as I can see, disappearing into a blondish haze.

"Now," Brendan says. His voice has a husky softness to it, like he finds a lot of things funny. "Look for the dark speck of a man moving in this direction."

I squint and look for the speck. "I'm not seeing it."

"Wait for the tiny dark shape."

"Maybe I see it. Like, about the size of a peppercorn."

The shape has changed. No longer a dot, more an i-shape or an exclamation point. A person shape. It comes close enough that I see motion, side to side... "Dad! It's Dad! That's his walk." I'm about to fall over from amazement. I grab Brendan's sleeve to keep my balance.

He says, "You, Darcy, are the power that's drawn him."

"I am? I have?"

"Darcy!" It's Dad, splashing through knee-deep water, coming to the inch-deep edge where we stand, wearing his baggy board shorts and Sierra Club tee, hair ruffled like he's been thinking.

"Dad, this is your friend, Brendan." I'm so thrilled that I get to introduce them. I can see this is the first time they've met face-to-face. Except I'm not sure Dad sees him. Dad's looking at me, with happy eyes and a relaxed expression that I've never seen on him. I take a quick breath and, for a second, have to look away.

"Darcy, how can you be here as if you're real? This is a place I make up—I imagine it when I meditate."

Brendan answers, "She's real, she is. Her body is well and alive at home, waiting for her spirit to return."

"You're alive too, right Dad?"

He nods, and I lean my forehead against his nearest shoulder. He loops both arms around me.

I can always come here to find him.

Without letting go of me, he turns his head toward Brendan. I sense without seeing that Dad has tears in his eyes. None of us speaks. We don't need to.

Whatever divorce could possibly do to make distance between a dad and his daughter, all that is undone now, permanently impossible.

Then I remember: Dad will forget this happened. Or maybe think it was a dream. Philomena said that's what happens. Then how is our meeting here going to do him any good? I press my forehead hard against his shoulder, sending him a message to hang onto this moment—don't let it go!

CHAPTER

THIRTY-NINE

I n the mailbox, where I'm expecting a few good catalogs, what do I find? Another letter from Tony. At least that's what it looks like, extra-fine-point pen printing. No return address. Like he doesn't want my mother to know he's writing to me?

Taking a seat on the front stoop, I tear it open. Another long one—Jeez, two pages.

Darcy — okay, the reason I'm writing you another letter. Shit, I don't know. Bored, I guess, from being buried alive. My latest chore, scraping moss off patio bricks. Tho they look better with moss on them. This make-work can't go on forever. I'd take off out of here if it weren't for the "legal consequences."

Tony in captivity is somewhat interesting. Not at all hostile. I'm okay with writing him occasionally, in whatever place he lands. I'll have a prison pen pal, a mother who is sleeping with the prisoner's father, a zoned-out monkish dad, and a boyfriend from another realm who may soon wreck my life on Earth. Perfect.

The front door squeaks open behind me. It's Mom. "I didn't know you were home." She sees what I'm doing. "You got a letter in the old-fashioned mail."

"From Tony. Llewellyn. Webb won't let him communicate any normal way."

"I see," she says meaningfully, making a point of asking nothing more.

"What does Webb think is going to happen to him, Mom? He can afford any lawyer."

She shakes her head. "Webb is angry—at Tony wasting himself like this. He feels he has failed, too, as a parent. He wants to be sure no one gets off easy, not Tony and not himself."

"But it's so insane that he's in this trouble, when there are horse races and casinos and you can buy a lottery ticket most anywhere."

"I know. But Webb says he wants Tony to 'know the cost of ignoring the rules'—also how much wreckage gambling can cause. Families lose their homes."

I picture Webb by the pool, jabbing at steaks on the grill, saying Tony has a good mind. Tony isn't the type for remorse, though.

"Could he go to gambling rehab?"

"Tony doesn't gamble. He thinks the odds are too much against consistently making money. Webb says he's exploiting the weakness of others, which is worse, in his mind, than if he'd been gambling himself."

Webb, I have to admit, has some good points.

"Mom, I have an idea. What if Tony's lawyer makes a suggestion to the judge: Tony could volunteer in a gambling rehab place for a semester or a year, do something like busing tables in the dining room. Being there, he'd hear some of the sad stories. And maybe he and his dad could pay for the stay of a gambler or two, which might help persuade the rehab center to take him on."

Mom is quiet, looking at me. "Pretty smart, Darcy. Interesting idea. I'll pass it on."

"One thing, though: Mom, don't say it was my idea."

She gives me another long look: "Okay. I guess I can understand that."

"Good. I mean, nobody would want it spread around that they're like some kind of judge, some school-principal-type person." I would lose all the cred I've built up from my radiant confidence, which I'm scared I'm going to lose soon, anyway. I almost dread prom. It's too important. I'm scared it will go horribly wrong. After wanting him for so long to be part of my normal life, now it's about to happen but in the most public big-deal way. Instead I should have arranged that he and I pop in for five minutes at the pizza place or wherever a few people are hanging out. There are a million ways for prom to be a disaster.

BACK ON THE ISLAND, alone this time, no Brendan or Risto. How I got myself here, I'm not sure. Maybe the intention— my focus on this place, this beach where the realms meet—is enough. I tried not thinking, but as soon you know you're doing that you're engaged in thinking again. It's very subtle, almost an accident when it happens. But it has to keep happening. Being here with Dad was so good—all human conversation should take place here.

As before, I stand in the shallow water that feels almost warm. It makes a nice rhythmic whisper as it comes and goes. My feet sink into the sand and I remember what Philomena said about being loose like sand. Standing here, I feel that ease. I sense myself swaying slightly with the movement of the water, though I don't know if I actually move. I feel like one of those lilies that never has to toil or spin, a Bible quote I saw in a gardening catalogue. I feel light and graceful and so at ease.

Down the beach, someone approaches, hardly more than a dark spot, getting larger as it comes closer. As before, it comes to take on the shape of a figure. I learned after Dad left the beach that the spirit—born or unborn—has to be willing to come. And most important, that we arrive with the physical appearance most familiar to the one we are coming to see. I don't have to worry about Risto's spirit showing up in some other body. Ever.

Now, all at once, Hawk is in front of me, a dozen or so feet away, out in the knee-deep water.

Good. We have unfinished business that bothers me, and I hoped my calling to him might bring him here. He's giving me a cold stare. The skin of my arms shivers. There's something scary about him, like he's wanting to hurt someone.

"Hi," I call out to him.

He doesn't say anything. Just keeps looking at me. I have to do this, but I don't want him to come any closer. Don't know what to say....

"So how—how are things with you, Hawk?"

He does a sarcastic laugh, looks out toward deeper water. "What do you think might help?"

He makes a hopeless gesture with both hands. I want Philomena here to tell him to be like sand, or maybe not that, maybe something else. I just don't know what.

"Things are going to get better," I say, though I'm only hoping. "Text me and tell me about the wind people or whatever."

He gives me a sort of nod, Tony-like, and the faintest hint of a smile. As he starts to vanish, I see a spark of light barely shining in him, just below where his ribs meet. I'm relieved to see it. He's a good guy underneath—I'm pretty sure that's what that means. But there's a lot of bitter feeling, of sneaking violent thoughts, on top of that. In this world, on this beach, I can sense that clearly. I wonder who hurt him so bad.

I walk back up the beach, flop myself face-down on the almost-hot sand. I realize once again that conversation and travel between realms is exhausting. I need to rest here in the sun, let the heat melt me to sleep.

RISTO and I lie nose to nose on my bed. All I had to do was picture him walking toward me on Brendan's beach, coming closer and closer, and then the two of us were here. I can do it. I can reach him and, if he wants, he can meet me. Like Philomena said, it seems like I've known this all along.

Now his hand is on my butt. I'm trying to say a couple of

things, but the way he keeps patting me there, I can't think. My mind is a puddle.

"Risto, do I need to write it down? When you need to get here? What you should say if somebody asks you where you're from? Is that possible, for you to have a piece of paper in your world?"

"All these informations I have," he says. The tip of his tongue brushes my lips again.

I have to remember to remind him later.

What am I supposed to remind him? I've already forgotten.

His mouth moving down my neck makes warm ripples out from everywhere he touches. Between my legs, I feel swollen, like my whole body is about to do a backbend—like I need to—my middle rising toward him, the rest of me falling loose and limp. We glom together, the parts of us fit. A charge running back and forth...him to me, to him to me... throat to throat, chest to chest, hot current running round and round...five, six seven places...until we're one explosion of light particles, each one spinning, full of feeling. When I open my eyes again, it's morning. He's not here. I can still feel him, a cloud of warmth around me.

Was that sex? Not exactly, but something like it, I'm pretty sure. Maybe what that book called chakra melding. Definitely, it was making love.

CHARLOTTE, coming down the hall outside the cafeteria, sees me and waves. I step over near the wall to get out of the traffic, so we can talk. She needs to know about chakra melding.

But now the crowd of passing students is fading into the distance, the sound of them dropping to a whisper like water rushing. We're on that beach, Charlotte coming toward me. I got us here without consciously thinking about it, because I needed to.

In cut-offs and a tank top, she's splashing her long legs through the water as she approaches. "Darcy," she says, as if we're getting together on a normal day at a normal beach, or back in the hall at school. How do I begin this conversation? It's not about Risto or chakras at all.

"Thanks for the haircut and color," I say.

"But you hated it. You're growing it out."

"I didn't hate it. It caused some complications, but that all got worked out. What's up with you? I feel like we haven't talked like usual. I've been distracted."

"You sure have."

"I'm sorry, Charlotte."

Her face changes, the way a small child's does when she's suddenly gotten what she's wanted. Joy shining off of her like there has never been a moment of anything else. I never saw her look completely this way, without any shadow or hesitation or mix of feelings. She evaporates backwards, still smiling.

And we're standing against the wall just outside the cafeteria, in the school-lunch smell of boiled green beans, tomato sauce, and cinnamon buns, knots of kids passing in both directions. The same kids as before. We must have only been gone for a second. Charlotte is saying what a great day she's having. Everything seems to be going right.

FORTY

T wo days until prom and already this week has been super extraordinary. Last night with Risto, plus what happened on that beach with Charlotte, Hawk, Dad, and Brendan.

The latest twist: Dad wanting to take a walk this afternoon. We don't take walks, therefore I know instantly that he's planning an important conversation. He picks me up after school, and we ride over to Lake Johnson, where we set off on the trail.

A few steps down the path, the air starts to feel damp, sounds of the road distant.

"What's up, Dad?" I'm not going to wait for him to bring up the topic. The way things are going, I'm feeling like an action hero, a goddess in charge. And I wonder if he remembers—wants to talk about—the moment on the beach.

He does his wry chuckle. "It's that obvious something is up?"

"Yes."

"I'll get right to it. I'm thinking—well, planning really, to maybe..."

He's hesitant. Not a good sign. "Planning to maybe what?"

"Go to Ireland to spend a month or so, in solitary contemplation. Meditating," he quickly adds, as if that's a word that would be more familiar.

Trembles radiate out from my stomach. I feel them all the way up under my scalp. This is not about the beach moment at all. I don't think he remembers it. Or maybe he thinks it was a dream.

We keep walking, our steps in tandem. He's keeping his stride as short as mine. "Solitary. So does that mean no Skype, no FaceTime?"

"For those few weeks, Darcy."

I don't like this. He's soft-pedaling it, which makes me suspicious. "One month or so, you say." I raise my voice enough to scare the birds. "Is this the start of you disappearing forever into a monastery?"

"I'm not going to disappear, Darcy. I simply need to feel complete silence for a bit."

I say nothing. If he wants silence, he can have some. See how he likes it.

A voice floats from the other side of the little lake. Another voice. A splash somewhere beyond the trees. The fire goes out of me. I don't feel like giving him a hard time. "Dad, you might find it surprising, but I can understand that." I know after our meeting on the other-world beach that I can always reach him, even if he doesn't know it. Still, I want him here. "Why Ireland?"

"I have in mind to go to Clonfert, where St. Brendan started a monastery—"

"I knew it! See, this is exactly what I've been saying: you're heading toward becoming a monk."

"There's no monastery there now, but I need to be where Brendan was. It's foolish of me, I know. As if a geographic location could bring clarity. The worst—the painful part—is weeks of no contact with my daughter. My time with you is already so reduced. I miss the everyday..." He gives me a sideways glance, looks as miserable as he did on the day of the announcement. Do I bring up the beach? If he has no memory of it, telling him will make me seem deluded, seriously troubled.

"You don't have to go all the way to Ireland, Dad. Brendan hasn't been there in fifteen hundred years at least. He died. He's on another plane of existence."

"I gather you googled him. I appreciate your being interested."

"Of course I did." That's true: I did google him—and I've met him.

An idea seizes me, a flash of glorious inspiration.

"Dad, you can accomplish what you want right here."

"How do I do that?" He's asking in a jokey way, but at least he's cheered up.

"I'm not joking. You can have me for your"—my brain scrambles for a word to describe it—"your spiritual, I don't know, friend?"

He semi-laughs. "Spiritual friend, is it? A nice idea."

"I'm serious." This way I can gradually introduce the beach and everything it means. Maybe he's not yet ready to remember it and that's why he doesn't.

"Darcy? When was the last time you attended a church service? Or opened a Bible? Your mother and I made an error in offering you no religious background. No opportunity to make a choice."

"Your parents didn't offer you any Sunday school, Dad. Both of them were atheists—yet God got in touch with you anyway."

"Being raised the way I was is one big reason this change has turned me upside down."

Upside down is the perfect description. He needs a spiritual friend as bad as I need him to stick around. "Dad, it would be good for you to have someone who has been raised like you to talk with about this stuff. That's me." I'm making this argument up as I go along. I have no idea what I'm going to say next, or how I'll ever present what I know in a way that's convincing and helpful to him. "Also, this could turn out to be my religious training. We'd need to talk about all this stuff often."

He's starting to soften. I can feel it. I hear in my head so much more than I used to. People's thoughts and feelings seem to turn light enough to float to me.

"Maybe we could do that when I get back."

"I'm not sure I'll be able to do it then. Things could have changed. You never know. The right time is now. You didn't already buy a plane ticket, did you? A non-refundable? I'm hoping not."

"You wouldn't so much as say grace at dinner at your other grandparents' house!"

"Like I said: things change." Although he doesn't really need this pointed out to him.

"Exactly what do you have in mind, Darcy?"

My mind searches again for a solid answer. Gives up. "There's no syllabus for the course, for either of us. No reading list or lab. We'll talk. It'll evolve."

"Evolve," he says, and falls into silence so deep that I half expect him to get down on his knees and pray about this decision. I can't tell where his mind is, what he's thinking. Then he seems to come out of a haze.

"To my astonishment," he says, "my gut tells me this is important, that it's the right thing."

"Good. Maybe Brendan is speaking to you from your gut." We're quiet while I'm staring around at the woods. "Does this mean you're not going to Ireland?"

He takes a breath. Stops. Starts again. "I can't say that, Darcy, but who knows? As you've pointed out, things do change."

"I guess that's good enough for now."

We resume our walking. Until that moment, I didn't realize we'd stopped.

CHAPTER

FORTY-ONE

Tomorrow night, this Saturday, is prom. Everybody in the hall between classes is antsy-electric. The place has the feel of a tornado on the way; I half expect my ears to pop. Ordinarily, I'd be scornful of the uproar, feeling left out. This time, I'm crazier than the rest of them. Sitting here tapping the point of a pencil on the desktop: lift it and let it drop, lift and drop, lift and drop.

The tiny sound is like a clock ticking.

SATURDAY MORNING. 6:22 a.m. Exhausted. Spent the whole night awake and trying to get myself connected with someone—anyone—from the other side who could help me make sure Risto gets here and knows what to do. Tried reaching him. No results. I trust him and his good intentions completely but I also know his limitations at this point. He has no understanding yet of schedules and human time; that seems to be the hardest thing to learn. So I kept on with my effort, tried levitating myself, but I lay there on my bed like wet cement for two hours and never lifted off the surface until I got up and paced around the room and went downstairs for desperately needed chocolate chip cookies. I seem to have forgotten how to do everything I've learned about flying, sensing messages, and all the rest. It's the stress I have put on us about getting to this dance.

I have the gold fiesta dress hanging on the hook on the back of my bedroom door. Turned out Katrina didn't want it anyway, which is hard to believe. It's like a blaze of light, continuously reminding me of what today is and that I have no idea whether to rely on Risto getting here. He'll be more upset than me if he messes this up.

This one dance shouldn't be so ridiculously important to either of us, but it's our public debut into the human world, and I'm scared it's going to blow up and ruin everything. Dad is going to get here at 7:30 p.m. with his treasured Nikon D4 camera, to save forever a moment that may not happen, a moment that may be a colossal disaster.

3:35 P.M. Charlotte is helping me with my hair. She's pumped, and although she's still in her yard sale movie star caftan, she's already done her eyes.

"I told you, Charlotte. I want nothing extreme." I feel like wailing. She has strands of my hair standing on end, and it's too long to do that now. "Make it soft and normal. I don't need to do anything radical that stands out."

Again, the wave of anxiety overtakes me.

"It's going to be perfect. I guarantee you. An undone-looking updo. Risto is going to show. You have nothing to worry about."

"If he doesn't—"

"He will."

"But if he doesn't or he evaporates at some point—"

"You evaporate with him."

"I could do that. Except *un*like him, I'd be leaving my zoned-out unconscious body behind. I'd be rushed to the E.R.—*again*."

Half an hour until Dad arrives. I have no flowers. I should have told Risto to bring flowers. Or bought them myself.

Otherwise, I am completely ready.

Waiting...

Charlotte, who decided Bink could pick her up here, is at the mirror, carefully fitting a tiara into her hair. "It adds a little sparkle. It's hardly more than a big barrette. Not a real crown or anything."

I could have gone with a gang in a limo, everybody loud and yukking it up. That would have been the best idea. Tonight's a big deal night for Martin, too. Although he has been walking around school with Jimmy in a semi-obvious way.

A shriek! My whole body jumps, but it's just Charlotte, therefore minor: tiara frustrations or mascara. My whole body goes weak and slumpy in relief.

Charlotte turns. Her face is whiter than Kleenex. Something's wrong— "Darcy!"

"What? What is it?"

"He was here. In the mirror."

I'm on my feet. "Risto!" I yell. Charlotte steps out of my way as I rush to the mirror.

"Risto!" My own face—frantic—is all I see there.

He was here. He came. Expecting me. But when he didn't see me he vanished. Oh, God! He's probably weirded out and won't show up for days. I call him again, quieter this time.

"It was like he came up out of water and melted backwards."

I can't venture out to try to find him. It's too risky. There's no sense of time passing where he lives; the dance could be over by the time we get back. Staring into the mirror as hard as I can, I see nothing but my face huge in front of me. I step back and back. The window light trembles against the side of my dress, a watery glimmering, and I see in the mirror the outline of him in the shadows on the gold. I think his name: *Risto. Risto!*

The shadow of him moves, as if he's turning back to face me. I hear his voice in my brain: *MyDarcyColvard, this location is correct? You are in your private chamber?*

I send my thoughts to him: *Yes. Come back. Please! I'm here.*

Instantly, he's standing in the room, completely physical and real, wearing a strange costume, made out of a lot of draping fabric: very Julius Caesar—not exactly a toga, but close. I don't care what he's wearing. I wrap my arms around him, around both his arms so he can't move. He's laughing. Then I feel his whole body tense. He's staring at Charlotte, who looks as if she might pass out from shock.

Risto's face is all confusion and alarm. "It's okay, Risto. This is my friend, Charlotte. We will go with her and her friend Bink to the fiesta. In a car."

"A car?" he says. In an instant, his fright has turned to excitement. "A vehicle? I have not entered a car. I have not navigated. This is greatly desirable."

He likes cars? This happens to guys before birth?

"Well, Risto"—and I still have not let go of him— "tonight you have an adventure ahead."

CHAPTER

FORTY-TWO

Charlotte, still in a state of Risto-induced shock, is on her way down the stairs. He and I wait in my room. The plan is that first, Charlotte will distract Mom and Dad, keeping them in the kitchen chatting, waiting for me to emerge for photos—and for my mysterious friend to arrive. I hope she's up to it. At least now she believes what she saw months ago with her own eyes.

Risto and I sit on the bed.

"You look wonderful," I tell him. "Very dressed up."

"For your best fiesta," he says. He looks—in a sweet, young way—proud of himself. He does look wonderful—and extremely odd. His version of formalwear is a variation of his knee-length shirt, but black instead of the usual white or beige. Plus a gold braid so shiny it could be the yellow part of a flame. My parents are going to be knocked into total silence —for one second, anyway. They'll have plenty to talk about when we leave.

"I must complete my preparation," he says, and crouches down, peering under the bed.

"What are you doing?"

He fumbles his hand under the bed, reaches behind the leg. What is he doing?

This is already out of control. Risto crawling around on the dusty floor, Charlotte taking too long downstairs—probably semi-firing on Dad if she's calmed down enough to act semi-normal. She mustn't forget to send me our signal.

"Eureka!" Risto says much too loud. "I have located." He rises, his eyes bright with triumph, holding out Mom's tiny silver condor that I gave him weeks ago. "My amulet. I have kept in safety here in your world."

"Good." I'm relieved that there was a reasonable reason for what he was doing. "We need an amulet." Which reminds me: in my underwear drawer I have the crumbled leaves, a box, and the book neither he nor I could read, all from his world. My info about his world so far hasn't come from any of the obvious, promising clues—unless the messages have simply soaked in and that seems to be the way it happens.

He sits again. My impatience rises. We have to get this going before I explode. "You appear resplendent, MyDarcy-Colvard." He's trying to calm me down.

"That's something else I need to mention, Risto. When we are around the others, please use only the first half of my name. Call me Darcy. That's what people here do. If you don't, they'll get confused."

He nods, gravely. "I am much fulfilling my education with you, MyDarcy."

MyDarcy. Yes. I've always liked that. But my stomach is more and more berserk with fear. There are so many ways this night—and my life—could shatter. What was I thinking? He needs much more education before he can do this.

From below, in the kitchen, come the two raps that Charlotte said would be the signal.

"Okay," I say to Risto, pulling at his arm. "Let's go."

I see no fear in him, which proves he has a lot to learn.

Step 1: We scoot down the stairs, fast as I can go in this dress and heels, with him close behind me.

Step 2: We pretend he's arriving outside on the porch. While he stands with me and watches, I open the front door, reach out and ring the doorbell, pause for one second and shut the door like I've just let him in. Count to ten, which Charlotte in the kitchen is also supposed to be doing.

We manage with perfect timing; here come the parents from the kitchen, the five of us arriving from two different directions in the living room. It's completely like Risto came up on the doorstep and I answered the door. Both parents smile expectantly, sociably. My heartbeat is jumping inside my head, like a frog in a box.

"Mom, Dad, this is Risto." I gather courage before I can say the rest. "Risto Bradley." It's not a lie. He is now named Bradley. Charlotte and I spent an entire night playing with names—nothing too flashy or too ordinary or too obviously symbolic would work. Did I think to tell Risto? He doesn't seem to have heard.

They're shaking hands: Mom and Risto, Dad and Risto. Behind them, Charlotte seems jumpy but pleased, as if this whole thing is a party she's throwing.

Both my parents are looking and looking at Risto, like they're wowed and fascinated and possibly perturbed. Of course they are. Who wouldn't be? When he arrived upstairs, I thought Charlotte was going to faint.

Dad does the have-a-seat-son thing, like he still lives here. Mom says, "That certainly is a striking outfit you have on, Risto. An imaginative twist on formalwear."

He nods with a serious look I haven't seen before. "Thank you, madam."

I see a bright spark of a laugh start in her eyes. She restrains herself.

"What year are you in school, Risto?" Dad says.

"My education is at a bare beginning," Risto says and casts a wonderfully warm look in my direction.

Dad laughs, no doubt thinking this guy is being witty and modest. My fear spikes again. The silence is growing.

"So have you always lived in Raleigh, Risto?" Mom says. Thank God she won't ask him anything that would show what part of town or anything socioeconomic; she goes overboard, judging people only on their personal, individual merits.

"Not always. I have been many places."

He's doing pretty well. I jump in to help: "Risto has spent some time in India."

"How wonderful," Mom says.

"Yes, it is of deep interest," he says.

Mom watches him closely, probably thinking: foreigner. I shouldn't have picked an Anglo name; what was I thinking? Should be Patel. Or Stephanopoulos.

"Must be quite a change for you," Dad says. "I imagine high school in Raleigh could be something of a let-down."

"But here in Raleigh lives MyDarcy," he says, bestowing upon my parents his glorious smile.

Dad looks rattled. Or suspicious. Or over-protective. Or scientifically inquiring. I don't know which. With his thumb, he starts nervously fiddling with a gizmo on his camera, which is tucked next to his leg in the chair.

The doorbell rings. It rings! Thank you, God! Charlotte walks in from the kitchen, where she has retreated, hiding. She'll help me make this work: I have an ally!

Dad goes to the door.

It's Bink, of course. I hear the blend of their voices coming from out in the foyer—deep murmur of guy sounds. Like Risto, Bink seems to have no fears of anything. However, he is a complete blank on what's going on. Or he better be.

Here they come, into the living room. Wow, Bink looks fabulous in his tuxedo, though not as good as Risto, of course. He's acting all stunned by how gorgeous Charlotte is in her pale green sheath, like he's been whammed back by a strong wind.

Risto watches with his sweet smile. I can imagine how this must feel for him. Like flying for me. I put my hand on top of his. He turns his smile toward me. Out of the corner of my eye, I see Mom notice. His hand feels so warm and real. This is happening. He's here. In my regular life. If this can happen, we can make anything happen.

"Okay," Charlotte says, her voice chirpy, like she's trying hard. "Let's get this picture, Dr. Colvard, so we can roll."

We assemble so fast for the photo, you'd think it was an emergency. Click, click, click! Dad snaps a bunch of pictures, like an old-fashioned newspaper photographer with an actual camera. And we're out the door.

This is all going so great. It's fine. It's absolutely perfect.

FORTY-THREE

In the lobby of the gym, people are milling around, girls furtively pulling at their dresses, touching their hair. Risto and I are about to make our entrance into the gym. A literal, actual entrance, through what looks from here like a tunneled walkway, the walls and ceiling shimmering blues and greens.

I want to hurry up, get in there. Not stand out here in the bright ordinary light, where everyone can see us way too clearly. I can practically hear them thinking, *Who's the guy with Darcy, and* what *is he wearing?*

Bink and Charlotte are ahead of us. They step into the tunnel. Risto and I are supposed to wait about half a minute, then follow. They charge ahead, and in practically the same moment, I feel a hand push me forward. Then Risto and I are standing in the arched entrance to the gym, next to "the herald," a junior student government guy whose freckled, bare chest is smeared with baby oil and green glitter, probably breaking a lot more than one law of the school dress code.

I barely remember to hand the herald the paper with our names to announce us. Because— what am I looking at? Opening ahead us of is like a magical cavern. This cannot be the gym. The whole space is full of wavering, silvery shapes as far as I can see. It's like there's no ceiling, but instead a shining, moving surface overhead. We're underwater, still breathing air.

And a Parthenon-type ruin on one wall—the name on it: Atlantis. Of course! The herald guy calls out: "Mermaid Darcy Colvard and her undersea escort Merman Risto Bradley." Reesto is how he says it. This is what Layna meant when she suggested "doing something with mermaids?" I had no idea.

Risto is looking one way and another, even more amazed than I am. "MyDarcy, I am vastly bewildered." We both stand here stupid, like we never intend to move. I am *so* glad I resigned from the decorating committee. What a disaster it could have been. This is *amazing*. Now I see where Chairperson Layna gets her confidence. She's earned it.

The merman-herald with the freckled green chest says, "Nice outfit, dude. Like a fancy-toga party. Like Atlantis. You fit right in." He's trying to get us moving.

"Come on, Risto." I pull at his arm. "Let's get out of the entrance. I'll explain."

Minutes later, safe at a table: glasses of blue-green punch in front of us. Risto holds one of the starfish-shaped cookies up like he's trying to picture it in the sky. Arnie What's-His-

Name, a student-government-type guy at the other end of the table, is watching, probably thinking Risto is stoned.

Which I can understand, because Risto looks like the most relaxed person here. Other faces range from somewhat uneasy—most of the guys—to intensely happy—that would be Katrina, who wound up getting a magenta dress with a bejeweled top that looks fantastic on her. Couples are dancing slowly, the band playing in a wavering, underwater way. Romantic, though I'm too nervous to feel the mood myself.

"Merman Martin Aldridge and Merman Jimmy Kingston," yells out the herald-guy. Martin! At exactly the same volume and tone of voice that the herald called out the names of everybody else. Martin's name flies at me like a magnet. I feel others twist to see my reaction.

"Oh, they look so beautiful," I say to Risto.

"Yes, so beautiful extremely." He doesn't see where I'm looking. He's still studying the watery decorations, watching the video of fish on the far wall.

Half-standing, I wave Martin and Jimmy toward our table. Martin sees me. They're coming over. This could be trouble: a real conversation. But I have to be supportive of Martin.

I pat Risto's nearest leg. Give it a rub. "You can do this."

Martin and Jimmy are sitting, looking giddy, now that their initial awkward moment—their grand entrance—is over. My awkward moment has barely begun.

"So where do you go to school, Risto?" Martin says. "I haven't seen you around." This is only his opener. Martin will ask everything my father would like to.

Come on, Risto, I say inside my head, squeezing his hand. *You can do it.*

"From astral, I come to Earth," he says.

Oh, crap. A thousand times crap.

But Martin is laughing. So is Jimmy. It must be the excitement of their debut.

"Okay, space guy," Jimmy says. "That's cool." Jimmy obviously thinks Risto is joking. It's also possible Martin and Jimmy have been drinking; they are so flush-faced. I wouldn't blame them.

Bink and Charlotte are back, both trying to look completely unsurprised by Martin's date. Good. The news of Martin and Jimmy deflects attention from Risto and me. The music is loud. It's hard to be heard unless you yell or put your mouth up against the other person's ear. That also helps us. If I can get us through the introductory info exchange every time, I think Risto can pass. After tonight, as he gets more educated, there will be less and less to worry about. Except for him finishing his human education and turning into a baby.

He whispers in my ear. "Let us perform the dancing, MyDarcy." He nods toward the center of the room, where a few couples are out on the floor, the band playing some retro thing nobody's ever heard before.

"Are you sure, Risto?"

He gives me a puzzled look. "What element exists to cause doubt?" I wish he'd say things more simply when it's obviously hard to hear.

"We've never danced." I love having my lips right against his ear. None of the rest of this matters.

"I dance exceedingly much."

Now I'm wondering who he dances with up on that mountaintop of bonfires and wrap-around ocean.

"All dance with frequency," he says, drawing a wide circle with his hand. "All of the everyone." He must be reading my mind. Or my face.

"Okay. But do you like this song? We could wait."

He pulls me by the hand. "These minstrels play for us a superlative tune." His English is having a setback, which means he's feeling stressed, whether he knows it or not.

We are out in the center of the floor in a spot where feet have danced away the soft fake sand—it looks like cornmeal. Risto, holding my hand, raises his other arm over his head, circling it as if he's waving a flag. He makes a loud yelp sound.

Oh, God. "Risto! We need to dance the way everybody else does."

He looks around. "Others are not dancing." He's right. Others have stepped back. I feel it. I can't bring myself to look. "Let's go sit. Please. We can talk and wait for a different song."

But he's pulling me by the hand as he starts out across the floor, doing something sinuous in time to the music. It's like a folk dance, what he's doing. I don't know how. Here we go—his legs slinging around each other and kicking, we're winding like a kiddie train in a park. I'm being hauled this way and that and all the time his face so radiant that no one could seriously believe he comes from Earth.

When the music trails away and we stop, he says, "Dancing is divine in its nature, MyDarcy." Everyone can hear him in the quiet, I know it. "It is the gift of all the gods and shapes the soul. Mr. Plato has uttered these words."

"Oh, Risto." I lean my forehead against his chest. He is wonderful—a boy who passionately dances, no matter who's watching—yet I want to disappear. I'm not wonderful enough myself to handle this situation, the attention I feel aimed at us. I'm scared to look around.

Some guy lets out the kind of woot-woot wolf howl you hear at ball games. I dare to look up. Those nearest us are smiling at us. They're not gawking or jeering. As we head back toward the table, I hear one of them say, "Bravo!" and another saying, "Very cool..."

And that's all. Not bad.

I should have relaxed from the start, trusted him to come through.

Risto and I are walking back to the table, when an ooh-and-ah sound starts up from the whole prom crowd. Everyone's looking at something behind us. A wall-sized curtain has opened, revealing—Oh my God!—a tank of water that reaches close to the ceiling. In it, huge live goldfish, koi, or carp, or whatever-you-call-them, are swimming orange and lovely.

Risto's face lights up with even greater joy. His eyes look like they're spilling light. "My home has come to grace us with its presence. Our water friends, so bright and festive..."

He sets off running. Across the floor and to the tank. Really he's flying. But low enough to pass.

Then—please, no—he scoots up the side of the tank, over the edge into the water. Without so much as a splash.

The crowd makes a sound like a huge rustling whisper,

people gasping and murmuring to each other, louder and louder as more tables notice. Out of the rushing sound, I hear the two most familiar voices: Charlotte shrieking, "Oh my God, Dar-ceee!" and Martin, "...un-fucking-believable..."

My heart is beating louder than the crowd. Sweat is all over me. All I can do is stare as Risto swims like an actual merman in that long shirt, his motion like no human swimmer that anybody has ever seen. He and the fish are playing tag, or some other, more exotic game.

I can half-feel, half-see from the corner of my eye as Charlotte makes wild faces at me—like she or anybody else can tell me what I could possibly do about this.

Then he's out of the water. Back at my side. Barely wet, only the slightest shine of dampness on him. I'm more drenched—from sweating—than he is.

"It is a perfection," he says. "The most delightful fiesta. I am happy I have come here with you, MyDarcy."

My throat feels so strangled I can't speak.

Finally I get out, "Risto. Everything is ruined."

"MyDarcyColvard!" He sounds completely surprised. Why bother to remind him to use just my first name? His cover's already blown. I lead him to two chairs over at a wall, far from our table, away from everybody. I look no one in the eye as we walk. I want to protect him from whatever they're thinking and saying. He is my love, no matter where he's from.

We've been hiding out here for about two seconds when people start coming over in twos and fours, saying stuff like: "Damn, man, that was gold medal!" and "I can*not* believe you did that. That was in*cred*ible!" Jimmy Kingston even tries to recruit Risto for the track team.

The reaction is a complete turn-around from everything I expected, everything I've feared. People are being so nice! I stay quiet and watch Risto smile with his sweet delight at what they are saying. It's like he's standing in a shower of love. I am so happy for him, so proud of him, so happy for us. Nothing is ruined. He's now officially part of my world, just as I am part of his. No more double life, just one big delicious future rolling out ahead. So what if he's going to be born as a baby at some point? I might be ancient or dead by then. Nobody gets a permanent guarantee, I have to keep reminding myself of that.

On the way home, Bink reacts to the aquarium episode by talking the whole time about his own heroic football plays. Risto whispers in my ear, "CarDriver Bink is a vain man."

We wait until Bink and Charlotte have driven away before Risto zips up into the air to my room and I go climb the stairs to meet him there. As I hear Mom stir, I yell, "Goodnight, Mom. See you in the a.m."

It's already a.m.—extremely so. But never mind.

We flop down on my bed. "It was wonderful, Risto—and it was scary. You were supposed to act like a *human*." I'm so happy now, all my fear behind me, that I couldn't possibly be mad at him.

"My heart fills with saddest regrets that you felt this moment of scary," he says, but he's smiling. He knows I have no regrets—because he understands me in a way no one else does, even though there's so much we haven't talked about yet. He knows my big feelings underneath my small worries, over stuff like how a dance will turn out.

He presses his forehead against mine, and I forget prom and the aquarium. I have one last thought as we melt into that chakra-melding-sex-like-thing. It really wouldn't have mattered if he'd flown up to the ceiling of the gym and turned somersaults. What was anybody going to do about it? Call the police? He's here. He's part of my whole life—at least until he's born. There's nothing anybody can do about it.

CHAPTER
FORTY-FOUR

L etter from Tony. I'm so used to letters from him that
I pour myself a slosh of lemonade while I'm flipping
open the page to read:

*Hi— Have left town. Thought u might want to hear how it
shook down. I've been deported 2 Florida. Until January I'm a
gambling rehab volunteer, so far vacuuming the place and
emptying trash cans. X-treme gamblers R not all who you might
expect. One ancient church secretary already did time for embez-
zling to play the slots. Being here way more interesting than my
house arrest. Heard u went to prom with a guy training for the
Olympics in diving. I guess things worked out better for u. I have a
different address U can write me here. The place has no electronics, for obvious reasons.*

Risto training for the Olympics!? Best possible rumor.
Meanwhile, Tony seems to be in training to be an okay guy.
He and Risto both, learning to be human. Maybe I'm doing
the same thing.

Later in the afternoon, Dad is at the door to show me the prom pictures. He looks disturbed. What now?

"Darcy," he says, walking in. "There's something here that makes no sense."

My face is getting red, I can feel it. "Like what?" I say with perfect casualness. We flop down on the sofa to look at his pictures together.

"I'll show you." He flips open his laptop. There, filling the whole screen, is a picture of us from prom night: Bink, Charlotte, and me, but where Risto should be is a hazy shape, inside of it a tiny silver spot, not at his heart or brain, but about where a pocket would be. The little condor—it has to be—his amulet!

I'm trying to think what to say. My mind is in slo-mo, my whole body going hot and cold.

"Every frame is like this," Dad says. "I don't understand it. There's no way to blame the equipment."

"Well, it is peculiar, isn't it?" I can't look at him.

"There's no precedent for anything like this. Nothing in the literature."

I force my eyes away from the incriminating screen, as if that will make it go away. I need time to think. A strategy. "Maybe it's like someone who makes watches stop. Nobody has figured out why *that* happens."

Silence from Dad while he stares out the big front window. The afternoon light hitting his face makes me think of how he was when we were at the edge of the water with Brendan.

Inside my head I call out: *Brendan, help! Risto, help me! Get Brendan!*

More silence.

Dad finally speaks. "I'm going to show this to a couple of transformational optics guys on campus to see what they think could have happened."

Oh, great. I can imagine...

"Darcy, tell me again how you met your friend. Rizzo."

"Risto. Let's hold off on showing the pictures around, Dad. It's only going to be embarrassing. Like I got ditched and I'm standing there by myself. Seriously. I'd prefer this to be private."

But it's like he doesn't hear me. "There's technology that can create invisibility. I mean, with a shield you can cause light to bend around an object so it appears not to be there. But it's expensive and difficult and even if your friend's clothes were made of that stuff, the rest of him would have been visible."

This is my fault. I should have remembered that the picture of Risto from the Taj Mahal evaporated. I should have refused from the start for us to be in any photographs. No one would suspect the reason. They'd think, *Oh, Darcy is just being odd—as usual.*

Another too-long moment passes before I say, "I guess it's one of those mysterious things."

These days, he might be able to accept a reason like that. I've gotten more okay myself with being uncertain and not knowing everything—I've had to.

He closes the laptop, but still has the two deep wrinkles between his eyebrows. He sits with his hands on top of his computer. "The light in this room *does* do some strange things," he says. "Always has, because of the bubbles and distortion in the old glass."

I never thought of that, but it's true. This light has moods of its own, one of the cool things about this old house. Maybe the house itself has helped to bring the spirits to us.

We sit and stare, Dad and I. Then, in the wide 4:30 p.m. shaft of the light, I see dust motes forming some kind of pattern. My skin starts to tense up, prickle.

Risto? Is it you? No, not now!

The motes are gathering into a human shape.

Don't, Risto, please.

I untangle my legs, ready to leap off the sofa and warn him away, but Dad puts a hand on my arm that anchors me where I sit.

"Wait." He's staring at the shape that grows a little fuller and thicker.

The shape is Brendan. I know, even though what I'm looking at is still barely more than an outline. I see him—and Dad sees him.

I think Brendan is speaking, silently and only to Dad. The air is full of a weight that feels like messages passing.

Then the shape is gone, only emptiness in the space where it was.

The light in the room has dropped into grayness, ordinary. Dad gets to his feet. He hasn't looked at me. He thinks he has a secret, a shocking secret. He's trying to get it together to say something routine, like, "I'll call you tomorrow," but his mouth isn't working yet. One huge change— his meeting with Brendan was here this time, not in the other realm. This time, it wasn't just a feeling of an invisible presence in the room. This time, Brendan was visible.

And Dad obviously remembers it.

"Dad," I say, clearing my throat, steering him by his arm toward the front hall. "I'll call you. We'll decide when to start our spiritual conversations."

He gives me a sharp investigative look. Pauses. "Darcy?" He takes a big, shaky breath. "I'm supposed to deliver a message: 'the two words, *oraham lasparay,* are Aramaic. One means beach. The other means edge or rim or shore.'"

That's the answer: the beach! *Oraham lasparay.* I asked Philomena if Risto and I could stay together. She told me in an ancient language to find the beach. My grumpy "fairy godmother" did that; she wanted to help me. And with Brendan's help, I've found it. Risto and I can stay together! The beach is where we can always meet—as Risto and Darcy—even a thousand years from now, no matter how many times either of us gets born.

Dad, who looks like he's been through a storm, watches me closely. I don't know what he sees as he looks at my expression, but my happiness feels like bubbly, sparkling froth rising inside my chest. Before I lose my nerve, I say it: "Dad, when we have our first spiritual discussion, let's talk about what just happened."

His eyes widen, searching my face. This—his passing me a message from a spirit—has to be the weirdest thing that's ever happened to him. His gaze is full of startled delight and amazement, the way he looked on that long-ago day in the kitchen, the first time I asked him a scientific question. We stand motionless for several long seconds, taking in what it means that we both know Brendan, stunned by the hugeness of what has just touched us. Then he gives me a nod and a Christmas-morning kind of look that tells me, "Yes, we're in this together."

And he heads out the door.

FORTY-FIVE

I can't get to sleep. Even if Risto were here, he couldn't help. This is not a Brendan problem either. It's a camera problem. A father problem. These are human complications and they require a solution that will work for other situations as well, because with Risto being part of my visible life, there are going to be a lot of quirks that I can't explain.

I don't want to go through stuff like this again and again, moments when he's an amulet-carrying cloud or who-knows-what. If that happens, everybody will start being weird to him, trying to find out about him or treating him like some kind of freak. Plus, there's no telling what he might say or do. Any of that could really affect our being together in the open.

Heaving myself up, I sit in the dark. I need to think about this logically. So what's my radical, far-reaching solution?

What do I do to hide the big mystery right in front of everyone's eyes?

I pull the spread up around my shoulders, like a superhero cape. It's chilly.

All the possibilities are preposterous: say he's from another country and has a learning problem and comes from a family of incredible athletes and has been jumping over tall hurdles and sailing up walls since he was a baby. It's too much to ask anybody to listen to, much less to believe.

What, then? He's a ghost? A hallucination? An alien? Not true, and just as bizarre as the truth.

The floor beside the bed feels sweaty-damp under my feet. I shift to a different spot.

What if I said: Dad! Mom! Risto comes from the astral realm. He is learning about human life, and he loves me.

What if I just did that? Told the truth, or something like it.

DAYS PASS, and Dad says nothing about the camera or the spiritual conversations. All is ordinary and routine. Then: big change! Last night, Risto wanted to schedule his next visit. Not just appear without warning, but make an actual plan. Of course I was thrilled. He's beginning to understand the concept of planning, of timing, of *when*.

"I choose to participate in additional Earth fiestas," he said. "A sporting contest is my hope."

So I told him about Martin's track meet today. Perfect! I was going anyway. Martin, my steady buddy again, texted me the day after prom, "If I were a dancer, I'd have asked u to dance." That's all he said, but it melted all the distance that was left between us.

Risto is due to arrive in the late morning—and not through the mirror or simply materializing in my room. No. He insists that he will, "Sound the entrance gong like CarDriverBink."

I've gotten us a ride to the track meet. It's his arrival at the house that's flipping me out. Unless we get out the door fast, he'll have to have another conversation with Mom, and there will be no distracting arrival of Bink to save us.

I don't want to go through the living-room-scene tension again, but when I tried to say no to his ringing the bell, he was disappointed and wounded. So we're agreed that he'll come to the door.

What if Mom asks him what took him to India? God knows what he might say—to sit with MyDarcy and talk about spirits on marble floor of most romantic Taj Mahal? I can't make up answers for him in advance; there's no way to guess all the questions.

Risto and I get out of the house with no problem—a great relief. Mom, who was on the phone with her agent when he arrived, stuck her head into the living room and said, "Hi, Risto. You two have fun." Friendly smile and then she's gone. Didn't ask who was driving. But I can't count on that kind of luck every time.

Today, though, my good luck holds. The track meet works out fine for everybody. Martin looks like that mythological guy with wings on his feet. He and Jimmy are so happy.

Our success, mine and Risto's on this second Earth adventure with no disaster, makes me intensely certain and confident: I'm going to work out a way for Risto to be here like normal, whenever, without parental interference and without me being anxious every second. So he and I can hang out and listen to music, go to parties and car washes and all the other human social activities.

Hawk said not to do any of this, to keep it all secret and not to risk people thinking I'm sick or something, but I'm not going to live like that. The way Hawk deals with his wind people and with his Earth life—he's lonely and sad.. The way he's acting is how I don't want to be. It has to be possible for a person to be in touch with the spirit world without being a scary weirdo or a monk. That's what I'm going to make happen in my life.

Mom and I sit in the kitchen, having a few Chips Ahoy Chocolate Chunkies for dessert. Dad is on his way to the house. I summoned him in the ordinary human way—by text. I have called a Family Summit.

He gets here quickly. I hear him hit the front step and let him in.

"Let's go out back," I say.

I'm well aware that the last time we did this, all three together, was the day I met Risto, the day the parents dropped their marital news, and the symmetry feels fitting. A sort of anniversary. We go toward our same three chairs. This time, the air holds the warmth of coming summer.

I still don't know what I'm going to say or do in this

moment. I decided minutes ago that I can't say the word "astral". They'd freak—though Dad is now starting to know Brendan. I can tell by his mixture of joyful moods and nervous secretiveness. He's more carefully watching what he says. Boy, do I ever understand!

The right words for this conversation will come to me; they're waiting somewhere within me. As we settle in, I call on help from Risto, Brendan, Philomena, Mom's muse. *Calling all helpers! Anyone! Be here, in my brain. I need you!*

Mom is making small talk, asking Dad about a grant proposal while they're waiting for me to speak. My mouth is dry. I'm halfway curious myself about what I'm going to say.

"You know the guy I went to prom with?" I ask.

They both nod eagerly, whipping their full attention onto me.

"He, Risto, is new here. His English is a little awkward. So it's not good to ask him a lot of questions or expect him to be completely average and predictable. I know you can tell he's a good guy... And here's the thing, you're both so open-minded. That's what's important. So when I see him again, if he comes over, what I most want is: could you treat him as you would Charlotte or Martin? Hang out and notice whatever you notice and come to your own conclusions. Don't overwhelm him with questions."

"Sure, honey," Dad says. He seems baffled at how little I'm asking. Who knows what he was worried I would announce. "We trust your judgment."

I want to say to him: *Dad, on the other plane, on the beach with Brendan, you already understand.* But Mom is looking dubious.

"I don't get why a little basic information would be such a problem," she says. "This no-questions business makes me wonder what it is he feels he needs to hide."

Dad shifts in his chair, then shifts again, his forehead painfully furrowed. They're not managing to present a united front. Really, they rarely ever did.

"It's not a matter of hiding, Mom."

"What is it a matter of?"

My eyes search the sky for some answer. "He's private. I have to respect that." The righteous tone in my voice—not good.

She goes prune-faced with disapproval.

"I don't want him to get scared away," I say.

She looks ever-so-slightly appeased. That's a motive she can understand. Does she worry about losing Webb? She probably *does* feel rejected by Dad. Still, she sits silent and grumpy, reserving her right to pester Risto with questions.

Her muse is who I need to help me now. Sophia. I picture her, red-haired in flaming yellow. As I strain to hear her voice, a swoosh of falling light catches my attention, over to the side of the yard, near the tree. Like a tiny meteorite, golf-ball-sized, the little orb sizzles for a moment on the ground, before it fades to nothing, same as the spark Risto dropped that first day. The parents don't seem to notice.

Directly above, a dark shadow sits in the tree. I see no one, but I sense the presence of Mom's muse, Sophia.

Now a stream of air sweeps across my face. I feel energy surge into my lungs and pores, catch a quick glimpse of fleeting shapes passing. They're not coming from overhead, not from Sophia. No. This is something different. As surely

329

as I know that Sophia is present, I know what these racing beings are. Hawk's spirit—the light that shone from him on the beach—is answering my call for helpers. We must have set up a link in that moment. He's sent his wind people.

Dad, changing the subject, is saying nice things about me. I hear him faintly. With all my force—and my invisible help from the wind people—I aim my thoughts to Sophia.

It's my only shot. I know she can communicate straight to Mom's brain. Nothing else will work.

Darcy, tell me, Sophia's voice unfurls in my mind like a silky scarf in a breeze. *Why this slow introduction of Risto's nature to your mother?*

So she won't freak out.

No response.

I try again: *So she won't think I've flipped out or that I'm in danger and somehow get in the way of Risto seeing me.*

No reaction.

So she won't worry, I simplify.

Yes, the voice whispers. *This is good.*

Of course. She's interested in what's good for Mom and her art, not me.

There is infinitely much you do not know, she says, *but I am going to assist in this situation. Worry would be bad for her. It is also true that the mystery your Risto brings into the home—the immensity, the grandeur of it—could be beneficial.*

Before I can thank her or ask what she'll do, her presence is gone from my mind, and I'm listening to Dad finish the sentence he started as the orb of light dropped from the tree. No more than two seconds have passed.

Mom's face—even her posture—has changed. She looks completely relaxed.

"It's not that I don't like Risto," she says, breaking in as if she hasn't heard Dad going on about me. "He seems like a nice boy, refreshing and imaginative, if a bit befuddled. I do trust your judgment—and my own deeper sense about all this. So you're right, I suppose we really have no need to pry into his whole life."

Sophia spoke to her! Mom has come around! I'm so surprised that I can hardly speak. I croak out, "Thanks, Mom," while inwardly, I add, *Thank you, Sophia! Thank you, conductor tree and wind people and Great Hawk Wing!* From now on, I'll think of Hawk by the name his shaman gave him.

Dad is looking gratified, as if the nice things he said about me are what changed her mind.

Quiet has settled over us. They're both looking at me in a new way, with a little added respect.

I feel content with the three of us sitting here, saying nothing, neither of them tense and agitated over being with each other. They both seem reasonably okay about the split these days. What happened was something nobody could have prevented. And the shock of it flung me out of myself to Risto and his world. Plus, I've learned some new ways of living my regular life. "Loose as sand," as Philomena would say, which means knowing most anything is possible and that bad stuff can turn out to be surprisingly good and that the universe is literally, flabbergastingly awesome.

Since we can all meet on the beach at the border of the realms, it doesn't matter so extremely much who's living where. Maybe they both know that, somewhere inside. I know I can always find Risto there, no matter how many times he's born. He'll be with me on Earth as long as he can be, but he'll be with me on that beach forever.

"Thanks," I say again, finally breaking the silence. "Seriously."

I feel so grateful and generous that I'm going to cut them both some slack—about Webb, about Dad's religion thing. I can do lots of stuff: write encouraging letters to Tony, be nice about Dad going to Ireland—as long as he promises he'll come back. "I really, really appreciate your going slow with Risto," I say to both of them.

Talking about Risto, saying his name to them, letting go of the secret, I feel a tremendous wave of relief. I can relax, stop hiding. The halves of my split-into-pieces life are completely pulled together into one. "I promise you'll really like him," I tell them. "He truly is an amazing guy."

ACKNOWLEDGMENTS

So many people read all or parts of this novel in progress and I'm grateful to every one. Among those who saw more than one draft are members of the invaluable writing group headed by Laurel Goldman. These readers include Joseph Burgo, Christina Askounis, Peter Filene, Angela Davis-Gardner, as well as early members of the group: G.C."Pete" Hendricks, Dorrie Casey, Linda Orr, Charlie Gates, and Georgann Eubanks.

I also received helpful feedback from other reader/critics: Judy Goldman, Marly Rusoff, Nicholas Stratas, Angella Pilkington, Eli Broun, Susannah Broun, Nancee Adams, Tammi Hernandez, Brooke Raymond, Mary Kole, Lee Smith, Dan Wakefield, Jesslyn Chain, Tabitha Gibson, and especially friend and long-time office partner Carrie Knowles.

Many thanks to editor Callie Rowland, publisher Tony Acree and others at Hydra Publications for bringing *My Life on Earth and Elsewhere* into the world.

A group of readers the age of main character Darcy met with me and offered feedback on excerpts of this novel. Thanks to the Mock Printz Book Club at Eva Perry Regional Library in Apex, NC. Present at that lively get-together were: Aparna Tharmar, Beth Griffin, Byron Qi, Caroline Diorio,

Caroline Galdi, David Foil, Emma Lynch, Jackson Brockton, Kaitlin Balding, Krista Wiese, Kyla Qi, Laia Nalian, Lori Glenn, Madi Lang, Matthew Cleveland, Taylor Nguyen, Maxwell Marshall, Meghna Iyer, Nimi Muminiy, Selina Lewis-Bartley, and Shubham Tyagi, Special thanks to Caroline Dee, Taylor Nguyen, and Amy Eaton, members of the group who read the full manuscript. And thank you to Valerie Nicholson, Cris Crissman, and Linda Winkler for bringing us together.

Several books helped better acquaint me with Darcy's "other worlds." These are *Out-of-Body Exploring* by Preston Dennett; *The Astral Plane: Its Scenery, Inhabitants, and Phenomena* by C.W. Leadbeater; and *Perfect Love: Find Intimacy on the Astral Plane* by D.J. Conway.

As always, I thank my dearly loved husband Bob Dick, a psychologist who uses clinical hypnosis and has deepened and expanded the reach of my own worlds.

ABOUT THE AUTHOR

Peggy Payne, a *New York Times* Notable writer, is author of novels about the intersecting of spirit and physical worlds. A Duke graduate, she grew up on the North Carolina coast and now lives near Chapel Hill with her psychologist husband, in a log house beside a pond in deep woods.

ALSO BY PEGGY PAYNE

Fiction

Sister India

Cobalt Blue

Revelation

Nonfiction

The Healing Power of Doing Good (co-author)

CPSIA information can be obtained
at www.ICGtesting.com
Printed in the USA
BVHW051527100423
662054BV00001B/1